Ruth's
REDEMPTION

Ruth's REDEMPTION

a novel

Marlene Banks

MOODY PUBLISHERS
CHICAGO

© 2012 by
MARLENE BANKS-BENN

This is a work of fiction. All of the characters portrayed in this novel are either products of the author's imagination or are used fictitiously.

Edited by Pam Pugh
Interior Design: Ragont Design
Cover Design: 1721 Media, LLC
Cover Image: Photos.com and InMagine.com

Library of Congress Cataloging-in-Publication Data

Banks-Benn, Marlene.
   Ruth's redemption / Marlene Banks-Benn.
      p. cm.
   ISBN 978-0-8024-0217-2
   1. Slavery—Fiction. 2. Southern States—History—1775-1865—
Fiction. I. Title.
PS3602.A664R88 2012
813'.6—dc23

                                                           2011033636

1 3 5 7 9 10 8 6 4 2

Printed in the United States of America

First I acknowledge my divine Source and heavenly Father to whom I dedicate this novel. Only through the saving sacrifice of Christ Jesus and the revealing work of the Holy Spirit was I able to come to a place of redemption, understanding, and purpose that led me to writing this story. To my God and my Savior . . . for His glory!

And I dedicate this novel to my parents, Bill and Phyllis Banks, in loving memory.

Prologue

Tidewater Region of Virginia, 1830

*H*er defiant dignity stood out even in this horrible cir-
cumstance. She was beautiful, standing tall, majes-
tically arrogant in spite of such indecent exposure. It was
obvious she wasn't like the others in the line. He could see it,
but more than that, he sensed it. Each of the women's shoulders slumped, their heads hung low, humiliation and defeat
apparent over every inch of them.

Some tried to cover their nakedness with their chained
hands to no avail. No one cared about their shame. They were
not afforded the privilege of pride or decency. To most of the
spectators, they were not human but stock animals on parade
for the highest bidder; assembled for inspection to be purchased for whatever the buyer desired.

*Dear Lord, when will this end? How long must my people
suffer this shame and bondage?* He prayed silently, holding
his anger in check, pushing down the urge to lash out. He

noticed her head was held high and her stance impudent even in shackles.

No one at the auction took pity on these women being sold like prime cattle . . . no one but him and God. His heart always ached at the sight of their uncovered bodies shiny with oil, pulled with chains and fettered in leg irons linking them all together. Waiting to hear from God, Bo stood in the back as he always did, out of sight of the others eager to make their purchases.

Some of the patrons poked and prodded the merchandise, ignoring their cries of discomfort and whimpers of shame and fear. One woman made no sound. Her eyes were fixed in a hostile stare at nothing in particular, her full lips tight.

Montgomery Dale, a wealthy farmer from outside Richmond, wanted to see her teeth. "Open up!" he commanded. After all, good skin, teeth, and a pink tongue meant you'd be getting a healthy slave. She didn't open her mouth.

"You heard me, you stupid wench, open up!" Her jaw visibly tightened.

Harvey Price moved over to her and struck her hard enough to rock her back. "You heard him! Open your mouth!" He took his hands and tried to pry her lips and jaw apart. She still resisted. He hit her a second time, trying again to open her jaws when, in an instant, she bit down on his fingers. He yelled and snatched his hands away.

"You bit me!" His fist slammed into her head. She did not open her mouth but her eyes shut tight from the blow. She bent over, groaning, and buckled to her knees.

"Never mind, I don't want a slave I have to beat to death to make mind. Waste of good money." Montgomery waved his hand as he walked away.

"I warned you, you troublesome . . ." Harvey punched her

in the face once more. She grunted from the pain and crumbled to the wooden platform. "Joe, get over here and loose her! Take her to the tobacco barn! I'm gonna teach this wench a lesson she'll never forget when she comes to. She won't bite nobody else when I'm done with her."

A thin, tall black man came from the rear of the stage holding a giant key. "Shame ya has ta whoop her, Mistah Harvey, she sho a good lookin' healthy one. Pretty as kin be an' got a good strong body. Shame ta scar up such a fine lookin' one. Dat'll bring down her worth, won' it?"

"Don't ask me no stupid questions, boy! Do as I say before I whip your black hide too!"

"Yessah, Massah Harvey, anythin' ya says, Massah Harvey."

Harvey grumbled, "Ain't nobody gonna buy her actin' like a stubborn mule. A good lashin's what she needs to teach her not to bite white folks."

Bo felt the strong stirring of his spirit. It was a forceful urging and he knew why. He made his way swiftly toward the front. Marshall Craig was watching him, his dislike for Bo apparent. Their farms were adjacent. Bo knew the man hated him, hated his being a free Negro and property owner, but there was nothing Marshall could do about it. A free black man productively working the land was an insult to a struggling white farmer. Marshall Craig opposed Mister Maitland and everything the man and his family represented. He despised all God-fearing men like Maitland, especially those who spoke out against slavery.

Ten years ago Jordan Maitland died, leaving instructions for his thirty-five slaves to be freed and a parcel of land given to Bo Peace. Bo continually produced abundant crops and maintained healthy farm stock on the flourishing farm he owned. He lived on this land with other freed slaves, working and living in agrarian prosperity. It was an industrious community of free blacks. Craig despised the idea of blacks running a farm on their own. He particularly disliked Bo, the man he considered the leader of the out-of-place coloreds.

Bo stepped up to Harvey. "I'll buy her, Mister Price, sir," he said quietly.

Harvey snapped his head around and looked at Bo. He knew this educated freed slave all too well. He talked too proper and was too blasted proud. Harvey didn't like Bo Peace but he didn't care about likes or dislikes, politics, humanity, or religion. All he was concerned with was making a profit. To him this black man's money was as good as anybody's. "You sure you want *this* one?" he asked.

"Yes sir, that one."

Harvey glanced at Joe then back at Bo. "Now I know she's mighty good to look at, boy, but you sure you want this here hard-to-tame wench?"

"Yes sir; how much you asking for her?"

"Let me see now . . . Seein' she's a strong healthy one with a breedin' history . . ." He rubbed his chin, which showed a week's worth of stubble, and his grin sported a missing front tooth. "I'll sell her to you for nine hundred fifty dollars." His grin widened. "She's awful fetchin', you know."

"Nine hundred fifty?" Bo knew a white man would pay less for a disobedient slave. That amount would take almost all he had to spend. He'd been hoping to purchase two slaves.

"That's my price. She's young and look at those hips . . . wide . . . made to have a passel of picaninnies. Valuable stock, she is and has a goodly caboose too, probably keep you warm and satisfied many a cold winter night to come. Shoot, appealin' as she is, I was tempted to try her out myself."

Harvey watched closely for Bo's reaction.

Bo kept his face emotionless. "Nine hundred fifty then is agreed."

Harvey slapped his back. "Good enough, glad to get this troublesome one off my hands. Joe, help get this ornery critter outta here and onto his wagon."

Bo handed Joe the two blankets he was carrying. Joe covered the woman even before unlocking her shackles. Bo observed all the women, sorry he couldn't buy every one of them. He dropped his head, not wanting his eyes to meet their pleading faces.

"Now look here, boy, you already see she's hardheaded, so no bringin' her back complainin'." Harvey snorted as he lit his pipe. "It's a deal that won't be bartered away for no reason, ya hear?"

"Yes, sir."

Aaron Philpot stepped up. "That's too much money, Bo. He's cheating you."

Harvey puffed smoke in Philpot's face and growled. "Shut up and mind your own business."

"Nine hundred fifty dollars in these parts for a hard-to-tame slave is robbery and you know it," Philpot insisted.

"Listen up you treacherous blabbermouth good doer, it's what I'm chargin' and what he's payin'. So git outta here causin' trouble!"

"I'm satisfied, Mister Philpot. It's as it should be." Bo took hold of part of the limp, wrapped body Joe was carrying down the steps.

One

Southampton County, Virginia

The autumn sun was just starting to warm up the late morning air when Bo pulled his wagon up to the front of the farmhouse. He was glad to be home after the three days away. Coral and Naomi were heading toward his house with baskets full of vegetables. They stopped, anxious to see the newest member of their little community.

"Good morning, ladies." Bo greeted them, tipping his hat before getting down from the wagon. "Where's Ike?"

"Out yonda killing me a fat hen for supper. We was just bringin' some fresh-picked turnip greens to ya house," Naomi answered cheerfully. She leaned back smiling, putting one hand on her chubby hip. "I was gonna surprise you with some dumplins but you got back too fast, a whole day early. You always gone four days to dem slave auctions. What happened?"

"I finished early before the auction really started. So I

started home right away." Bo looked back at the buckboard. "I could use a little help." The slave woman stirred in the blankets and straw bed made to keep her as comfortable as possible. Her moans were soft, indicating she was in some pain.

Coral ran to the wagon wide-eyed. "Lawd have mercy, what you done gone en done, Bo? She looks all battered up. You do dis ta her?" Naomi came up behind Coral to peek.

"You know good and well I wouldn't do such a thing to a woman. It was Harvey Price's doing. He was so mad he would have killed her. That's why I bought her. He was going to whip her something fierce if I hadn't. The Lord had me get her out of there as fast as I could."

Coral frowned. "We gotta get her to bed. Looks like she was run over by a wagon 'stead a toted here in one."

The women set their baskets on the porch and helped get the wobbly moaning slave into the house. The confused newcomer struggled as they tried to console her.

"We ain't gonna hurt ya, chile. We's trying to help ya." Naomi spoke gently, settling her on the bed.

"I think there're some clothes left in here she can wear." Coral rummaged through drawers in the shabby wooden chest.

"I think a good hot bath would help," Naomi added sympathetically.

Bo nodded. "I'll get Johnny Boy and Ned to fill up the tub."

"Get some Epsom salts too. From the looks of her she'll need it. What's her name?" Coral asked.

"The paper says Ruth." The slave woman opened her eyes at the sound of her name.

"Is that your name, honey, you's called Ruth?" Naomi smiled at her. The woman closed her eyes without speaking.

"That's a nice name," Bo said.

"How old is she?" Naomi wanted to know.

"Paper says born twenty years ago."

"You didn't ask her?"

He shook his head. "She wouldn't talk to me. Hasn't spoken to me the whole way here. I tried to fix her up but she wouldn't let me touch her either. Best I could do was cover her in more blankets when she was sleeping. Maybe her jaw's so swollen she can't say anything. I'll get water brought in, then I'm going to Branche's to get some supplies. You tell me what she needs before I leave. Tend to her for me, please. She might take to womenfolk better." He left the room.

Naomi admired Ruth. "She sure is fetchin' ain't she, Coral? Look at those pretty eyes. You ever seen such mysterious-looking eyes like dem before?"

"Yeah, she's kinda odd lookin', but real pretty. I s'pect she look even prettier when de swellin' goes down."

"She'll be a real beauty once she gits de blood off her an fixed up an healed. Dat mean ole Harvey musta hit her somethin' awful, an in de face, too. God's gonna deal wit dat man in glory. He's evil as a snake," Naomi said. "She's still real fetchin', you kin tell. Wonder if Bo sees what we sees?"

"Oh, he sees all right. He's a man, ain't he?"

"He only got one slave dis time; wonder why?"

"Got a feelin' dis here gal be a handful fo him, so one is enuff."

Bo's mind was filled with thoughts of the slave woman all the way to Branche's Mercantile Emporium. To him she was breathtakingly beautiful beyond any woman he'd seen since his wife. He had so many questions about this proud and pretty slave named Ruth. The ownership paper gave only a sketchy history. Ruth Leese was born west in the Blue Ridge

14

Highlands of Virginia. At birth she was owned by Henry Leese, who sold her at age thirteen to Edward Stanley for breeding stock. Stanley sold her to Jock Price in Kings County, Harvey's equally obnoxious slave-dealing brother. The large Stanley Plantation was known for its vast number of slaves.

Bo wondered why Mister Stanley had sold Ruth. *Most likely cause she's willful.* Bo knew full well Harvey wasn't put off by insolent behavior. A heartless and intrinsically cruel man, Harvey eagerly broke down hard-to-handle slaves, and he would have broken Ruth or killed her trying. He didn't care about damaging the merchandise as some dealers did. He was determined to show any slave who challenged him who was in control. Bo shuddered to think what the poor woman would have had to endure if Harvey had exacted his brand of punishment on her.

"Is that why You told me to buy her right away, Lord?" he asked out loud. The affirmative answer came quickly to his spirit. Pulling his wagon to the rear, the only entrance nonwhites were allowed, Bo noticed more wagons and horses than usual. A cluster of slaves huddled outside the store next to the apple brandy barrels. He knew Rooster Slocum was somewhere in the crowd when he saw the fine-looking carriage belonging to his owner, Seymour Slocum. As he approached the men, the circle opened. Rooster stepped from the center. "Afternoon, Bo, ya come jes in time."

"In time for what?"

"To hear 'bout the goins on at the meetin' house two Sundays from now."

"What goings on?"

"There's gonna be a prophet talkin'. Name's Nat Turner."

"I hear he's a mighty man a God," Sammy added.

15

"Why's he coming here?" Bo asked, unimpressed by the accolade.

"Don't know, but Buck says he's got somthin' awful 'portant ta tell all us slaves and free Negroes in these parts. So be sure ya git there."

"Don't I always come to worship the Lord?"

"Ya do," Rooster replied dryly. "But this ain't bout worshiping no Jesus. This here bout us an' our living here and now."

"What he gotta tell us we don' already know?" Luke asked, scratching his thick raggedy beard.

Rooster pondered before answering. "Don't know exactly but whatever it is must be mighty 'portant 'cause my cousin Booney sneaked over to Mistah Connelly's all the way from Calhoun's place at night to give us the news. He's comin' wit dis here Turner fella to tell us. The prophet comes from the Moore farm."

"Do Preacher know?" Cass, a short stocky brown-skinned slave asked.

"He should. Booney was goin' ta him afta he left us."

"What about Mistah Abernathy?"

"He's still in Tennessee visiting his wife's sick kinfolk, an' a good thing. I don't think this prophet wants no white folks at de meetin."

"Good thing he ain't here; he always snoopin' round askin questions bout what we's doing," Cass grumbled.

"He don't mean no harm, I don't reckon. He always been good to us slaves, ain't he?" Sammy said.

"Yeah, him and his abolition talk and friendly ways mean well but he's liable ta git us all strung up while tryin' to free us." Cass and a few of the men chuckled.

John Moore asked, "What if Rebin' Purdy and Miss Polly come?"

"Booney knows what ta do in dat case."

"All this secrecy sounds mighty peculiar," Bo observed, scratching his head. "What difference does it make if Reverend Purdy and his wife come to Sunday meeting? They always come when they want and we always welcome them. We wouldn't have a meeting place if it wasn't for Purdy."

"This is different," Rooster snapped.

"Different how?"

"Just wait en see."

"De meetin' house is on Purdy's land. We can't stop em if they wanna come," Cass added.

"We won't. We jes wait till dey leave."

"Wait fo' what?" Cass wanted to know.

"Stop askin' so many fool questions. Jes be der dat Sunday and fin' out . . . all of you. And don't say a word ta nobody bout dis exceptin' us. No word a dis can leak out to de white folks."

"What about John Lightfoot and Harry Deer Runner?" Dudley Cramer asked.

"No Injuns either; nobody but us. Maybe later we tell dem but not now. Don't know if we kin trust 'em."

Bo spoke up. "I trust John Lightfoot."

"You trust everybody," Rooster replied, frowning. "Dat's yo' problem. Ya too dang trustin' and too easy on white folks. Too holy for your own good and too easy swayed."

"Swayed how?"

"Never mind, jes keep dis to yo'self. Cause if ya don't . . . and dis goes for all a ya . . . it could mean mo' den a whippin'. It could be de hangin' tree."

Two

She sleepin'," Naomi whispered when Bo walked
into the farmhouse. "It was the devil gettin' her ta
see we ain't goin' hurt her. She a feisty little somethin' an'
strong as a bull. Coral almost got the musket."

"What?"

"Afta we wash her, she gets dressed, den grabs the big
knife and was fixin' to run away. I s'pose she'd stuck us if we
tried ta stop her."

"How did you quiet her down—take the knife?"

"We jes pray."

"She prayed with you?"

"No we pray fo' her . . . and fo' us. She a stubborn one, dat
gal, and mean. She thought we was touched when we start
callin' on Jesus ta hep. Afta we pray, she settle down some an'
we tol her we want ta hep her and how blessed she is ya
bought her. How kind ya is and how ya did it to keep her from
bein' beat ta death by dat no 'count Harvey."

"Did she talk to you?"

"Pawshal."

"What did she say?"

"She wanna leave here and be free. I think she mean it."

"I'm sure she does."

"What you gonna do wit her?"

"Same as with the others, I reckon."

"You's givin' her her freedom?"

"Yep, after she works awhile for me buying her freedom, she can do what she wants."

"What work she gonna do round here?"

"I don't know yet."

"She ain't no field-worker, I tell you dat. Her hands barely calloused."

"You're right, I don't think she did much fieldwork." Bo sat down on the bench by the door.

"What work she do befo'?"

He didn't want to talk about it. "She did other things."

"She a house slave?"

"Yeah, in a way."

"In what way?"

He breathed hard reluctant to answer. "She was a breeder and worked in the house too."

Naomi's eyebrows lifted. "Was she now?" Her lips turned up into a smile. "So what now?" she asked.

"She can keep house, cook, wash clothes, and tend the gardens," Bo pointed out.

Naomi snickered. "Thank the Lawd cause ya sho needn' some hep round dis place. Since Minnie married Tote and went up noth ta Pennsylvania wit dem Quakers, yo house a regular wreck."

"Yeah, I guess it is messy."

"Dustier den a barn round here and a right toe up mess. I

19

had ta clean 'fo I could cook a proper meal. Do you ever wash yo eatin' bowls?"

"If I'm not too tired from working all day, I do."

"What you be needn is a wife, Bo Peace. I was telling Ephraim jes yesterday. Ephraim, I says, Bo need him a wife real bad."

"I know, Naomi. You've told *me* the same thing over and over."

"Well, why ain't ya got one yet? Been years since Baby Gal passed on. How long you gonna grieve? Lawd, boy, you got ta get on wit livin'. Baby Gal wouldn't want you grievin' all this time for her. She loved ya and she want you ta fine somebody else to be ya wife."

Bo sighed. "Yes, Naomi, I know."

"It be bes fo' ya to hurry while you's still a fit man."

"Yes, ma'am."

"She remind you of Baby Gal a bit?"

"You think so?"

"Uh-huh. She real pretty jes like Baby Gal." Satisfied with her meddling and hoping she'd planted an idea in Bo's mind, Naomi changed the subject. "Ya bring de goods like I ask?"

"On the wagon with the candles and sugar you wanted. I got those licorice whips you love so much too. Johnny Boy's taking you home in the wagon with your load when you're ready to go."

Naomi grinned. "You's such a good man, Bo, a real thoughtful fella."

"There's a price for my goodness this time," Bo suggested with a smile.

"What price?"

"Promise me you'll look out for this one. I think she'll

need a lot of help and somebody to look after her. You know, another woman nearby."

"Das all?"

"That's it."

"Why da special interes' in dis one?"

"I don't know, but if she needs anything, you see that she gets it and I'll make it worth your trouble."

Naomi looked at Bo curiously then put her index finger to her mouth. "If ya ask me, she be needin' a friend mo' 'en anythang."

He knocked on the door lightly. *Ruth has been asleep for hours,* he thought. There was no answer. He cracked the door open to find her sitting in the chair looking out the window by the bed.

"Good, you're awake," he said in as friendly a tone as he could muster.

She looked at him but didn't answer. Bo looked deep into her cold eyes framed by her blank expression. The eyes were big, slanted, heavily fringed with long, slightly curled lashes. They were a clear light brown, the color of Mister Maitland's fine European whiskey. They reminded him of Baby Gal's eyes so much . . . too much. Her light-toned reddish brown skin was flawless except for the bruises Harvey's blows had inflicted. Dark wavy hair was plaited in two braids and hung down below her shoulders. Her features were delicate and regal, even with her rigid posture. She was breathtaking to look at . . . breathtaking and heartbreaking.

"Naomi made some chicken and dumplings and turnip greens with corn bread. She's a good cook. You haven't had anything since you got here, she said. You hungry?"

She gazed at him without responding.

21

"If your sore jaw's able to chew, come sit and eat supper if you want." He closed the door.

Later it surprised Bo to see her standing in the doorway watching him eat, wearing Baby Gal's best muslin blouse and skirt. A pang of memory stabbed his heart at the sight of the clothes. She was a little taller and thicker than Baby Gal in most places, smaller in the waist but wider around the hips. Trying not to stare, he kept his attention on his bowl, eating heartily and enjoying the tasty meal Naomi had prepared. Ruth stared at him stone-faced and silent. The food's aroma had beckoned her out of the room.

Bo finally stood up. "Ruth; isn't that your name?"

She nodded.

"Sit down, I'll fix you a bowl."

"I kin get my own," she answered softly. "You keep eatin '."

"No, you're still weak. Sit down so you can get your strength back. I'll help you."

Puzzled, she sat in the chair across from his.

"You like chicken and dumplings?" he asked, attempting to make small talk. She nodded again. He was thankful she responded at all. He took a bowl and started spooning food in it.

"Chicken and dumplings are one of my favorite meals, and Naomi's is about the best I ever ate. Her turnips are good too. You're in for some good eating."

He set the bowl in front of her and took his seat again. He noticed her wince a few times at the first mouthfuls and then started hungrily, devouring the food without saying grace.

Ruth watched Bo closely when she thought he wasn't looking at her. "Is there something you want to say to me?" he asked, after catching her snatch her gaze away several times.

"You's a free man?"

22

"I am."

"Dis here yo place?"

"It is."

"Ya rich?"

"Not at all, just blessed of the Lord."

"White folks let ya have all dis and buys slaves?"

"There are some free black men around here. A few of us have a little property. We exist, but there aren't many of us. As far as buying slaves go, all Harvey cares about is money. His greed for money doesn't worry about who's spending it as long as it gets in his pockets. Some slave dealers won't sell to Negroes or Indians but he doesn't care who he sells to if they have money."

Ruth narrowed her eyes. "How ya do dis ta ya own kin? It ain't right."

"I buy my people to set them free as much as I can. That's what God has blessed me to do."

"God . . . you baleeve in da white man's God?"

"I believe in our heavenly Father, yes. I believe Christ Jesus is the Son of God, my Savior, and I believe in the Holy Spirit."

"I don't," Ruth announced before shoving a dumpling in her mouth.

"Why not?"

"Why should I? All dat talk 'bout a God; ain't nobody saved me or da rest a our kind from workin' from sunup to sundown for nothin' but da lash'. I run away twice and was drug back both times. Whas God doin' to save me or da rest a us?"

"God will move in His time. I know He will, and then all our people will be free."

Ruth stopped and looked at Bo like she pitied him, then

23

shrugged. "Guess if I had all dis and was free, I'd figure like you."

"I wasn't always free. I was a slave until ten years ago."

"How ya get free?"

"My master died and said for all of us to be freed. His sons honored their father's wishes."

"So I's free now too since ya bought me? Das what dey tol me."

"Yes, you are. All I ask is that you work off the cost I paid for you, and then you can leave with my blessing and any help I can offer."

"Fair enuff, I reckon."

"I think you'll do well keeping house, cooking, and cleaning. I have several small gardens you can tend to. That will keep your days full."

"Where I live?"

"We'll build you a small place close to the gardens. Until then you can stay with one of the other unmarried ladies."

She stuck out her lower lip. "You plan on havin' your way wit me and breedin' me? Cause if ya is, you's wastin' ya time. I ain't fit for breedin' no mo'."

"Didn't Harvey say . . .?"

"That snake lied through his teeth. He knows I ain't breedin' no mo'. His brother told him and Carter did too."

"Who's Carter?"

"Massah Stanley overseea." She looked at Bo's inquisitive expression. "I run away fo' I was full wit chile so nobody knowed but me I was carryin'. That slave catcher and Carter caught me and I fought em hard. Dey beat me bad. Later when I was givin' birth somethin' was wrong. My baby died and I almost did too."

"I'm sorry your baby died."

Ruth looked at him, her beautiful hollow eyes boring into his. She straightened her back. "I ain't sorry; better off dead den livin' a slave. Better off never bein' born. Das why I run away. I hate havin' mo' babies born to be property like I is. Wish I never been born."

Her sad words and the feelings that accompanied them were all too familiar to Bo, painfully familiar. "Why did Stanley sell you?"

"Cause I ain't never have no mo' babies since I run away. Massah Stanley sold me off sayin' I ain't no breedin' use to him no mo'. He got him a new breedin' gal to take my place. I's pawt of de trade."

Bo was angry. "Harvey Price is a low-down, lying skunk." He caught himself and stopped.

"So you ain't want me fo breedin'?"

"No, not at all, I detest such things. Chickens, horses, and cows are to be bred, not human beings."

"So you ain't mad I ain't fit?"

"Of course not; why should it matter to me?"

Distrust crept across her face. "Then you musta just got me for ya own."

Bo's frustrated sigh was heavy. He put his fork down. "Ruth, I want you to understand something. God has set you free from a life of uncompensated servitude and abuse to your body and soul. I will never use you in that way . . . never."

"Dat what Massah Stanley say, but ain't stop his sons from havin' me fo dey own when dey wanted or dat rotten overseea."

The thought sickened Bo. "I promise I will never misuse you. I'd have to answer to God for treating you like an animal or dishonoring your womanhood. I know it's hard for you to believe, but I want to help you, not hurt you. Help you get used to being free and help you feel like a lady in spite of all the mistreatment."

"You sho talk like one of dem high-acting white men. You had schoolin'?"

"I was taught by Mister Maitland's wife. She was a fine strong-willed lady, a schoolteacher before she married. She bravely taught her five children and me along with several other children of the house slaves all together in one room."

"You got it mighty fancy fo' a slave. Why you have it so good?"

"God's plan, I believe. My mother was a house slave for the Maitlands. My father was blacksmith and tended the horses. They're both dead now. Yellow fever took them in 1812 not long after the war started . . . took my two brothers and sister too. Killed my whole family . . . everybody but me for some reason. After they were gone Mister Maitland took special interest in me. I suppose because I didn't have any close family left. He was a devout Christian who wrestled with the ungodliness of owning slaves. Before he died, he realized without doubt it was wrong."

"He a preacha?"

"Not formerly, but he read Scriptures and taught the Bible to everyone on the plantation, including his slaves."

"You use a lot a dem fancy words. You can read, huh?"

"Yes. Would you like to learn?"

Her eye perked up. "You teach me readin'?"

"I've taught others. Why not you?" He got up with his empty bowl and put it in the pan on an oblong table. Ruth's countenance seemed more relaxed. He glanced back. "I think if I'm going to teach you to read, you'll need a Good Book of your own."

Ruth looked up at him and nodded. "Whatever ya say, Massah."

"Don't call me that!" he snapped.

She jumped, startled. "Well you is. Ain't you's my massah since ya paid fo me?"

He closed his eyes and breathed out. "I paid to set you free, not to be your master. Just like Jesus paid to set you free."

She rolled her eyes. "What Jesus pay wit? And if He did, why ain't I's free befo' now?"

"Christ Jesus paid with His life. You can be as free as you want if you believe that and confess Him as your Savior and Lord of your life."

"I knowd plenty a folks say dey baleeve but dey still slaves."

"You can be free in Christ even when you're a slave. Free from the wages of sin, free from eternal damnation, free in your mind and heart."

"Hogwash. I's wanna be free in my body. Free ta come en go as I please. Free ta live like a human stead a animal." Ruth rose with her empty bowl, taking it to the pan. "I wash dose," she offered.

"You sure you feel up to it?"

"Gonna earn my keep an git my freedom. What do I call ya if not massah?"

"My name is Bodine. Folks call me Bo. Bo Boy Peace is what they used to call me when I was coming up."

"Bo Boy? Das a funny name."

"My father's name was Bodine Peace because his first master was Arthur Peace up in Maryland. Momma named me Bodine too and called me Bo. To make a difference in the names, they called me Bo Boy."

"Oh, I gets it. Where da bucket fo watta?"

"I'll get you some hot water. It's heating over in the fire-place. You wait here."

Ruth's hands went on her hips. "I ain't hepless, ya know. I can carry a kettle a watta."

"You took a lot of punching from Harvey. Aren't you aching?"

"So' and tenda in places but I's been battered mo den dis befo'."

The thought bothered Bo but he shook it off. He looked at her swollen nose, jaw, and eye and the two bruises on her face. The thought of the brutality incensed him. "I got some dry goods for you to make yourself a dress," he said, wishing that would be enough to offset the horror of the beating.

She looked down at the muslin skirt. "Who dese clothes was?"

He moved to the fireplace. "My wife's," he responded sadly.

"You got a wife?"

"She died four years ago."

"Dat why you took up wit dat ole woman?"

He was poking the wood embers. "Old woman?"

"Naomi, ain't she yo woman?"

"No, no." He chuckled and turned facing her. "Naomi and Ephraim belong to each other. They're married. You'll meet him soon enough."

"I's see she real taken wit you."

"Naomi thinks it's her lot in life to meddle in my affairs for some reason. She's a good woman who looks out for me, so I let her."

"She round here fussin' like a mother hen. I thought you and her . . . never mind."

"She's my wife's mother. We're kind of kin."

28

"Oh."

Bo lifted the boiling kettle from the hook and took it to the big pan with the wooden bowls. "Naomi thinks of me like her son. She had two boys who were sold away from her and she's never seen them since. Don't know where they are now. I think her heart grieves for them sometimes and she soothes it by staying close to me." Steam rose as he poured hot water into the pan. "Naomi and my wife were very close. She really misses her." His countenance displayed his sadness.

"You miss her much?"

"Very much."

"What her name was?"

He stepped back from the table, pulling the kettle away. "We called her Baby Gal but her given name was Nellie."

Ruth noticed his tenseness. "She pretty to look at?" she asked, adding cool water from the barrel next to the table into the pan.

"She was." He looked at the beauty standing before him. "She was beautiful beyond words." A far-off daze followed by silence made Ruth aware of the emotions he was feeling. Understanding he was bothered by her questions, she left well enough alone as she pondered this odd situation. Bo Peace was a peculiar master, a peculiar man indeed. He wasn't brutish like most men she was used to. He didn't look at her as others did; like she was a piece of meat and they were hungry wolves. He talked kindly to her and acted concerned. He said he was setting her free and wanted to help her. Could this be true? Was he what he claimed to be? Few men were, from what she'd experienced.

Three

The candlelight began to throw a luminous glow around Ruth when the fireplace light faded. Bo sat in his thatched chair trying to read the Bible and attempting to ignore the constant disturbance of her presence. The more he looked at her, the more he saw likenesses to his deceased wife. He couldn't concentrate for stealing glimpses that turned into gazes that became outright stares. Even bruised and swollen, she was enchanting.

Ruth sat on the bench, fussing over the material he'd given her to make a dress. She seemed oblivious of his watching her. He noticed her face scrunch up several times as she bent over the table twisting the cloth this way and that.

"I can get Naomi to help if you need it," he offered, watching her confused moves.

She looked over at him. "Dis here is some real fine cloth. I ain't never had no dress outta fine cloth like dis."

"It's just cotton."

"I ain't never made me no dress outta smooth cloth 'fo.

Missy had cloth like dis for her clothes but not us. We had burlap and sack frocks."

"Does it matter, the kind of cloth?"

"I reckon not, but don't wanna mess wit such fine goods."

"Don't worry, I'll get Naomi to come help you. You know, we need to decide where you're going to stay until your cabin is built."

Ruth looked around. "Cain't I stay here?"

"It wouldn't be proper for an unmarried lady to live in the house with an unmarried man."

She blinked. "I s'pose not . . ."

"Something wrong?"

Ruth sighed softly. "I ain't use ta bein' called no lady." Her gaze avoided his face for a minute. She was ashamed of her confession. "You readin'?" she asked, smiling to throw off her embarrassment.

Bo understood she was trying to feign happiness and be friendly. "Yes, I'm reading the Good Book. Would you like to hear some of it?"

Ruth chuckled. "Ya sho ain't much talkin' like any slave I ever knowed."

His body stiffened. "I told you I'm not a slave. I'm a free Negro."

"Ya say ya *was* a slave, but ya don't sound like ya ever was ta me. Ya sound like one a dem educated white folks."

"Does it bother you the way I speak?"

"Naw, it done bother me none but . . ."

"Go ahead, say what's on your mind."

"It makes me knows how truly ignant I is. Missy use ta call all us slaves in da house bone ignant creatures. I hated it when she do dat. Weren't our fault we ain't never had no schoolin'. They say we couldn't learn so what was we to do?

31

But dat ain't true causin' you learned and otha slaves I knowed learned ta read a little."

"Do you want to learn, Ruth?"

"Uh-huh."

"Then I'll teach you anything I can that you want to learn. You'll do better on your own if you can at least read some." He saw her frowning. "What's wrong now?"

"How's I gonna live on my own? How's I gonna survive?"

"Some of the slaves I've freed stayed here on the property and worked the land for shared profits . . . sharecropping. We're a village in our own right. It's what God meant for me to do with this blessing—to build a village of African men and women who love the Lord and live with dignity, being examples of God's freedom."

"So all yo' free slaves live here?"

"Some moved up north in hopes of better prospects. A few went to work for Mister Maitland's family for pay and a cabin. You can decide what you want to do when the time comes."

"How long fo' you set me free?"

"I don't set you free, Ruth, God does. You were legally free the moment I paid the price Harvey wanted. If you're willing to work off the cost for one year, that will be fair enough. If not, it doesn't matter; you can go whenever you like. I won't hold you. I'll ask George Maitland to get the free man's declaration ready. He's an attorney; he'll make sure it's good and legal."

"I need papers?"

"Yes, you do. If you're captured without that declaration saying you're free, they will put you back in chains and take you down to Georgia, Alabama, or Mississippi. That's where they take a lot of slaves from around here these days. Things are so poorly in this area they don't need so many anymore.

Harvey brags about shipping slaves from Norfolk to the Georgia turpentine plantations. That's a slow death sentence for any slave."

Her eyes narrowed into slits. "That no-good, low-down lizard. I hope somebody cuts his evil head off and . . ." She saw the disapproving glance Bo gave her and stopped.

"Let me tell you a story," he said quietly.

Bo closed his Bible when he finished reading. He had given Ruth the main details of the story and read parts of it from the Bible. She sat silent. "What do you think of the story about Joseph?" he asked, breaking her reflective quiet.

She paused before answering. "I never heard a such a thing. Ya own flesh 'n blood tries ta kill ya den sells ya off ta slavery. Dem brothers musta been some kinda mean. Den he wrongly accused of attackin' his massah's wife and throwed in prison. And end up in charge a everythin'. Hard ta baleeve."

"God can do the unbelievable. He can change the unjust things in this world anytime He wants."

"Den why ain't He free all us from slavery?"

"He will. I know He will."

"How long folks s'pose ta wait?"

"It was many years before Joseph's dream came true through his deliverance."

"I don't understand. We been bearin' dis load for a long time. If God is so merciful like folks say, He shoulda done somethin' long time ago."

"Our heavenly Father *is* merciful. I have no doubt of that. His timing is not like ours. A thousand of our years are but one day to Him."

"A thousan?"

"That's what the Bible says."

33

Ruth looked thoughtful for a moment. "Ya baleeve everythin' ya read in dat der Good Book?"

"I do."

"I think it's a lot of hogwash."

"So you've said. I hope you'll change your mind one day."

"Josiah at the plantation use ta say da Good Book ain't nothin' but a bunch a made-up stories ta make us slaves mine our massahs."

"Did this Josiah ever read the Bible?"

"He couldn't read but he refused ta listen ta any of it from Preacha Smith."

"Who was Preacher Smith?"

"He was a white man who use ta travel 'round and have church meetin' with the Indians and slaves. He read from da Bible and preach sermons on Jesus and how God is so all-powerful. Folks would be singin' and shoutin' and fallin' out. Made me sick. I went sometimes but I ain't like it. I just went to git away from Missy bossing me 'round fo a spell. Da white folks ain't come to Preacha Smith meetin'. They went to the big fancy Sunday meetin' house up on the hill wit Rebin' Snodgrass."

"Why didn't you like the sermons?"

"I ain't see why dey all cited 'bout some God who ain't studyin' 'em. Dey still slaves and dey shoutin' 'bout it like fools."

"They weren't shouting about being slaves. They were rejoicing in the goodness of the Lord. Praising God jubilantly."

"Why, dey still in slavery. What's ta shout 'bout?"

"Hope."

"Hope fo' what? Mo' hard work and whippins?"

"Hope for freedom. Hope in Christ for enough grace to endure slavery and for an eternal life as free men and women where no man will take a whip to them."

"Ya soun jes like Preacha Smith."

34

Four

Seven Years Earlier

Thirteen-year-old Ruth stood trembling behind her mother, tears trickling down her face. Etta was crying, pleading to Henry Leese between sobs. Henry, a portly balding man, stood firm and unaffected by the woman's tears and desperate wailing.

"Don't take my Sugar Babe from me!" Etta screamed, grabbing onto him and falling to her knees. "Oh, please, Massah, don't sell her off, Massah, please!"

"Now, Etta, stop all this nonsense. What's done is done."

"Not my girl, not my sweet Sugar Babe!"

Henry backed up from her grasp on his leg. "If you don't stop all this, Etta, I'm going to have Joe take the whip to you."

His wife, Selma, stood on the porch dabbing her tearing eyes. "Oh, Henry, how could you? How cruel to do that to my Etta."

"Selma, you stay out of this! Don't you go getting all weepy on me. This is business, and it's not up for debate!"

Selma stomped her foot. "Why, Henry Leese, you're a beast, an absolute beast!"

He pointed his cane at her angrily. "Get in the house or shut your mouth, woman! This don't concern you, so keep quiet!"

Selma covered her face with her handkerchief, murmuring softly to smother her sobs. "You awful beast."

He had no pity in his heart, only impatience toward what he deemed female emotionalism. "Now you calm down, Etta, I mean it. I won't tolerate much more of this."

Ruth's eyes were stretched in fear. "Momma, don't cry no mo'." She bent down and helped her mother to her feet. "Don't cry, Momma, I's be awright at da new place. Please stop cryin'. I gonna go wit no fuss. Iss awright, don't carry on so Massah get the whip put on ya. Stop cryin', Momma." Ruth helped her mother up.

"Listen to the girl, Etta, she's smart," Henry said, patting Ruth's shoulder.

Etta whirled around hollering, "Ya promised! Ya said ya weren't never gonna split my Sugar Babe and me! Afta ya stole my boys from me ya swore ya wouldn't do dat wit her!"

Selma stepped off the porch, glowering at her husband.

Henry cleared his throat. "I know I said that once, but things aren't so profitable as they once were. I have to run this place as I see fit." He moved next to his wife, whispering, "I'm getting more than top dollar for this gal to breed with Stanley's prize buck, Jasper. She'll make fine strapping children for Stanley."

Etta overheard what he said to Selma and desperately grabbed hold of his arm. "No! Ya can't do dat, not ta my baby! Not dat!"

Henry snatched his arm away. "Now get hold of yourself,

Etta, and get on back in the house. I'm warning you." He looked over at the silent man sitting on top of the wagon. "Deacon, take Sugar Babe to Stanley's now," he ordered then looked at Ruth. "Kiss your momma good-bye, gal, and get on the wagon."

"Yes, Massah."

"Oh, Lawd, don't take my baby!" Etta pleaded, grabbing hold of Ruth. Ruth fought back her emotions with all her might. She could have fallen down under the weight of her fear and sadness, but she defiantly stood tall and held herself together. She kissed her mother and pulled away quickly, climbing into the wagon next to the old gray-haired slave.

Ruth looked back worried at her mother's loud lamenting sorrow. "Ya won't whip Momma, will ya, Massah?" she asked.

Henry sighed dismissively. "No, I'll let her cry herself out," he said, shaking his head. "You just mind Mister Stanley like you have me, you hear? He's your master now."

Ruth nodded, trying to push down the lump in her throat and not cry anymore. She was afraid her mother would get more upset and get the whip. Selma took hold of Etta but the distraught mother collapsed to the ground out of her mistress's arms. Deacon started the horses. Etta screamed like she was on fire. "Sugar Babe, oh Lawd, my Sugar Babe! Don't take my Sugar Babe from me!"

"I's gonna obey Massah Stanley, sir, just don't whip my momma," Ruth called out as they rolled away. She stared at her mother on the ground by Miss Selma's feet, crying her heart out. It was a scene the slave girl called Sugar Babe but named Ruth would never forget or ever get over.

The Stanley plantation was twenty times the size of Henry Leese's farm. It was the biggest in the valley; bigger even than the Indian village in the mountains. The ride was long. Ruth broke down and cried after they were some distance from the farm. She cried off and on most of the way, although Deacon tried to pacify her. It was deep dusk when they arrived at the plantation. The slaves were slowly migrating out of the fields. "I's never seen so many slaves in one place, Deacon. This Massah Stanley, he real rich, ain't he?"

"Richest in de county."

"Wit all dese slaves what he need me fo?"

Deacon looked at Ruth with profound sadness. Then he forced a smile. "He ain't got nair a slave as pretty as you, Sugar Babe. Massah tol' me dat Mistah Stanley saw ya years ago when ya was just a little un. He said he ain't never seed no prettier picaninnie in all his life. Shucks, Massah says you's about the prettiest gal in all de valley, colored or white."

Ruth folded her arms across her chest. "I wish I wasn't pretty. Then I could stay wit my momma."

They were approaching a grand house on the hill. "Ya a woman now, Sugar Babe. Time to act like it. Ya ain't no little girl no mo'. You's a fully growd woman as of right now, so member dat."

Ruth stared; the tears she could no longer hold back rolled down her face. "I don't wanna be no growd woman. I wan my momma."

"Ya want ya momma whipped?"

"Naw."

"Then ya do jes like dese here folk say or dey'll complain to Massah Henry and he'll whip ya momma. Ya hear?"

"Yessah."

Ruth was entrusted to Gabby, the head of household slaves on the Stanley plantation.

Gabby was one generation from West Africa and had wonderful stories to tell about her home. She wore lovely store-bought dresses that her mistress no longer wanted. She talked kindly to Ruth on her first day and gave her a bath and found a shapeless frock for her to wear. Gabby told Ruth she would be Miss Molly's personal slave, and that she'd be learning household tasks also. Molly was Edward Stanley's spoiled thirteen-year-old daughter.

When evening of the second day arrived, Ruth was taken out of the house to the stables. A mean-spirited man named Carter hurried her along. "I's gonna sleep out here tonight?" She was confused.

"That's right."

"By myself? Where Gabby?"

"Where she belongs, in the big house."

"What 'bout Miss Molly?"

"Miss Molly will be fine without you for a night, but don't worry, you won't be by yourself." They entered the barn and walked to a stall with a high pile of hay. Ruth pulled back. Crouched in the corner was a big ugly beast of a man. He leered at her, showing only a few rotting teeth in his mouth. She was terrified. "Go on in, honey, and meet your new friend, Jasper." Carter grinned, pushing her inside the stall.

"I want Gabby! Take me back ta Gabby! I s'pose ta be fo Miss Molly!" she screamed, horrified.

"Git in there! You be with Miss Molly and Gabby tomorrow. You're staying with Jasper till morning. He's gonna make a woman outta yah," Carter told her with a lecherous sneer.

"I don't wanna be no woman!" Ruth started crying.

Jasper moved up closer to her. "I declare, she every bit pretty as Massah say she is. I ain't never had no fine lookin' lass like dis one." He grinned and pulled Ruth to him.

"Get away!" she yelled flailing her arms and trying to kick at him.

"Ya better stop now, gal," Jasper warned her, scoffing. "Ya don't wanna git me riled up now, do ya?"

"Don't touch me!" Ruth kicked him hard in his shin. Carter chuckled. Jasper grabbed at her, still laughing. Ruth smacked his hands away and tried to scramble from his grasp. "You better be nice to ole Jasper, gal, or der be the whip for ya," Carter threatened, snorting back a laugh.

Ruth froze. Remembering Deacon's warning about her mother, she squeezed her eyes shut tight as Jasper's smelly sweaty body enfolded her.

"Enjoy your night, Jasper." Carter left the barn, chuckling.

Jasper was a big man, strong and muscular. His dark brown skin was covered in scars. His nose had been broken and was oddly crooked. She pounded on his chest to ward off the dreadful assault but it didn't faze him. He was too strong. Ruth wailed for help repeatedly before finally realizing no one would come to save her. Exhausted, she could resist no further. Mercilessly pinned down, she closed her eyes and endured his forceful assault. "That's right, little girly, let ole Jasper do his work and make a woman outta ya." Even his hot smelly breath was disgusting. Her cries of pain fell on deaf ears because Jasper never ceased his frenzied pursuit of pleasure.

When it was over she crawled into the corner. Whimpering, hurt, and humiliated, she tried to cover the blood. She was full of loathing she could do nothing about. She hated Jasper; she hated Mister Stanley and Mister Leese for selling her. She hated Carter, but more than anything, she hated life as a slave.

"What's your name, girly?" Jasper asked.

"Ruth," she answered, sniffling.

By morning she had endured two more episodes of Jasper's forced invasion on her body. Ruth was mentally, physically, and spiritually shattered. She felt weak, torn apart, and dirty. His touch haunted her mind, making her skin crawl. He lay sleeping in the hay snoring loudly while she huddled in the corner wondering if death would not be a better fate. Once Ruth looked up and noticed a pitchfork leaning against the wall some distance from the stall. A powerful desire rose up in her to exact revenge on the person who had hurt her. She wanted to kill Jasper for what he had done. Thoughts of what would happen to her mother if she did doused the urge. She felt utterly helpless. Is this why her momma had carried on so? Did she know the dreaded fate awaiting her daughter? So this is what it's like being a woman. She remembered Deacon's advice that she was no longer a girl but a woman from now on. *Dat animal Jasper killed Sugar Babe. I's a woman now. Der is no mor' Sugar Babe cause dat's what Momma and people who cared 'bout me called me. Nobody here care 'bout me. I be my birth name from now on. I Ruth cause Sugar Babe is dead.*

➤ ➤ ➤ ➤ ➤ ➤

Ruth slept fitfully, dreaming of the misery she experienced at the hands of Jasper. The vision was so vivid she cried out in her sleep, physically fending him off with her arms flinging and legs kicking. As she fought out her nightmare, her feet tangled in the blanket, causing her to fall on the floor. Stunned awake in confusion, she saw the candlelight coming toward the door. The door opened and a male silhouette stood in the doorway.

"What's happening?" Bo asked, staring down at Ruth on the floor. "Are you hurt?" He placed the candle on the chest and rushed to help her up.

"Don't touch me!" she yelled, kicking out at him.

"I'm trying to help you get off the floor. What's wrong with you?" He reached down and took her by her shoulders.

She struggled against him as he lifted her; slapping at him trying to run her nails along the side of his face. "Git way from me, ya dirty pig!" she screamed almost maniacally. "You ain't gittin' ya way wit me no mo'! I's kill ya first!"

"Ruth, it's me, Bo Peace. What is it?" He shook her hard enough to jar her senses. She stopped with a frozen glare then the empty eyes returned. "Ruth, you awake?"

"Bo Peace?"

"That's right, it's Bo. Who did you think I was?"

"Jasper," she whispered.

"Jasper?"

"I's dreamin'. I's sorry."

He took his hands off her shoulders. "I heard you screaming and then I heard a thump. I didn't know what was happening. Did you hurt yourself?"

Ruth straightened her sleeping gown at the neck self-consciously and walked away from Bo's inquiring gaze. "Naw, I ain't hurt'."

"Well, as long as you're not hurt . . ." He turned to pick up the candleholder from the chest by the door. "I'll say good night again."

"Good night."

"Do you want to tell me about it?"

She looked away. "Naw."

"Well, good night then." He closed the door behind him. Ruth sat on the edge of the lumpy bed. Tears rolling down her face. She wiped them with her hand. "I's free now. Free from nobody havin' me fo dey own no mo'. Free . . . free and dat mean from bein' used by you too, Bo Peace."

But he ain't forcin' hisself on me like the others? Why?

Five

Mara was pulling sweet potatoes when she spotted Naomi going across the field. She threw down the sack and took off running toward the creek through rows of tall corn to intercept her before she reached the big oak at the beginning of the trail. "Naomi! Naomi!" she shouted, running out of breath before she was visible.

Naomi turned, eventually seeing Mara coming out of the cornfield. "I declare, why ya in such a dither?"

"I called to stop you." Mara was panting, bent forward, hands on her knees.

"Ya all outta breath an fo' what?" Mara was still trying to breathe normally. "I's in a hurry, whatcha want?"

"I see you're carrying your sewing basket. You going to Bo's to do some mending?"

Naomi huffed impatiently. "What if I is?"

"I could go along to help with the mending and cleaning or anything he needed me to do."

"I ain't mendin'. I's helpin' make a dress fo de new slave

he bought en freed. She's doin' the tidyin' up round der now so he won't be needin' yo hep."

Mara's eyes widened. "She?"

"Yep, a woman."

"A little girl or a grown woman?"

Naomi grinned devilishly. "She ain't no youngun, dats fo sho. She fully growed an pretty as a picture." She chuckled at the expression on Mara's face. "Makes me tink of my sweet Baby Gal."

Mara's mouth puckered. "Humph, and just where is this full-grown *woman* staying?"

"None a yo' business, but Ruth be stayin' wit Mae till Bo builds her a cabin."

"Her name's Ruth?"

"Uh-huh, pretty name, ain't it? An I tell ya, she even prettier den her name. Gotta hurry, can't stand here chattin' wit ya all day long." Naomi walked away smiling.

Mara stirred the black kettle of lye soap more forcefully than necessary, exerting her anger as she muttered under her breath, thoughts of this Ruth woman roiling in her mind. She flipped a crinkly lock of sandy brown hair from her face. Jethro came up behind her. "Ya gonna knock dat kettle over if ya don't ease up." He chuckled.

"Go away and leave me be!" she snapped.

"What bee got under yo' bonnet?"

"Never you mind."

Jethro pouted. "Oughtn't talk so mean fo' no reason."

Lisbeth Polk, a gray-haired, dark-skinned woman, was walking toward them carrying an empty bucket. "Jethro, why ain't ya gettin Moe dat water he ask fo?" she hollered before she even reached him.

"I's goin', just talkin' ta Mara a spell."

Lisbeth waved her free arm. "Ya always talkin' ta Mara. Mara got work ta do and so does you. Get goin' with dat water." Jethro grumbled some unflattering adjectives about Lisbeth and moved on. Lisbeth wiped her forehead and stared at Mara. When she plunked the bucket on the ground, Mara ignored her. "You oughtta put dat man outta his misery en jump de broom wit him. He 'bout ta split in two over ya."

"Let him." Mara stirred harder.

"That's mighty ugly. Why ya don' wanna couple up wit Jethro? He's a good man."

"I just don't, that's all."

Lisbeth's eyes bore into Mara. "I knows why. Don't tink I don' know what ya up ta. You pining over Bo, ain't cha?" Mara kept working without responding. "You tink he's gonna git lonely nuff one day en come git ya and whisk ya off ta his farmhouse." Lisbeth swung around to the other side of Mara, facing her directly. "You'd let po' Jethro slip on by, waitin' fo somethin' ain't never gonna happen. Bo don't want ya, chile, when ya gonna see dat?"

Mara stopped stirring and looked furiously at Lisbeth. "Old woman, you better get from out of my face. How would you know what Bo wants? You don't know what you're talking about. Always up in folks' business instead of minding your own. You're nothing but an old black busybody! You don't know about me or what I want, and you sure don't know what Bo Peace wants! So get on away from me and leave me be!"

"Humph, I knows Bo don want yo' snooty light-skin tail. I knows dat." Lisbeth stuck out her tongue, picked up her bucket, and sauntered away.

Naomi brushed Ruth's hair gingerly. "I use ta take such pleasure in brushin' my Baby Gal's hair like dis but hers wasn't as straight en long." She peeked over Ruth's shoulder, watching her stitch the seam as carefully as she could. "You's doin' just fine. Ain't no different than that old tough burlap or muslin we's use to fixin'."

"I only has one sto' bought dress in my life. Missy Molly gave me a dress she outgrowed but it were too tight. I could hardly breathe in dat thing."

"Dis gonna look so pretty on ya. The color goes wit dose purty brown eyes. How ya hair git so long en purty and yo eyes so light?"

"Momma was born in de mountains with de Sioux Injuns. Her folks be Sioux slaves. She was African and Monacan. When de Sioux moved west, she were sold to Massah Leese. Dey don't genly sell off der slaves but times were so hard dey couldn't feed 'em. Momma said my poppa was kin ta Massah Leese. Dey was brothers by Massah Leese's poppa. Massah Leese git the farm from his family when ole Massah Leese die. I never seen ole Massah Leese causin he was dead fo' I was born. Them Leeses come from somewhere called Scotland. So I's all mixed up, I reckon."

"Sho looks pretty on ya. Ain't no shame in being mixed up, since we's all got mixed up wit dem white men having der way whenever dey want. Hardly a pure African left ceptin' when dey first come off de boat. By the next generation or two we's sho nuff washed down with some white blood in us." Naomi noticed Ruth's body tense. "Bo got a spinning wheel and rack in de barn. It was Baby Gal's. She sho could spin up a purty piece of cloth if I say so myself. I get him to bring it in here and you can make your own cloth. Plenty a cotton over in the north field ta use. Ya know how ta pick cotton en spin?"

"I saw it done befo' but I ain't never did it myself."

"Nothin' to it; I'll show ya how."

"Naomi, do you know this woman Mae I's gotta live wit?"

"Sho, Mae's a real nice person. You'll like her."

"Why I can't stay wit you?"

"We's had too many folks staying wit us. So Ephraim put his foot down and say no mo'. When Ephraim done made up his mind, no amount a beggin's gonna change it. The man's bullheaded as they come. Say he likes us being alone fo' a change."

"Ya like havin' a husband?"

"Sho do."

"He good to ya?"

"Real good."

"Ya love him?"

"Course I do. Me and him jumped the broom a long time ago."

"What it be like?"

"What what be like?" Naomi was pulling Ruth's dark wavy hair together, tying it with a ribbon to put up in a fancy style as she used to do with her daughter's hair.

"Lovin' a man?"

Naomi stopped, looked down at Ruth, and looked out the window. "It hard ta say really. Different fo' different folks. Some fall crazy in love and knows dey gotta be together right away or dey can't stan it. For others it come slow, dey take a little time and get ta see if dey really likes a body. Den ders folks like Ephraim and me. Liked each other good nuff so we jump de broom and den grows closer mo' and mo' as time passes. You's young; don't ya worry, it gonna happen."

47

"I don' wan it ta happen."

"You don't?"

"I wanna be free, and belongin' to any man ain't being free. Don't wanna jump no broom either. Ya just tradin' one massah fo' another."

"Dat's a pity cause ya miss all of what God wans for His chillun not havin' a man a yo' own."

"I don't care 'bout what God wans. I wan my freedom."

"You's got it now, honey. You's free as any colored gal gonna git in dis man's world."

"Am I? I gots ta carry round some paper sayin' I free or dey puts me back in chains. Some slave catchers don' care bout no paper. Dey takes free folks and make 'em slaves again. How dat bein' free?"

"Things ain't all time gonna be like dis."

"Now ya sound like Bo."

"Bo's real close to the Lawd, ya know."

Ruth looked out the window. Not far from the house, she could see the horse and cart and Bo digging up white potatoes. It was an unusually warm, early September day. Bo's muscular arms were glistening with sweat. *He handles the hoe like a weapon, like a warrior,* she thought, with his big manly figure bending over, striking at the dirt first, then pulling up potatoes out of the ground. His kinky black hair shone in the afternoon sun. She thought about Bo's eyes; dark, deep, and expressive, set in a face that was rugged with a strong chin; and yet he was gentle. Ruth looked long and hard at her liberator; a man like none she'd ever known. Stirrings she couldn't identify made her finally look away.

Naomi watched with interest. "I say lovin' a man is one of de sweetest feelins der is fo any woman."

"What do it feel like?" Ruth asked in an almost inaudible whisper.

Naomi got a dreamy look on her face. "Well, like everythin's right with dis world even when ya knows it ain't."

"My momma said she loved my poppa, but he ran away and they caught and killed him."

"I reckon it near broke yo momma's heart."

"S'pose so, but I don't see why. He was runnin' ta freedom en left her behind . . . en me too."

"It were fer ya own good, chile. Hard goin' through dem woods en swamps. He had mo' a chance by hisself."

"Dat's what Momma say but I don't see how he leave his kin in slavery and go livin' free in peace."

"Maybe he come back fo' y'all."

"That's what Momma say too, but I don' believe it. If he gits to freedom and he come back, they a hung him jes like dey did Jud. Dey hung po' Jud from dat big ole cypress so's we could all see. Left him der ta rot fo days to warn de res a us what happen if we run away."

"Lawd, have mercy, I knows what that like when a runaway gits caught. Enuff ta tear a body's heart out dey chest how dey do them po' folks fo' just wantin' ta be free."

"Sometimes I think better ta be dead den live a slave."

Naomi looked at Ruth sorrowfully. "I knows, chile. I feel dat way myself but de Lawd give me strength to carry on."

Ruth made sure Naomi didn't see her roll her eyes. The Lord, again; she didn't want to hear about the Lord. "Ya friendly with Mae, Naomi?" she asked, changing the subject.

"Sho am. Mae's a kindly woman, salt of the earth. Ya be fine wit her. Sides, Mae don't have no man. You be good company fo her."

"Can't I stay here?"

"Lawd, no, Bo wouldn't hear of it. That man so propa he won't do nothin' ta cause folks ta talkin'."

"I don' care what folks say 'bout me. Most don' like me no how."

"I's not one fo puttin' much store in folks' pinions either, but Bo makes a point ta live righteous befo' God en de world."

"He talks like a preacha."

"Cause he thinks like one."

"He a strange man."

"Ya think so?"

"I wan ta stay here, Naomi. I don't wanna stay wit Mae. Women don' like me much. Always sayin' mean things ta me and lookin' at me like I was dirt neath der feet."

"Mae won't act like dat, chile. She a good, God-fearin' woman."

"Don' matter. Deys no different; dey don' want me round der men folk. Dey look down on me cause . . ." Ruth fiddled with the needle and thread.

"Go on, spit it out."

"Never no mind."

"Cause yo so purty and dey's jealous. Cause ya was a breedin' slave and made to lay wit whoever massah say ya lay wit. And if that weren't bad nuff, you was a house slave too. Field slaves take offense to house slaves, ain't that so?"

Ruth looked back at Naomi. "Dat's right and dey hated me mo' than most even dough some of 'em tried not ta sho it. Nobody ain't had no say where we work so why begrudge me? I ain't ask ta be bought for breedin. I ain't want to . . . I hated it . . ." Tears filled her eyes and she turned away. "I hated it . . . I hated all a it . . . dem pawin' all o'er me . . . hurtin' me."

Naomi set the brush down and stood in front of Ruth. "Don't think bout it no mo. Ya don't have to suffa dat shame no mo in your sweet life. As far as folks liking you go, people have bout as much sense as mules, maybe less. They don't know how ta feel de right way 'bout things dat bother dem too much. They ain't hate you because of you. Dey hated what ya reminded dem of; de way white folks mistreat us and how we have ta do whatever dey wan us ta do like animals. Dey hate livin' like dey has ta live and not bein' able ta do nuthin' bout it. Bein' mean to ya was jes de way dey git out some anger en sho how dey feel. Can't show it ta massah or any white folks so dey shows it ta each other . . . ta you."

"It ain't right." Ruth's tears fell.

"No, honey, it ain't right. Women envyin how ya look ain't right cause ya can't help how ya look. But you oughta know colored folks is fighting inside demselves 'bout so much. Wantin' freedom and a life better den what we have. Holdin' in fury en bitterness en not bein' able ta lash out at de ones who imprison us. We takes it out on each other cause we ain't able ta do no better. Fury boils inside us till it overflows."

"I stay to myself on de plantation mostly. De other house slaves pay me no tention 'ceptin' Gabby. I had ta tend ta Miss Molly. She was a awful willful brat and got on my nerves orderin' me 'round all day. It woulda been nice to have somebody friendly ta talk wit."

"Don't ya talk ta Jesus?"

Ruth's body tightened. "No."

"Ya shoulda. He de best friend a body kin have."

"Ya believe dat?"

"I sho do."

"I don'. Ain't no Savior who kin let folks suffer like He let us suffer be a friend a mine. What kind of savin' is dat?"

"De Lawd knows we suffers and He's workin' on it. Look at us, we's free now and someday all our peoples gonna be free."

"Is I free, really free?" Ruth wanted to know.

"Yes, chile. Bo don't own no slaves afta he buys 'em. He give 'em all der freedom."

"Freedom ta stay where I wanna?"

Naomi smiled knowingly. "Why you wanna stay here so bad? It ain't propa."

Ruth shrugged. "I don' know why. I jes feel like no harm come ta me here long as I's wit him."

"Ya never felt that way before?"

"Wit my momma I did, but I shouldn't have cause I's taken from her en ain't never feel dat way no mo'."

"I try ta tell Bo ta let ya stay. See if he change his mind. It ain't gonna be easy cause he stubborn as a mule when he wanna be."

Ruth looked back out the window, emptiness inside her longing to be filled. For the first time in years, she felt an odd sensation of hope. Naomi walked to the bench by the door and sat down to her sewing. "Bo's a fine lookin' black stallion, ain't he?" she said with a cackle.

Ruth's face warmed and she looked down at the sewing on her lap. "I s'pose so."

"My Baby Gal thought de sun rose and set wit dat man. Sometimes I think dats why she died so young. She love Bo too much."

Ruth looked up. "Too much?"

"Mo then she love anythin' or anyone else . . . even de Lawd maybe. Ain't s'pose ta love nuthin' mo' den da Lawd."

"Was she beautiful?"

"If I says so myself, she was de most fetchin' gal in dis here county, but I's pawshal."

Ruth gave a weak smile and looked down again. Slowly she fixed her eyes back out the window. Bo had moved farther down the row, but she could still see his figure and the horse and cart. Naomi cocked an eye. "Gonna have a lots a vegetables ta take ta Branche's dis year." Ruth didn't hear Naomi so she gave no answer. "I says we's gonna have lots ta sell. De corn's good 'n tall en real sweet. Should be plenty for eatin' an sellin'."

"Uh-huh," Ruth murmured, never taking her eyes off Bo. "Lawd, chile, ya's gonna stare a hole in dat window lookin' at dat man."

Ruth's head snapped around to Naomi's chuckle. "I's lookin' at the garden not at him."

"Sho you was . . ."

"I was too," Ruth protested.

"Bo's a mighty special man. A gal be blessed ta have a man like him."

Ruth's neck stretched and her head went up. "What's so special bout him otha den bein' free en havin' dis place?"

"Well . . . dat's just a little bit a what Bo Peace is, bein' a free farmer wit land. De Lawd has His hand on Bo's life. Kept him alive when fever took all his kin. Kept him livin' fo' a reason I'd say. God's got a plan fo' his life, I reckon. Bo's a godly man and kind to a fault. He loves de Lawd wit all his heart and he special to de Lawd cause de Lawd tell him things, important things."

"Dat sho is silly, de Lawd telling him things. Tell him what?"

"Well, things like what ta plant and when ta harvest and things like dat ta keep dis farm producin' when others are failin'. De Lawd keeps Bo's farm thrivin' no matter what conditions is like. Everybody knows it too. Dey can't figure out how he do it but dey see it, an dem white folks hate it something fierce."

53

"So he a good farmer. Lots of men good farmers who don' believe in yo Jesus."

"He ain't jes a good farmer, he a truly blessed farmer. God got His hand on whatever dat man do. God talks ta Bo and guide him 'bout all kinda things."

"Like what 'sides farming?"

Naomi looked to the window, blinked, and looked back at Ruth. Her smile was wide. "He told Bo ta buy *you* at de slave auction."

Ruth's expression humbled immediately. "Oh."

"Yep, Bo a special man, awright. He special to de Lawd and special to us who knows and loves him. He humble; ain't gonna say so hisself but he real special."

➤ ➤ ➤ ➤ ➤ ➤

The afternoon sun felt good on Bo's back. The cart was full almost to overflowing. It had been a good year indeed. There was plenty for sharing, eating, and selling. He threw the hoe on top of the potatoes and took the horse's reins, leading him toward the house. He mentally ran down his other chores to be done. He'd go to Branche's tomorrow, then start putting up posts for the new fence on the northwest pasture. He was hoping to buy another cow come spring. Ephraim and Johnny Boy went fishing and should have caught plenty. He was trying to keep his mind occupied and not think about Ruth. He hoped Naomi had taken her down to Mae's by now. Ruth was taking up far too much of his thoughts and emotions. Her beauty flashed through his brain often, and her hollow eyes made him sad to think what she'd endured that damaged her soul so much. He didn't want to think about her. He didn't want to feel for her any more than he felt for all the slaves he bought and freed. He didn't want to be drawn to her beauty or have pity for her hardships. She was cold and empty inside, gutted by the life she'd had to live. He understood, but he didn't need to tackle all that. He didn't want to have the desire to hold and comfort her, to spend time with her and show her love. He didn't want to care for her too much . . . but he did.

He stepped into the farmhouse, finding Ruth with her back to him adding wood to the fireplace. She turned, smiling. "Good, ya brought in some potatoes fo' supper." She walked toward him looking like an angel of loveliness. Her hair was fixed up pretty with a ribbon hanging down like Baby Gal sometimes wore. Ruth's face was beaming.

"I thought Naomi took you to Mae's."

"She already gone home wit Ephraim. He come en git her afta fishin'. Left some big ole perch and catfish. Be mighty tasty wit potatoes, parsnips, turnips, and onions. Did you bring onions?"

She took the small sack of potatoes out of his hands. Bo was speechless, staring at the bowlful of parsnips and turnips on the table. She looked at his face, knowing what was on his mind. "I'll git dis goin' in no time."

There was something very different about her, more than just the hair. She had swept and cleaned up; everything looked neat and in its place. It made him uneasy but delighted at the same time. "I . . . um . . . I'm going to take the rest of the potatoes to the barn."

"Naomi said ders some cabbage coming up out der. Ya bring in any cabbage?"

"Not till the beginning of next month before they'll be ready. Tell me, why didn't you go down to Mae's?"

Ruth smiled sweetly like he never thought he'd see her

smile. "Naomi didn't have time ta take me so she say I stay right here fo now."

Bo frowned. "She did, did she?"

"Yep, sho did." She dumped the potatoes in a basket on the floor by the fireplace, picked up the basket starting toward the door.

"Where are you going?"

"To de well ta wash dis dirt from dese here potatoes."

"Oh. Well, I'm going to the barn."

"Ya already tol' me."

"So I did." He rushed past her out the door and off the porch, then he grabbed hold of the horse and headed to the barn on the south end.

"I have a good meal ready fo' ya dis evenin'," she called as he made his way around the rear of the house. He looked toward the door at her standing and holding the basket with a smile on her face. She looked so pretty, almost like she had a spark of life inside those hollow eyes. He knew he was undeniably drawn to her. *What's happening, Lord?* he prayed, panicky.

Bo was riding fast toward her cabin when Naomi saw him approaching. The dirt was kicking up hard enough to tell somebody was in a hurry. She shielded her eyes from the sun with her hand to see who it was. It was Bo and she knew he'd be furious. The smoke coming from the chimney gave off a pungent smell of garden herbs and fish from the stream. She stood up from her corn shucking, smiling but ready for battle. "It fo' yo' own good, Bo Peace. So I's ready," she muttered.

He stopped right in front of her but didn't dismount.

"Hey der, Bo." She was grinning impishly, waving an ear of yellow corn. "Didn't reckon I see ya over 'ere today."

I bet you didn't.

"Afternoon, Naomi." His voice was tight.

Naomi continued smiling, straightening her sunbonnet and brushing corn silk off the big apron covering her sweeping skirt. She was waiting for Bo to make the next move, just in case she was wrong about the reason for his visit or his apparent mood.

"This morning, didn't you agree you would take Ruth to Mae's cabin for me?"

"I sho did, but Ephraim come so soon and . . ."

"You know it's not right for her to stay there with me, Naomi. Why didn't you make sure she was settled in with Mae like you promised?"

Naomi looked guiltily down at the ground. "Well, ya see . . ."

"She's in the house fixing supper right now."

"I knows." Naomi shuffled. It was harder than she'd thought but she had to get it over with. "She doesn't wanna be wit Mae. She wanna stay wit you, and I don't see no reason why she cain't."

"No reason." Bo threw his leg over his horse and jumped down hard. "You know she can't live with me."

"Why not? The gal's scared. She don't want no strangers round judgin' her en bein' mean ta her. She been through enuff."

"Who's going to be mean to her? Mae's a goodly woman. She'd never be mean to Ruth. You know that."

"She jes don't wanna be with nobody else. She told me so. She ain't trustin' of folks much and throwin' her ta Mae won't help matters none. Ruth a real spooked gal, and if she gonna trust again she need ta stay put somewhere for once. I wouldn't bother makin' her no cabin either if I was you. Let her stay wit ya till she heals en leaves fo' good . . . if she leaves."

"Are you touched? She can't stay with me!"

"Why not?"

"Stop asking that when you know good and well why not!"

"No need ta be hateful 'bout it."

Bo took a deep breath. "I'm sorry for hollering. It's just that I expected her to be gone to Mae's and now . . . It's no good her staying at the farmhouse with me. It's not decent. You should know that."

"Ya plannin' on acting indecent wit 'er?"

"Of course not but . . ."

"Too much temptation?"

"I am human. I'm a man after all."

"That ya is and it be high time ya member dat."

Bo was troubled by the inference. "That's not the point. A respectable lady doesn't live with a man she's not properly tied to."

"Den take her fo yo' wife."

"What?"

"I said marry up wit her, jump the broom."

"That's insane, I can't do that!"

"Why not?" Bo looked at Naomi, evidently unwilling to speak his mind.

She put a hand on her hip. "I knows ya ain't acting like this cause she use ta be a breedin' slave. Cause if ya is, let me remind ya yo' own momma was breeded fo' she was sold and come ta Massah Maitland's en yo' daddy, Bodine, jumped de broom wit her."

"I know, I know. It has nothing to do with that."

"Den couple up wit de gal."

"I should have known you were up to no good trying to matchmake. I don't know that woman. She doesn't know me, and she's not ready to *couple up* with anybody."

"Ain't she—or is it you ain't ready?"

"What do mean, me? I'm still grieving my wife, why would you ask . . ."

"Bo, ya need to let Baby Gal go. It be time ya git pas her dyin' since it been years since she gone. As much as it grieves me ta say so, ya gotta git on wit livin' cause she ain't comin' back and ya wastin' time. Ya needs a wife and dat der gal Ruth is good as any far as I see. She mighty taken wit ya too."

"She is?"

Naomi saw interest in Bo's eyes. "Sho is."

"But she's nothing like Baby Gal. Baby Gal was warm and loving. This woman is hard and hollow inside." A pained expression overtook his face.

"Don't go thinkin ya gonna git another Baby Gal, cause ya ain't. God only make one a my precious baby. So stop lookin' for another one of her and pay 'tention ta what's in front a ya. Ruth might be hollow now but if ya fills her wit yo' sweet ways, she kin be as full en lovin' as anybody."

"How do you know that?"

"Cause she a woman and we gals need lovin' en care. She ain't had dat in a long time. Why ya think she so hard en empty? Dey drain all de love outta her. Used her like a barnyard hen."

"How do you know so much about her life in just a few days?"

"You forget I's a woman too. Ain't always been old and gray. I been a slave in my life a lot longer den ya ever was. I knows enough bout women living her kinda life. She ain't the first breedin' slave I come cross. She needs something to undo all the hurt she knows. I kin feel it, dat gal's cravin love . . . en a home she can be free en safe in."

"'Cravin' love' . . . I think *you* are touched. She doesn't

59

want me to come near her or try to help her at all, let alone love her. She wants her freedom and that's it."

"Don'tcha see? She wounded. Ya know how wounded creatures be. We was wounded befo' or did ya forgit? We had time ta heal, en all she needs is time ta heal. She mo' wounded den we ever was. She was used inside and out. Bein' used for breedin' leaves a hole in the soul. Give her time."

"Fine, but not in my farmhouse."

"Why not?"

"Stop asking that."

"Ya might as well stop runnin' from what gonna happen anyhow."

"What?"

"Don't act like ya don't feel it too. Like de Lawd ain't leadin' ya dat way."

"What are you jabbering about now, Naomi?"

"You ain't de only one de Lawd tells things to. Every now and den He says a little somthin' ta me."

Six

*B*o was quiet all evening. He ate dinner and avoided small talk. Ruth, on the other hand, was uncharacter-istically chatty. She'd talk about the gardens or some other aspect of the farm.

"That's a real nice horse ya had pulling the cart," she said after a lengthy lull in conversation.

"He's a good workhorse," Bo replied, thinking the fish was quite tasty, but he was too out of sorts to enjoy it. Ruth was a surprisingly good cook. He chewed aimlessly, staring anywhere but her direction.

"How many horses ya got?" she asked.

"Three."

"Massah Stanley had lots a horses, purty high-breed ones. I use ta spend all the time I could steal away to be wit dem animals."

Bo looked at her curiously. "You like horses?"

"I love horses. Dey was my only friends on Stanley's

place. Folks use ta tease me fo' spenin' so much time wit horses, but I didn't care."

"I like horses a lot too." He remembered Naomi's words at that moment and looked at her hollow eyes, trying to calm his anxiety. *Could she possibly be . . . ?*

"How's the supper?"

"Awful good. You're a very good cook, I see." He smiled at her for the first time that evening.

Ruth was relieved. She'd felt the distance earlier. She knew it was because she was still at his house instead of Mae's cabin. Bo hadn't mentioned it again about her going to Mae's, and she could feel the tension. She watched him closely, trying to read his mood.

I gots ta make him wants me ta stay.

"Naomi said ya got venison in the barn. I can make a mighty good stew with some vegetables tomorrow."

He looked up. "Tomorrow? Oh, tomorrow . . . I have to go to Branche's to sell Mister Chesley my corn and potatoes."

"I make it while ya gone."

His eyes dropped to the table. "Ruth, I think it would be best . . . I think you should go to Mae's tomorrow. I'll take you in the wagon with Johnny Boy and me in the morning. We'll leave you off on our way to town."

Ruth's smile faded. "Awright, if dat's what ya wan." She was perfectly quiet clearing the table and washing the dishes. She excused herself from listening when Bo started reading the Bible.

"You sure you don't want to hear me read from the Bible tonight?"

"I's sho." She went into the small bedroom and closed the door.

Bo continued to read, but lost concentration when he

thought he heard her crying. To think he made her cry ate at his heart. He closed the book, blew out the candle, and sat listening to the dying cook fire's crackle and night creatures' serenades. Naomi's lecture replayed in his head. He prayed for wisdom and peace about many things . . . especially about Ruth.

Bo was sleeping restlessly, but started awake when he felt something against his body. The room was dark except for the moon's light coming in from the window. "What?" He rubbed his eyes, still half asleep and confused. The moon threw enough illumination for him to see Ruth when he looked over. He felt her warm sensuality next to him and sprang up in the sitting position. "Ruth?"

"Yeah, it's me."

"What are you doing in here?"

"You kin have me fo yo own. If ya like me, den kin I stay?" Ruth was uncovered and sat up, reaching for Bo.

"Oh, no not this . . ." He hopped out of bed in a shot. "Put some clothes on . . . now!" he ordered and fled into the other room. He was only trembling from the shock, he told himself as he poked at dying embers. He was wrapped in a blanket, since September days were hot but the nights were chilly. Bo's heart was thumping wildly, mind swirling. *My Lord, what is she trying to do? Why am I being tempted this way?*

He got the fire reignited in the big fireplace and added another log. *She has to go. That's all there is to it. First thing at daybreak she's off to Mae's cabin.* The more he thought about it, the more frustrated he became. Part of him desired her, part of him knew it could not be . . . should not be. Then he was angry. She was stirring up what he'd worked so hard

63

to suppress. *If Naomi had done what I asked in the first place
. . .* Now he was angry with her too.

Ruth sat on the side of the bed trying to figure out what
had gone wrong. *What I do? Why he leave like dat? Is he gon'
throw me out now witout my freedom paper?* She was confused and humiliated. It had always worked before when she
wanted something. She used her womanhood to convince
Carter to talk to Massah, and he got Massah Stanley to not
send her in to that animal Jasper anymore. And when Wilbur
Stanley wanted his way with her, she'd gotten many extras
such as more food and candy, or a pretty bonnet, and once
even some perfumed bath salts. When there was talk of putting
her in the fields, she was extra good to Wilbur to stop that from
happening. Then when she ran away and they caught her, she
would have been lashed if she hadn't let that disgusting Merle
Oakes and Carter have their way with her all night.

She had learned how to get her way if she had to, but this
man . . . *this one is different,* she thought. No man ever rejected
her that way . . . no man. Slave men fought each other to be
with Ruth. How could Bo not want her? After all, his wife is
dead. He's alone and he should want a woman.

*What I did wrong? Now he hates me. He looked at me like
he was disgusted . . . he thinks I's ugly!*

She left Bo's room, padding quickly in her bare feet to the
small room next door. Her head was down and she was just
inside the door when he called out to her. "Would you come
here, Ruth?"

She walked slowly into the big room. He sat in the thatched
chair in front of the window. He'd lighted a candle, and the fire
was starting to throw heat. The room felt comfortable, but she
was miserable. "Sit down, please," Bo requested kindly.

Ruth sat in the wooden rocker. She couldn't look at him. Bo closed his Bible and sighed. "Why did you come to my bedroom?"

"I tol ya, so you could have me fo yo own." Her head stayed down.

"Ruth, look at me." His voice was still calm. She looked up. "Did I give you the idea you had to give yourself to me for any reason?"

"Naw." She looked away. "I thought ya let me stay if ya could have yo way wit me."

Bo closed his eyes. "You do not have to do that now. Don't you understand? You do not give yourself to any man unless he's your husband. Don't give pieces of yourself away like that. The Lord delivered you from having to live like that anymore."

"Yessah."

"God meant for a man and woman to be together as man and wife under an acceptable commitment."

"Yessah."

"You make yourself less than what you are when you do what you did . . . and for what? Mae is no devil. She's a good woman and will treat you right."

"Yessah, I knows you ain't like me and ya think I's ugly. Ya ain't want me."

His mouth opened but he quickly shut it. His grip on the Bible tightened. "I never said I didn't like you. I don't think you're ugly at all; just the opposite, you're very beautiful."

"Den why won't ya . . .?"

"It's a sin against God. We're not taken in matrimony."

"White folks say we can't marry no how, and they don' hold no sto' in jumpin' de broom. None of 'em care bout us bein' in matchamony."

"I do and you should too because *God* does. It's sin any other way."

"If you really thought I was purty, ya wouldn't care 'bout it bein' no sin. Preacha Man didn't when he had his way wit me."

"Who's Preacher Man?"

"Slave dat called hisself a preacha, but he act mo' like a tomcat in da barnyard."

Bo cocked an eye. "Oh, really."

"He said if I fought agin him havin' his way, he'd see to it dat I go ta hell when I die. Kin he do dat?"

Bo's face contorted angrily. "No, he cannot. Where is this so-called preacher now?"

"Dey hung him." Ruth flinched. "Dey claim he force hisself on a white woman and dey strung 'em up en cut off his privates, but I think it was a lie. Dis white stranger come through and was de guilty man, but he slipped off that night so dey blame ole Preacha Man cause he was always talkin' 'bout freedom."

Bo nodded. "He forced himself on you?"

"Uh-huh, sometimes when he was of a mind to."

"Dear God . . . Ruth, you don't have to live like that anymore."

"I knowed I ain't fetchin' to ya." Her head dropped in shame.

"That's not true."

"Is it cause my face bruised and still a little swoll?" Her hands lightly touched her face on each side.

His heart palpitated. He wanted to hold her face himself and comfort her with kisses, but he didn't dare. "Even with the swelling and bruises you're pretty."

Ruth got up and went to Bo and sat at his feet in front the chair. She looked up at him like an innocent child. "Please, don' make me go away. I wanna stay here wit you. Please, let me stay."

"It wouldn't be right. People would talk and you'd be shamed."

"Don't matter none, I already shamed."

"Not here you aren't and not now; this is a new beginning for you—a new life without bondage and shame so you can live like the Lord wants you to live. You don't want to scandalize yourself, do you?"

Ruth grabbed tight to his knees. "Oh, please, please don' throw me away. I be good, I promise I be good. I won' shame ya . . . I won'. Jes let me stay." Tears fell down her cheeks.

Lord, she doesn't know what she's asking of me.

"It isn't decent, Ruth, for a man and woman not joined by God to keep living together in this house."

"Please don' make me go be wit Mae."

"Why does it matter so much if you stay here or in Mae's cabin?"

"Dis like havin' a home here. Like de shack we had on Massah Leese's. Momma and me live dere, just de two of us. It was near de big house. They took me from dere and I ain't never feel like I was home since . . . till I come here. I . . . I wanna be wit you."

Bo's heart sank into a sea of emotion that was taking him under quick. He could hear Naomi hammering in his ear with her opinions.

Lord Jesus, what do I do?

After minutes of sitting hearing Ruth whimper and feeling her clutching his legs, he answered, "All right, you can stay but only under one condition."

Her face lit up. She squeezed his knees. "Oh, thank ya! I be good. Ya see, I be real good."

"But you haven't heard the condition." Bo thought of Naomi.

"I don' care, I do anythin', jes lemme stay."

"Anything? Are you willing for us to marry?"

Ruth was stunned. "Marry?"

"That's right."

"Ya would take me fo yo wife?"

"I would."

"Ya would couple up wit me jes sos folks wouldn' talk agin us bein here together?"

Bo got a strange look on his face that confused Ruth. He looked away from her inquiring stare. When he lifted his eyes back to hers, he took a long breath and said, "That's part of the reason, yes."

She wanted to persist, but let it go. She was still shocked at his proposal, and he looked strained himself. He waited for her response, telling himself he must be losing his mind.

Ruth's astonishment gradually waned as happiness and expectation took its place. She stared at Bo, and saw a good man. They were being drawn to each other in an indescribable pull. "Awright, I do anything ya wan ta stay here wit ya . . . anything."

➤ ➤ ➤ ➤ ➤ ➤

Cheasley Branche was a cantankerous tightwad and a man who surely took advantage. He also was one of the few merchants in Southampton County who would trade with freed slaves. If not for Cheasley, Bo would have had to go all the way to Richmond to sell his goods, since free blacks—as well as Indians—were limited to where they could do business.

Branche's Emporium had grown from the trading post Cheasley's father had founded into a large establishment that supplied the smaller general stores in Suffolk, Southampton, and Sussex Counties. Cheasley was a businessman first and utmost. He didn't care where products came from as long as he was assured to make a good profit. He bartered to the point of tedium, determined not to pay a cent more a bushel than he needed. After his shrewd purchases, he'd sell the very same merchandise for an outrageous price . . . always according to his mood.

He was known for justifying his greed when arguing about his questionable ethics. "It's the nature of business—buy and sell to make a profit," Cheasley often declared. He knew freed slaves and Indians had no other option but to deal with him, so he made it beneficial at every turn, and this unscrupulous practice paid off handsomely.

Bo's head would ache from bargaining by the time an agreement was reached. He had to hold in his resentment and pray "without ceasing" when dealing with Cheasley Branche. He walked around, spotting additional items he needed while Cheasley filled his shopping list; blacks weren't allowed to handle any goods themselves, so as not to give offense to white customers.

Bo noticed Lester Mayfield when he walked into the store. The middle-aged white farmer looked haggard and drawn, his spindly body slumped. Bo knew Lester could barely support his wife and ten children. He took off his hat and nodded to Bo, then went to Cheasley and whispered to the man.

"Forget it!" Cheasley howled. "No more credit till you pay what you owe!"

Lester looked around, embarrassed. "I'll pay; I promise, I'll pay."

"You said that two months ago."

"Things been hard on us, Mister Cheasley and with Adelaide down expecting again . . ."

"Again? She's expecting again?"

"Yes, sir."

Cheasley snorted shaking his head. "You two breed like rabbits. I declare, it's unbelievable."

Lester straightened up. "You don't have to be insultin'."

Cheasley slammed down the boxes in his hand. "I'll tell you what's insulting—you not paying your bill, that's insulting! Then you have the gall to come in here asking for more credit? Now that's really insulting!" His voice rebounded through the store.

"I do the best I can. Don't I always pay you in the end?"

"Taking too long this time." He turned his back to the farmer and went back to filling Bo's order from the shelves.

Bo was looking at a nice woven circle rug for Ruth so her feet wouldn't have to touch a cold floor when she got out of bed in the coming winter months.

"Things are bad all over. You know that," Lester muttered.

"Ain't my problem. I can't go giving out my merchandise to every dirt farmer who's got it rough. I got a business to run. I got a wife and children to feed too. I'm a business, not a charity."

Lester looked down, rolling his hand around inside his hat. "Just one more time," he whispered.

"I already told you, no!" Cheasley repeated.

Lester turned to walk away when Bo stepped up to the counter. "Mister Cheasley, you can put what he needs on my bill."

Cheasley turned around facing Bo. "You mean you paying for him?"

"Yes, sir. Whatever he needs I'll pay."

70

Cheasley scratched his head. "Do I hear you saying you're paying your money to help this white man?"

"I am, yes sir."

Lester stopped with his hand on the doorknob and looked at Bo. Cheasley looked at Lester and motioned for him to come back. Lester walked back to the counter with his hat still in hand. He shook Bo's hand vigorously. "I'm grateful, Bo, mighty grateful. I'll pay you back. Just wait till I'm done after full harvest, and I'll pay you back every penny."

"I'm sure we can work something out. You do what you can when you can, and if you can't ever give it back, I don't care. Take care of your family first."

Cheasley gaped at Bo. "Why?" was all he said, shaking his head.

"I do what's pleasing to God. I bless folks because the Lord in many ways blessed me. God doesn't bless anyone based on color. This man needs help and I can help him and his family, so why shouldn't I?"

Cheasley snorted. "Cause he's white, for starters."

"Lester has never done me any harm. He's a man who loves the Lord from what I know about him, and God loves him."

"How you know God loves him? What do you know about a white man's God?"

"There's one God, sir, and He's not a white man's God or a colored man's God. He's a human being's God, all of us together."

"Nonsense," Cheasley spouted. "I don't fool much with religion, but no way our God fools with you coloreds."

"You're wrong," Lester interjected. "Bo is right, there's one God of this world and He's all our God. Jesus came to save everybody; whosoever would look to the cross of salvation,

71

not just white folks. Whosoever—and that includes Indians, coloreds, and Jews."

"Jews!" Cheasley's jaw tightened. "Now I know you're both crazy."

Lester stepped closer to the counter with a serious face. "Ain't crazy, it's what's taught in the Good Book whether you like it or not. You ought to read it sometime and maybe you'll get more understanding."

"Bah, it's just religious fanaticism. Got folks all mixed up talking silly." Cheasley looked at Bo. "Why you really helping him?"

"The Lord told me to help him because he's one of His children."

Cheasley's fist pounded the counter. "Well, I'll be . . . I done seen and heard it all. A freed slave helping a struggling white man cause he hears voices telling him to. And the voice is from God no less." He frowned at Lester. "And you . . . you oughta be ashamed that he's doing so much better than you. Bo here pays for his purchases on the spot most times, and his bill is paid up on a regular basis when he has one. Never thought I'd say this to a white man about a colored, but you should be more like him." Cheasley walked to the shelves in the corner, shaking his head and mumbling. "What are things coming to when white men are in worse shape than coloreds? Folks saying God's for coloreds and Indians . . . and Jews of all people; what's this world coming to?"

Seven

$\mathscr{J}$t was almost midmorning when Bo and Johnny Boy got back to the farm from Branche's. Naomi, Coral, and Mae were in a dither and had converged on his house.

"'Bout time ya git back here." Mae was outside sweeping the porch. She hurried to Bo and Johnny Boy at the horse-drawn wagon, flailing a broom. "You gotta get bathed and dressed fo' de preacha gets here."

"Bathed?"

"A course, ya can't take a new wife with de dirt off de road all ov'r ya. Git down to de creek en wash."

"The creek? It might be chilly in the creek this time of year," Bo protested. Johnny snickered.

"Ruth's in de tub full a hot water inside, so ya have ta use de creek. A little col' water won' kill ya. Jes stay in dere long nuff ta git de dirt offin' ya. Don' go swimmin'."

"We have to unload the wagon. I've got some wool for Naomi and . . ."

"Never ya mind 'bout all dat. Ned kin take care a it. Ya

gettin' hitched, boy! Go git ready! It be time fo' ya know it."
Mae's huge smile was not to be argued with.

"How did you find out? I only told Naomi this morning on
my way to town . . . never mind." He started off the wagon.
"Where did you say Ruth was?"

"In de house and ya can't see her till time, so git. Go to de
barn round back. Ned's waitin' fo ya with ya Sunday-go-ta-
meetin clothes."

Bo sat back down on the wagon seat and drove off. When
he reached the south barn, he saw Ned and Ephraim baling
hay. They greeted him with big smiles and pats on the back.

*Lord, am I hearing You right? Is this what You really want
me to do?*

The last wagon pulled off and horses rode into the dusk of
the rapidly descending sun. The marriage ceremony was over
and their cheerful witnesses all gone. Bo turned and looked long
toward the house. He was elated yet somewhat apprehensive.
Thick black smoke billowed from the front chimney. He watched
it for a few minutes, trying to collect himself. The evening chill
began to wrap around his bones, sending him inside the house.
Ruth was standing near the fireplace. The flames licked the logs
and threw the only light in the room. She turned to Bo when he
shut the door and placed the bolt on it. She was breathtakingly
beautiful in spite of the almost diminished bruises.

Naomi and the other women had spruced Ruth up. They
put a few small late-blooming flowers in her hair. She was
wearing the same white satin and lace dress Baby Gal had
worn when he'd jumped the broom with her. Isabelle Maitland had given the dress to Baby Gal. It was bought in Richmond, her very expensive and highly fashionable debutante
gown from years ago. Baby Gal had looked beautiful in it. He

74

remembered how she stopped his heart when he first saw her. But this was not Baby Gal, this was Ruth, his new bride. She was even more lovely than Baby Gal, if possible; taller, fuller, and more sensual. He kept pushing away the rightful feelings a man should have for the woman he just married.

She's my wife now . . . my wife . . . it's proper to feel this way about her.

"Chilly tonight; I start a fire in da bedroom," Ruth said and glided to the door of the room.

"Ruth?"

She turned and looked at him.

"Are you happy we got married?" he asked, uncertain.

She nodded.

"You're beautiful," he told her, relieved.

Her smile was wide. "I ain't never had no dress dis purty."

"The dress is pretty too, but I meant you. You're beautiful even without the dress," he said. She blushed and went into the larger bedroom.

He followed her, taking the log out of her hand. "You'll dirty your clothes. Let me do this. You go change while I make the fire in here."

She looked into his eyes and he saw what he thought was a glimmer of life, a spark of some kind flickering in the hollowness of her soul. That was more encouragement than he expected. He pulled her to him without thinking and kissed her. Her body stiffened. His other arm enclosed her waist. Mounting desire filled him almost instantly. Her stiffness dissolved as he whispered, "Ruth, I promise I'll be good to you" in her ear. She allowed herself to respond to his tenderness.

What was it about him that was so different? she wondered. He was, after all, just a man like all the others, but he wasn't like the others. He wasn't unfeeling or indifferent. He didn't look at her with animal-like stares, but his gazes seemed to be filled with kindness and caring. When he said her name it was a sweet song to her ears. When they united as man and wife, Bo was tender with every caress and sweet with each word, but his strength and passion were evident. Best of all, his intentions were honorable. This man was so unordinary in everything he did from handling the land and his animals to how he loved her. All Ruth had ever known was to crawl away from intimacy, feeling dirty and used by men who didn't care for her as a woman or even think of her as a person. All she had wanted to do was escape as fast as she could from their unsavory remarks or attempts to repeat their vile acts. Not this time. She snuggled close to him, feeling safe and warm. He kissed her forehead and looked at her like no man had ever looked at her before. Was this love? Was this the thing she'd heard women giggle and talk about, swoon and sway over? The thing Miss Molly used to sing about and read in those books, daydreaming for hours?

How was it Bo could make her feel so cherished when he knew her past? She wanted a physical connection because she felt she owed it to him. For so long, she felt that it was the one constant in why she existed, that and giving birth, which she could no longer do. Now she was confused. Things were different somehow. What was changing and why did this man care about her? This man . . . this man who was her lawfully wedded husband. Her husband. The reality of it was strange, almost unbelievable. She never before wanted to couple for keeps. Almost everything about Bo Peace and her life with him so far was unbelievable.

Bo's mind wandered back to months earlier when he prayed for the grieving to cease. He was weary of mourning and ready to love again; to love without guilt about betraying Baby Gal. He wanted freedom. He needed release from loneliness and sorrow. Bo had asked God to either send him the woman or take away his feeling of discontentment. To his amazement this prayer was answered through Ruth. He twirled a lock of her wavy hair, smiling, but noticed her deep concentration in thought.

"Is something bothering you?" he asked.

She shook her head.

"What are you thinking about?" he pressed.

"What it be like to be free."

"You already are free. I told you . . ."

"I mean really free. Free ta go where I wan."

"You are free. I don't own you. I'm your husband, not your master. Remember that. Try to believe that because it's your new life now as a free Negro woman."

"Maybe when I get da freedom papers in my hand, I . . ."

"If it makes you feel any freer, I'll get it written as soon as possible, but since you won't be needing it to leave now, I don't see the rush."

Ruth glanced at Bo. "I ain't gonna need it fo' a while, but den when my year up . . ."

"Your year?"

"I owes ya a year for buyin' my freedom, don' I?"

He stroked her cheek affectionately, smiling. "That was before we jumped the broom. You owe me nothing now except to be my wife. You're free now so we can be together till one of us dies. I don't hold you indebted to me for anything, my sweet." He kissed her nose.

Ruth closed her eyes as the realization washed over her. His touch clouded her thinking, but she pushed her determined thoughts to the surface. "Ya means I ain't free ta move on afta my year is done?"

Bo's eyes widened. "You can't still want to leave in a year." His voice was choked.

"I still wants my freedom."

"Your freedom? You *are* free. I keep telling you that."

Ruth slid from under his arms and sat up, pulling the cover over her. "Ya tol' me I be free ta go if I wan in a year. My debt be paid and I could do what I wan."

"Yes, but that was before we got married. You're my wife now. You belong here with me forever."

"So's I ain't free really?"

Bo's hurt showed on his face. "You are," he said, yielding to her relentless stare. "You are free to do as you want even though we're married . . . you're free, Ruth."

"Den I's free ta leave in a year?"

"You want to leave in a year?"

"Uh-huh; I wan my freedom."

Bo moved away from Ruth. "Then I'll have the papers made up and you can go whenever you like."

She touched his shoulder. "Ain't no hurry. I gonna stay my year en cook en clean fo' ya like I say I would. I ain't gonna owe no man when I gets my freedom."

He grabbed her shoulders. "I told you, you don't owe me anything! You're my wife, not my slave!"

Ruth was shocked at his outburst. "I knows, but I's still beholdin'."

"I don't want your gratitude," Bo growled, releasing his hold.

"If it wasn't fo' ya buyin' me, I ain't be free at all." Ruth moved closer and touched Bo's arm. "I's mighty thankful to ya . . ."

78

Bo jerked away. "That's not what I want from a wife."

She moved closer to him. "What do ya want?" she purred.

He looked at her, his countenance showing his disappointment and resentment. "I want a wife who wants to be with me because she has caring feelings for me. A woman who'll spend the rest of her life by my side."

Ruth froze and blinked stunned. "You's cain't want dat from me . . . not me."

"Why not? I pledged myself to you, didn't I?" *Lord, why is this happening?* Bo pleaded silently.

"But I thought we married so folks ain't think po'ly of us livin' here wit each other."

"That was just a small part of why, Ruth. I wanted you to be mine. I wanted to have a home with you. I thought you wanted a home to call your own. A life to live free and proud like our folks always dream of but most of us don't get. I thought you wanted to stay here with me always. That you cared for me."

"I be what ya wan, I will. I be yo' wife till my year is up."

"I don't want a wife for a year! I want a wife for life!"

"But ya knowed I wants my freedom. Ya knowed it."

"You can have your freedom as my wife."

"It ain't freedom if I have ta stay here."

"Then go! You don't have to stay here at all! You can leave when you get ready, because I don't want a wife for just a year out of obligation!"

Ruth's mouth drew in and her nose flared out. "I pay my debt, I tol' ya . . ."

"When will you understand there is no more debt when I took you for my wife?"

She began to tremble. "Why ya mad wit me?"

"Because I thought you wanted to stay here with me as

my wife. I lost one wife and now I'll lose another. I would never have jumped the broom and made my vow of marriage before the Lord if I knew you would walk away."

His sorrow pulled at Ruth's heart. "Why ya want ta keep me fo' a wife? I ain't fit. Ya knows what I been."

"You are fit as anybody. Being a slave who had to breed was not your fault or your choice. Just like being slaves wasn't any of our choice. When I look at you I don't see a breeding slave; I see a beautiful woman I wedded for life. I didn't jump the broom just to make things look good. I chose you because the Lord let me know you were the answer to my prayers."

"I ain't no ansa ta nobody prayin'."

"You were to mine, or so I thought."

"All my life I wanna be free. Now I is, en I can't give it up ta be no man's wife, dats mo' bondage. White women wit a husband ain't much better off den slaves if ya ask me. Mean ole men bossin' em around all de time."

"Being married to me would not be bondage. Married folk are committed to each other by *choice*, to build a life together and be comfort for one another. That's not bondage. God brings folks together to be *happy* with each other, not enslaved."

"Humph, ain't what Missy Olivia Stanley say." Ruth's head tilted. "She say marriage was worse den being a slave. Das what she tol us slaves in de house all da time."

"Not when the Lord is in the center of the marriage, it's not. Not when two people care deeply for each other."

"What you sayin'? Ya care deeply fo' me?"

Bo looked her in the eyes. They'd gone cold again, no spark of warmth. "I do."

Ruth swallowed hard. "How kin ya?"

"Why shouldn't I?"

"We jes knowed each ottha days ago."

"I know, but God moves swiftly when He wants."

"You don' know me much."

"I know enough, and the joy of it is getting to know each other better."

"I ain't able ta make ya a good wife forever."

"Why not?"

Ruth paused. "I don' baleeve in de Lawd like ya do."

"You will. He'll show Himself to be faithful to you and that will open your eyes."

"I don' wan Him showin' nothin' ta me. I jes don' wanna be tied down, I wan my freedom."

Bo's eyes darkened. "Then you'll have it like I said. You are free to leave whenever you want. I'll have the declaration made up as soon as Mister George gets back from Philadelphia. He should be home by the end of harvest."

"No hurry. Got a year fo' my time is up."

"You don't understand. Once he writes the paper, you don't have to wait a year. You can leave immediately." Bo slid down, staring at the ceiling.

Ruth looked wounded. She sat up on the bed and turned away from him.

"If you're so bent on leaving, I'd rather you just leave when you get your papers. And until then, please sleep in the other bedroom."

"But I's grateful and willin' ta . . ."

"I don't want your gratitude, I told you! I want a wife, a real wife, not a one-year agreement! Now go. You can have your own room." He turned on his side with his back to her. He felt her finally get out of bed and heard her leave. The door closed softly. He waited till then to let the tears fall.

81

Eight

or several days, word circulated about Bo Peace's marriage to the mysterious slave woman. Some folks didn't believe it; others did but were surprised, and some acted like they expected him to remarry. "After all, Bo is a man, ain't he? He's just a man and we know how men are 'bout a pretty face," Janey Parsons commented, standing outside the meetinghouse. Her head dropped and twisted sideways. "I notice de newlyweds ain't at Sunday meetin'. Bo never misses Sunday meetin' lessen he sick. I reckon too much enjoyin' de new wife keepin' him home."

Emma snickered. "You's shameless, Janey."

"It's de truf. Man been witout fo' a long time. He won't turn her loose till spring."

They both snickered this time.

Emma covered her mouth then took her hand away when she saw the preacher waving at them. "Good preachin'!" she shouted at him, then asked Janey, "Why so secret when Bo jumped de broom?"

Janey withdrew her arm from the waving position. "Weren't no secret from dem on de farm. Dey was all dere, sos Betty tol' me. But 'tween me en you I heard she low class."

"Low class how?"

"Don't know jes yet but it gonna come out sooner or later. Must be somethin' scandless cause he ain't wed her here at de meetin' house like he done Baby Gal."

"Hard ta think Bo would jump de broom low class after havin' such a sweet decent gal like his first wife."

"From what else I hear, they was already livin like dey was coupled. Gettin' de milk fo ya buy de cow." Janey winked again.

"Bo Peace, livin in sin wit a woman? Dat's hard to imagine. He's such a decent actin' fella."

"Who kin understand even de best of men?"

"Did the preacha say a piece over em and den dey jump de broom?"

"Dat's what Betty says."

"Well, den deys wedded right and proper."

"Bo been by hisself fo' a while now. I ain't shocked he's so taken wit some purty slave gal he bought."

"She must be mighty purty ta turn his holy head that way."

"Ain't no man dat holy when it come ta dat. Ask Preacha Jones's wife, she tell ya."

"Ya oughtta be shame talking like dis on sacred ground, an bout da preacha too."

"Ain't lyin' on him. De preacha's wife always complainin' bout his high nature. Dats what she calls it." The women looked over at the preacher and covered their mouths, laughing uncontrollably.

Emma slapped her thigh several times tryin to restrain her laughter. "Stop blasphemin' en git back ta Bo and dis woman he married."

"I heard she de spittin' image a Baby Gal, and ya knows how he was bout her."

"Lawd knows yes, he was a fool in love wit dat chile."

"Well, he better get his fill of his new bride by next Sunday sermon. We's havin that important preacha Prophet Turner comin'."

Three Days Later

The women stopped and stared as Naomi and Ruth approached the stream. Nanny poked Lula, who winked at Ethel and Betty. Mara had her back turned and didn't see them coming. Emma nodded her head to indicate to Janey which direction to look. At the last instant, Ethel whispered to Mara, who turned around immediately.

Naomi watched their faces carefully. Ruth was nervous. She hadn't expected so many others to be at the stream washing clothes. Naomi stopped by the bank, and they set the basket of clothes on the ground. Nanny dropped her garment and stood up. "Well now, who dis lovely chile wit ya, Naomi?" she asked, grinning.

"Dis here Ruth, everybody, Bo's new wife."

"Mighty good meetin' ya, Ruth." Nanny shot a look at Mara.

Mara was bent over staring up at Ruth through slitted eyes.

"My name's Lula. Glad ta meet cha."

"I's Emma and dis here is Janey, my sister."

"Nice ta meet y'all," Ruth said softly.

"Pleasure meetin' de gal dat got Bo Peace to jump de broom. Hi, my name's Ethel." Ethel nudged Mara but she was like a statue. She didn't utter a word, just kept staring. "Neber mind her, she in a bad way today. Dis here is Mara."

"She all da time in a bad way." Nanny chuckled. "Mara, ifin ya ain't speakin', stop starin', tain't polite," she snapped. Mara dropped her head and returned to scrubbing clothes with zeal.

Betty put a calming hand on Mara's shoulder before asking Ruth, "Where's ya from, honey?"

"Shenadoah Valley, by de mountains," Ruth answered. She and Naomi each took a piece of clothing from the basket and bent down on their knees by the cool water.

"Lotta Injuns up in them mountains, ain't it?"

"I reckon so," Ruth replied. She was uncomfortable being the center of attention. She self-consciously touched her face. The swelling had gone down, but she knew there was still some remnant of bruising.

"Ya got Injun blood in ya?" Ethel asked.

"Yes, ma'am."

"Dat why her hair so long and purty," Naomi quipped as she flipped Ruth's long braid. Ethel rolled her eyes. Janey and Emma exchanged envious glances.

"Bo, he a special man," Nanny muttered. "A messenger of de Lawd, he is."

"Sho is, he a saint," Emma added, nodding.

"Bo buy ya off de slave block?" Betty asked bluntly. Ruth's eyes were lowered as she nodded. Satisfied her fact-finding mission was complete, Betty went on. "Ya sho is blessed he git hold a ya en married ya. Den I guess ya already knows ya blessed seein' dat farmhouse en all."

Lula held up a pair of wet britches for her inspection. "Bo been duckin' womenfolk round here fo years. How ya git him ta jump de broom so fast, honey?"

Naomi cocked an eye looking at Lula. Emma dropped down on her haunches as if waiting to hear the response. Betty froze in place, staring at Ruth. Mara even looked up from her laundry. Emma, Janey, and Ethel were holding their collective breaths watching Ruth's reaction.

Ruth was flustered, but not about to give those hens the pleasure of knowing it. She raised her head, smiled, and said with dignity, "Some women has ta hog-tie dey men ta git hitched up wit 'em. Dat ain't how it was 'tween Bo en me. When two is meant ta be together, den time ain't a matter." She looked around at the skeptical faces and continued calmly. "Bo tol me I's de answer ta his prayin'. So I ain't had ta do a thing ta get him cross dat broom. Twas all his doin'. He a man who know what he wans." She dropped her head back to her washing. Naomi grinned at the gaped mouths. Mara turned her furious face away. No one said another word for quite a while.

➤ ➤ ➤ ➤ ➤ ➤

The venison stew was hot and succulent, but Bo pushed it around in his bowl, uninterested in its savory meat or the fresh vegetables. He'd been brooding since the unpleasant news on their wedding night. Ruth tried to be pleasant and accommodating, but he wasn't responsive to her efforts. He stayed out in the barns or fields and gardens most of the time or elsewhere on the farm at other cabins. It was obvious he was avoiding her. There were no more tender hugs and sweet kisses. He dispensed only polite comments when necessary and an occasional cordial remark. He looked sad all the time.

Guilt plagued Ruth every time she looked at his drawn expression. Had her plans to leave in a year caused this unhappy withdrawal? Was this really her home . . . a real home she'd be walking away from?

Lack of conversation made the meals unpleasant, but she was determined to keep trying to cheer things up. She missed the relationship they had started developing, the closeness, and his kindness and concern. A hundred times a day, Ruth blamed herself for ruining it.

As they sat at the table having their evening meal, she looked over at Bo staring vacantly past her and said, "Naomi said there's a big harvest party the end of next month." He nodded. "She said there's a big dance at the big ole barn behind the Sunday meetin' house." He nodded again. "Ya goin' ta de dance?" she hinted.

He shrugged and looked at her. "Why?"

"I jes wonderin'. I might make a purty frock if we's goin'."

"No need for you to worry about the Harvest Dance. Mister George will be back by then. I'll have your papers and you can leave. So you won't be here." His look was cold.

"Naomi said it's always such fun . . . I wanna go . . . I mean, I was thinking ta wait till spring at least ta leave."

Lord, why is she torturing me? If she's leaving I wish she'd just go!

"Why wait?"

"I ain't got nowhere ta go en it be winter soon. I needs ta make plans on how ta live on my own. I's hoping ya let me stay till . . ."

His expression softened. He sighed at the compassionate urging of his spirit. "Of course you can stay if you need to. I would never throw you out in the winter cold, but I want you to know it's your choice. You are free to stay or to go, whatever you want. I'm not holding you here against your will. You are free. Do you understand?"

"I understands." They ate the remainder of the meal in silence.

When they had finished eating, Bo went to the thatched chair and picked up his Bible for the first time in days; he'd been too upset to read it. He'd been going to bed as soon as supper was over or he'd sit by the window and stare out into the dark. Tonight he opened the book and read to himself as Ruth prepared to wash the dishes. "Will you read to me?"

He looked surprised but nodded. "I'm reading about Moses," he told her. "Moses was a Hebrew who was spared from certain death by his mother putting him in a basket and floating him down the river. He was found by the pharaoh's daughter."

"What's a pharaoh?"

"A pharaoh is a who. That's what the Egyptians called their king."

"Oh."

"Moses was raised in the pharaoh's palace like royalty." Bo went on to tell part of the story, then read some of the exodus from Egypt. He read about all the plagues and of the Israelites escaping through the sea. Ruth was fascinated and asked questions as she listened and washed the dishes. When she finished, she sat at her favorite spot, on the floor by Bo's feet, as he continued reading to her.

"Das no true story, is it?"

"Yes, it is."

"Cain't be."

"Why not?"

"The sea partin' and sticks turning ta snakes, dat all make-believe. Cain't really happen."

"With God it can. All things are possible with God."

"How ya know?"

"It says so in the Bible. In the book of Mark, chapter 10 is one place it says that."

"Ya mean all dose things really happen?"

"They did. This Book is true and I know that without a shadow of doubt."

"How ya know?"

"In my spirit. My spirit lets me know things."

She frowned at him. "Yo spirit? Ya always talkin' bout yo' spirit."

"It's the Holy Spirit inside me."

"If God kin do anythin', why ain't He put a end ta slavery?"

"He will. All in His good time."

"Ya said dem Hebrew folks was slaves?"

"For four hundred years."

"God freed dem?"

"He did. They walked right out of Egypt."

"Why God take so long?"

"I don't know, but whatever God does is perfect even in His timing although we don't always understand it."

"When I use ta go da Sunday prayer meetin', I heard stories but never baleeve 'em. Dey sound made up as dose fool stories Miss Molly use ta read ta me 'bout knights in armor en giants. Plum silly if ya ask me."

"The Bible has a story about a giant too. I'll read it to you tomorrow."

"And ya says it truly happened?"

"When you come to know the Lord, it will all make sense and be more real than even living in this world is now."

Ruth looked at Bo strangely. "You's a different kinda man, but if I kin be made ta baleeve, you's da one kin do it." Ruth smiled, stood up, and moved to sit on his lap.

"What are you doing?" *Lord, I can't be with her like this if she's going to leave me.*

"I wanna be close ta ya. You's my husband, aint ya?" She wrapped her arms around his neck.

Bo struggled to dislodge her but she held on tight. "You have to let go," he complained.

"Why ain'tcha wan me no mo'?"

"Ruth, let go."

She tried to kiss him, but he fought against it. "Let go right now."

"I's yo wife, ain't I? Let me be ya wife."

"No, not like this!" *Oh, Jesus, help me.* "Ruth!" He grabbed her arms tightly.

She stopped and stared at him, looking wounded. "Ya hurtin' me," she whimpered.

He let go. "I didn't mean to hurt you, but you have to stop this. I've tried to explain to you that our relationship won't be like that if you don't commit to being my wife as God intended a man and woman."

"Ya mean fo'ever?"

"Yes."

"Fo me ta stay here?"

"That's right. I really want you to stay but I won't force you to. If you're going to leave me in the spring, that changes things . . . I can't go through losing another wife."

"But I ain't gonna be dead."

"It doesn't matter if you are still alive. You won't be with me. Might as well be dead for all the good it does."

Ruth wrapped her arms around his neck and kissed Bo. He tried to turn away, but she was determined. She slid off his lap and stood in front of him and held out her arms. It struck fear in her heart that he would never again feel the way he had on their wedding night. She was desperate for him to hold her again. She wanted to be his wife . . . at least at that moment.

Bo rose to his feet. He was torn. She was so beautiful! And after all, she was his wife. "Tell me you won't leave me," he insisted.

Her heart pounded. She thought about his love for her. Then she answered. "I won't." She whispered the words, not looking at his face.

He turned her face to him and looked into her eyes. Was there a spark of interest or was he imagining it? He didn't believe her words. "You really want to be my wife?"

"I do; I wanna be yo' wife." She wanted him to comfort her as he had before. Tears started spilling out because she had no strength to hold them back. She felt his arms go around her.

He kissed her head lovingly. "I'll always be good to you, I promise," he said before he swept her up into his arms. Then her face fell into the bend of his neck while she was still crying. "I love you, Ruth." He said it over and over. It was like a dream she never wanted to end. That night she fell asleep in his arms, oddly contented but confused about his decision to comfort her—just to comfort her and allow her to rest, abstaining from making love.

This was all new to Ruth, but she felt a peace she'd never known before.

Nine

The prophet's imposing presence at the meeting-house caused Bo some uneasiness from the moment he observed him. Nat Turner was a short muscular man who appeared to be around the same age as Bo. Prophet Turner sat during the service and watched the congregation sing.

Mister Purdy and his wife were not present. Their conspicuous white faces were regularly seen at the Negro church. The meetinghouse was on Purdy property, a privilege they granted the Negroes out of an undercover abolitionist sympathy. Fortunately the white folks had a big do at their own church this day, celebrating the marriage between the son of one of the county's wealthier plantation owners to the daughter of one of the county's most socially prominent families.

After the time of boisterous and joy-filled singing, the congregation settled down to hear the sermon by Prophet Nat Turner. Bo was impressed that Turner was well-versed with an accurate knowledge of the Scriptures, but still there was something that bothered him.

Rooster sat in the front, which was not his custom. He was smiling and nodded in agreement with the prophet the whole time. The texts of this long sermon were from the books of Joshua, Judges, and 1 Samuel. Turner spoke of men taken from humble means and called to do mighty deeds in the name of the Lord. He told of Joshua, who came out of Egypt with Moses and who was chosen by the Lord to bring down the walls of Jericho. He explained how Gideon was low man in a family of no repute trying to hide wheat from the Midianites when God called him into service. Lastly, he spoke of David, the shepherd boy who was the least thought of among his brothers. He shouted the story of David killing Goliath and told of how the warrior spirit came forth in David at a young age to protect his sheep.

"God called the shepherd boy to put down his staff and take up the sword," Turner repeated several times. Bo wondered during the impassioned sermon what important thing the prophet had come to say. The story of these biblical heroes was not new to them. Then Nat Turner closed his Bible and began to connect his sermon with the real reason for his visit.

"I am a simple slave who works dawn till dusk on a dirt farm in Southampton County. Ever since I was a child my mother told me stories of our family's place in Africa, our homeland. I come from a proud bloodline of royal African lineage. My grandmother and mother taught me my people's ways but they also taught me how to listen to God. We are not always going to be enslaved to the white man to toil and work for nothing till we drop. God is going to deliver us all!"

The congregation cheered thunderously.

Ruth looked at Bo, amazed. *Dis man*, she thought, *is smart like Bo, kin read, and speaks propa like Bo. Dey call him prophet so maybe Bo's a prophet too.*

Nat quieted the crowd and continued. "*One man* took action to free the Hebrews. *One man* led the fall of the Jericho wall. *One man* garnered the troops to defeat the Midianites . . . and *one divine Man* saved our souls. But we will not see freedom if we wait for white people to see their sin and set us free. We will never taste the sweetness of being free men and women till we take action!" Low murmurs floated through the air. "Brothers and sisters, we have to get over our fears and take the brave road to get what we deserve. Jesus came to set the captives free! God says we all should have liberty!"

"Dat's right! We should all be free!" Rooster shouted, throwing up his fist.

"Free as any white man!" Pappy Seymour called from the midsection.

"Know, my brothers and sisters, freedom has a high price. It could mean your very lives," Turner cautioned, then scanned their faces before saying, "but isn't it worth dying to be free if just for a while? Or do you value your lives of uncompensated servitude and mistreatment more? Some things are worth dying for, like freedom to live as human beings and not be treated like mindless critters! The right to be free is worth everything, including our very lives! Even if not for us but our future generations, we must unite in this cause!" He waved his Bible in the air. "Wasn't Christ Jesus crucified for a greater cause than Himself?"

"Yes, hallelujah, hallelujah!!" Lula yelled, falling sideways on the bench.

"Praise God Almighty!" Preacher Jones shouted from behind the prophet.

"I am not afraid to be martyred for my people's freedom, and I bid you not to shy away from it if the time comes for you to further justice!" Nat Turner's eyes were popping with passion. His voice thundered through the room. Bo watched the people around him as some waved their hands and shouted in agreement; others nodded and whispered among themselves. The vibrant speaker had captured the congregation's attention, and the crowd seemed to be in harmony with what he was saying.

Bo's spirit, however, was not peaceful with what he was hearing or seeing. "What is this man proposing? What does he want us to do?" he whispered to Ruth.

"I don' know, but he right," she answered, smiling.

Nat Turner went on. "God calls men to stand up and organize soldiers to revolt when the time is right. I will say no more at this time, but heed my words, friends, there will come a time of reckoning when slaves become warriors for freedom. We will be brave soldiers and strike a blow for posterity!"

"What means pos . . . posterity?" Ruth asked.

"Future generations," Bo answered, looking worried.

"You's so smart," Ruth gushed, linking her arm inside his.

"We Africans are a strong, mighty people. Why have we allowed the white man to dominate us in this fashion? The time draws near to rise up in the name of almighty God!" Turner waved his Bible again. "Sooner than you know I will say to our captors, as David told Goliath, 'This day will the Lord deliver thee into mine hand; and I will smite thee, and take thine head from thee; and I will give the carcases of the host of the Philistines this day unto the fowls of the air, and to the wild beasts of the earth; that all the earth may know that there is a God in Israel'!"

Bo sat perfectly still, not making a sound, as the congregation around him erupted, wildly clapping and roaring.

Ruth too was clapping. She leaned over and asked, "Is dat da story ya read ta me bout da boy killing da giant?"

95

"It is. It's David and Goliath."

When the clamor diminished, the prophet continued. "Let us learn the power of a God who loves liberty. We'll fight under the guidance of the Lord against this evil they call slavery! In the spirit of Toussaint-Louverture and Gabriel Prosser, we will fight! In the way of Jeremiah of the Good Book, like 'fire shut up in my bones,' freedom burns in my heart! God is calling us to take up arms. The African will be free—or die trying!"

His eyes swept the audience. Voices rose again filling the room as he took the seat across from the preacher. Bo looked over at Ephraim and Naomi, who were clutching each other's hands fearfully. He glanced at Michael Combs, who sat on the bench at the other side of the aisle. Michael was looking equally dismayed. Ned and Johnny Boy were clapping and whistling. Tommy from the Gaylord farm caught Bo's attention and shook his head somberly. Almost everyone else was joyful and making affirming sounds or motions.

Rooster stood up and faced the mostly raucous group. His gaze fell on Bo. "I tol' ya dis important, didn't I?" he said grinning. "Prophet Nat's gettin' us ready ta fight fer freedom."

"Freedom!" Nanny's husband, Claude, yelled. "Freedom! Freedom!"

The prophet got to his feet again and held up his hand. "All successful movements need a good leader. This area needs someone who has knowledge, is young enough and healthy, someone trusted by whites to travel around if need be for your leader under me."

The man sitting next to Rooster sprang to his feet. He was Booney, Rooster's cousin, a very light-skinned, medium-height man with a thick build. "Gotta be somebody we kin trus'," he added.

Rooster immediately spoke up. "Dere's only one man fo de job: Bo Peace. White folks love em and he kin read real good. He's de smartest colored round here cepin' fo Preacha. Smarter den plenty white folks en he's 'bout as trustworthy as dey come."

"Yeah and he free. Kin come en go like he wanna," Cass chimed in from the second row.

Booney searched the room for the one they called Bo to rise. "He here?" he asked.

"Sho, right over dere." Rooster pointed to Bo. Nat Turner looked hard at Bo, as did Booney and the preacher waiting for a response.

Bo rose slowly. He looked down at Ruth. She was grinning proudly. He looked back at the prophet then to Rooster and Booney. "I'm sorry, but I can't oblige." He sat down and avoided Ruth's puzzled expression. Low murmurs were heard.

"Why not?" Rooster asked. "You's always talkin' 'bout us people bein' free one day."

"I'm no leader or organizer," Bo said flatly.

"What ya mean? Ya organize all dem freed slaves on yo farm."

Bo was feeling pressured. All eyes were on him, including the prophet's and especially Ruth's. "I just can't right now, that's all."

"We need ya, Bo, ya know we ain't educated like ya is. Most us slaves cain't read a lick."

"Leave him alone; he got a new wife ta tend ta," Ephraim snapped.

"Ain't dis mo' important?" Cass asked, looking at Bo accusingly.

"Not if you's already free en don't care 'bout nobody else gettin' free," Jeb Tate said, folding his arms across his big belly.

"That's not true!" Bo retorted. "I care about all slaves being free, and every one of you know I do. I buy slaves just to set them free. How can you rightly say I don't care?"

Prophet Turner sat down staring at Bo. "If his heart isn't that of a warrior, we can't use him. Is there anyone else? Who else can read besides Preacher Jones? You need someone who will be able to read my letters of instructions."

"I can," Mara said. "I can read just as good as him. We were both taught by Miss Isabelle."

"We need a man," Booney said, dismissing her. "Anyone else?"

Newton Grimly stood up. "I'm a warrior from Africa! My mammy said so! We was from a warrior tribe!"

"Aw, Newt, ya can't read a thang," Rooster pointed out.

"I might cain't read but I kin fight like de devil," the big burly man insisted, flexing his muscles. He pumped his fist into the air and declared, "I's a warrior! Got African warrior blood in me!"

Mara added, "I can fight too . . . if I have to."

Rooster huffed. "Newt, sit down, and Mara, we cain't have no women organizin' things, so you sit down too."

"Might need her if she kin read," Booney said. "But not as leader."

"We need every able-bodied man and woman for one task or another," the prophet advised.

"What xactly we plan on doin'?" Michael asked.

"Fight, a course!" Rooster said, smiling. A few laughed.

"Fight who en wit what en why?"

"Ya boneheaded or something? Didn't ya hear Prophet Nat? We's fightin' fo' freedom, fightin' de white folks."

"Fightin' how?" Michael stood and looked at the prophet,

not Rooster. "What we gonna do? Jes leave en dare em ta stop us? Or is we attackin' dem first?"

Good questions, Bo thought.

Nat Turner folded his hands reverently in his lap. "God will reveal in time what form of rebellious action to take."

"Sound mighty mysterious ta me," Michael grumbled as he sat down.

Preacher Jones got up and walked forward. "This is the Lord's house. We are people of God and we don't attack unless we have to. I'm sure Prophet Nat is not saying we should go round attacking the whites for no reason. He will have a plan as given to him by God. For now we must pray for guidance and strength. The prophet will come again, and by then hopefully we will have a leader amongst us."

"What 'bout you?" Ben Smiley called out.

Janey said, "Dat's right, you's already a leader anyhow." People started murmuring among themselves.

Preacher Jones looked around. "I am a man of God."

"Ain't dis God's will we fight fo' freedom?" Cass yelled.

"Indeed it is!" Prophet Turner shouted back.

Rooster threw his arm out and pointed to Preacher Jones. "Den he's our man, a man a God. Who could be better?"

"You agree, Preacha?" Ben asked.

"Well . . . um . . . I . . . I have no objections at the moment but . . ."

"Good, den we all agree de preacha is our organizer." Rooster sat down.

"He weren't done talkin'. Let him say his peace," Michael said.

"Something else ya wanna say, Preacha?" Booney asked, taking a seat next to Rooster.

"Well . . . um, just that if at any time I think this interferes

99

with my place as a minister of the gospel . . . well then, I'll have to step back. I am a man of God first."

"So is Prophet Nat, ain't he?" Mara remarked loudly.

Nat Turner stood up. "Any insurrection against our enslavement will be deemed by God. I do not say these things idly of myself but of the spirit that moves in me. *I am a slave!* I know the restrictions bondage inflicts and I suffer the indignities of being a mere beast of burden. I have known since childhood there was a purpose for me beyond this life of servitude. My mother and grandmother taught me from my youth to prepare for becoming great, even in these hostile surroundings. I ran away from my master and was well into freedom for thirty days but returned to my master under the guidance of the Spirit."

"Ya got free en went back?" Luke Myers asked incredulously.

"I surely did because God told me to go back. My purpose is not just to free myself but strike a blow for all slaves and free as many as possible in my lifetime. Mine, like Christ's, is a wide-reaching mission. I have to deny myself for the greater good. Sacrifice for God's purpose."

"Ya really 'scaped en went back to yo' massah?" Emma asked in awe.

"Yes, madam, I did. Many can attest to the truth of what I say. I was spiritually chastised for my narrow vision of acquiring freedom for just myself. I was obedient to God when I returned. I now have a more widespread destiny, which includes my fellow slaves."

Bo looked at Ruth. Her mouth hung open and her eyes were glued to the eloquent speaker.

Ten

Ruth wasn't talking much during the ride home. Bo was troubled, and his mind bounced off thoughts of all he heard and saw, especially from Nat Turner. When he finally pushed it aside, he realized Ruth looked sullen. "You're mighty quiet."

She barely looked at him when she flicked a smile. "What's wrong?" he asked.

"I ain't like what happen tanight."

"Me either. That prophet isn't preaching Jesus, he's preaching slave revolt."

She frowned. "Is dat wrong ta wan freedom?"

"No, it's not wrong to want freedom, but getting it through violence is not the way of God."

"Dat's not what de prophet say. He say dere plenty times God tol His people ta fight, ta wage war en kill up de enemy."

"Yes, in the Old Testament there was."

"So it awright ta fight fo' freedom."

"In the New Testament when Jesus came, He told us to

love our enemies, to forgive, and don't do evil for evil but do good for evil."

"Foolishness."

"You think so?"

"I sho do. How ya spose ta love folks who torture ya en treat ya like dogs?"

"Jesus did," he said softly. "They crucified the Lord. Tortured and nailed Him to a cross of wood. Some of His last words were to ask the Father to forgive them for what they were doing." Ruth didn't say anything. Bo's words surprised her. "I want freedom for all slaves as bad as anyone else, but it has to be God who does the freeing."

"But He ain't doin' it."

"He will."

"Folks tired a waitin'."

"What will a revolt get but bloodshed and harsher treatment for slaves?"

"Ya don' believe de prophet?"

He didn't want to get into a deep discussion, but he wasn't going to lie to her. "Nat Turner . . . I don't know. He may be a man of God; I can't dispute that but I can't swallow some of what I heard him saying."

"I thought ya put so much sto' in de Good Book like he do?"

"I do, but what he gets out of it is not what the Lord is telling me when I read it."

"Dat makes no sense. Ain't it de same Book?"

"Yes, but the Bible speaks to us through the Holy Spirit. People sometimes read into it what they want because of the foul spirit in them or their strong fleshly desires."

Ruth shook her head. "Too much figurin' fo' me. If God wan folks ta know what He wan, He oughta come right out en tell 'em."

"He does, but not like we expect."

"Why ain't ya willin' ta lead de folks fo' freedom?"

"You disappointed that I'm not, aren't you?"

"Yeah, I thought ya be glad ta hep. Why ain't ya?"

"Ruth, this may turn out to make a lot of trouble for a lot of folks. I don't know where it's heading or how it's going to end. I can't get caught up in the fury to attack white people just because some so-called prophet says he's called by God to do so. We don't really know this man. It could be a trap."

"Ya don't like him, do ya?"

"I don't dislike him. I just don't know him and I won't trust my future—our future—and all I've been blessed to hold together on his word. God will have to lead me directly to involve myself in this business."

"Sound mo' like ya scared ta me."

"You're wrong; I'm not scared but I'm no fool either. *You* sound like you're ready to go running off to revolt with the man."

"I is."

"Are you serious?"

"Sho is."

"You would risk your life in a rebellion just because of what he said today, a total stranger?"

"Not jes what he says but what I feels. I hate white folks fo how dey treat us en I don' wanna live under dey cruelty no mo'."

"You don't have to, I told you . . ."

"Maybe I is free but what bout all da others? We gotta hep dem get free too, don't we?"

"I do what I can. I pray for God's help, and He blesses me to free a few each year."

"What if ya kin free mo' slaves all at once? Kill up a bunch of white folks en put de fear a God in der hearts like de prophet says."

103

"Do you hear yourself? You're talking about taking human lives."

"How many a our folks lives dey take? How many lives dey ruin even dough we's still livin'?"

Dear God, is her heart so full of hatred? "When the Lord delivers us, I believe we won't have to revolt violently. We need to let God fight this battle for us. The Hebrews didn't wage war to get out of Egypt. God moved on their behalf."

"Dose fairy stories don' hep us none."

"They're not fairy stories, they're the truth of what the power of God has done. It's Him showing Himself to us in ways we can understand."

"I ain't understandin' much a nothin' I hear from it."

"Perhaps your heart and mind are closed." He glanced her way and caught the eye roll. It made him smile. She was even more beautiful when she was feisty and stubborn.

"All I knows is lots a folks livin' but wishin' dey was dead cause a slavery."

Bo looked at his wife thoughtfully. "You're talking about yourself, aren't you?" *Naomi's right; she is wounded and it's turned into hate. Lord, help me soften her heart and show her how not to hate but to love. Guide me to show her Your love somehow.*

"I wish I was dead plenty times."

"I felt that way when I was younger before I knew my Savior . . . hopeless."

"I 'spose ya' freedom changed dat."

"It changed while I was still a slave. Jesus gave me hope even in slavery."

Ruth looked at him strangely. "Jesus yo' answer ta everythin', ain't it?"

"Thankfully, yes, He is."

Eleven

A huge fallen oak blocked the road. Bo had to take an alternate route to get home. He got quiet again and this time it was Ruth wondering what was wrong.

"This trail takes three times as long to get us home and winds too close to the swamp," he complained.

"Da swamp?"

"Yeah, it's a small part of the Great Dismal Swamp that comes inland."

"Ya talkin' 'bout de Black Water Death Swamp?"

"It has been known as that in slave quarters."

"What wrong wit being a little near de swamp if we ain't in it?"

"I don't go too close if I can help it."

"Scared?" Ruth asked sarcastically.

Bo tightened his jaw. "No, I'm not scared. Do you think I'm a coward, that I'm afraid to die?"

"I ain't mean nothin'," she said, thinking she may have gone too far. She hadn't meant to insult him and she didn't want him mad at her. She hated the thought of Bo being angry with her.

"I'm not a coward," he insisted.

"What wrong wit bein' near de swamp den?" she asked, hoping to move the conversation away from the subject.

"Slave catchers . . . they lie in wait around the swamp because runaways head for it to avoid capture. Some say escaped slaves live in the swamps because no one wants to go in there after them. It's too dangerous, so slave hunters wait close enough to get them coming or going. Lots of seedy characters move around and about the swamp too. Everything from highway robbers to men just looking for something to satisfy the evil inside them."

They rode on in silence. Bo looked around cautiously, eyes darting, head turning at every suspicious sound. It made Ruth nervous. She wished they had waited for the rest of the congregation that was going their way, but Bo was anxious to leave the charged-up atmosphere. He didn't want to stay at church talking with the others . . . and prophet Turner.

The terrain thickened with willows, bald cypress, and tupelos still lush in the Indian summer climate. The marsh to the right was distinctly visible, but the ground under the wagon was still firm and the path clear. An eeriness hung in the air till even the birds' singing sounded morose. What Ruth wasn't aware of and Bo knew all too well was that many people had met their end or recapture in the vicinity of the swamp, and the spirit of fear and death clung heavy there.

Ruth asked, "Is dey lot a wild animals round here?"

Bo looked at her fearful face and grinned. "Only a few bears, wild pigs and bobcat, weasels and otters, lizards and snakes."

Ruth's eyes popped wide. "Bears and bobcats out here?"

"What's wrong; you scared?" He chuckled.

His retaliatory remark did not amuse her, and her rigid demeanor resurfaced. "No, I ain't scared." An odd sound from a cluster of white cypress trees startled her and she scooted closer to him.

Bo put one arm around her. She leaned in as close as she could get. "Don't worry, I won't let any ole bear, wild pig, or bobcat eat you . . . even if you do think I'm a coward."

Ruth started to reply but saw that his attention was focused straight ahead. She looked way in the distance and saw figures of some kind on the road, but they were too far ahead to distinguish.

"Get in the back," he ordered, slowing down the horses.

"What?"

"Get back there under the blankets. Get between the bales of hay, hurry."

"Why?"

"Don't ask questions or argue, just do it." He'd come to a stop.

"Whas wrong?"

Bo jumped off the seat and moved around to the rear of the buckboard. "There's folks up ahead." As Ruth swung herself over in the seat and slid down from her place onto the buckboard, he pulled the blanket off the bales of hay. There was a musket in the middle. He grabbed it in one hand. It was similar to the one hanging over the big fireplace, but she knew that one was still there. There was another that hung over his bed but it looked different from this one too.

This must be the one from the barn, she thought. From the start she'd wondered how a black man could have gotten hold of so many firearms and why he had them. Ruth scrunched between the bales and he pushed them closer to her. "When we get up there don't you make a sound. I'm covering you with these blankets."

"But why . . ."

"I don't know who's on this road and I want you safe. No matter what happens, stay under there and wait for me to tell you to come out. Do you understand?"

"What if ya need my help?"

He gave a half smile. "I won't. Let me handle this my way." He put the musket in her hand. Have you ever shot one of these?"

"Naw."

"Then just hold it for me. I have the pistol behind the seat but if I need it, keep ready. Lie very still when I get up to those men."

"What if . . ." She paused.

"What if what?"

"Nothin'."

He read her fearful face. "If anything happens to me and they find you, cock back this hammer, aim at their face or chest and pull the trigger. It's already loaded." He kissed her on the forehead. "Don't be afraid, 'cause Jesus is with us." He pulled the blankets to cover her. Ruth didn't feel assured being told Jesus was with them. Jesus hadn't stopped any other bad things from happening to her that she could tell.

Bo saw four white men as he got closer; no one he recognized. The men guardedly watched his approach, spreading out across the road to block the path. He knew this meant trouble.

Lord Jesus, keep us under Your wings and protect us from evil.

He slowed the horses to a halt. The skinny older man on a gray horse rode up beside the wagon. "What's your name, boy?"

"Bo Peace, sir."

"Bo Peace, huh? What you doing back here near swampland, Bo?"

"Der's a big ole tree done fell down cross dat der road back a spell. Has ta come dis way ta git home, sir," using his select slave vernacular.

"And just where is home?"

"Maitland's farm right outside Jerusalem, sir."

A second man rode up next to the first. "Where you comin' from?" he demanded. This man's hateful spirit was evident from his flaring nostrils to his cold eyes and thin, pursed lips. He rode the biggest animal in the group, a large black-and-white spotted horse.

"Sunday meeting, boss."

"Aw, let him go, Wally, he's no runaway. Runaways don't ride around in big ole wagons like this," the third man called. He stayed put, but his brown stallion kept dancing in place while his rider held him in place.

The fourth man let his horse trot to the rear of the wagon. Bo kept a calm demeanor despite his growing nervousness. "What you got back here?" he wanted to know.

"Jes some hay bales, sir." Bo kept his eyes down and did not look any of them in the face.

"Aw go on . . . git!" the first man said, turning his horse around.

"Yessah," Bo replied and started a slow movement forward. The men opened up but Bo knew not to take off too quickly. As he drove on, he could feel their stares on his back. He was not at ease yet. When he was out of earshot after a good distance, he heard hooves coming behind him. Without turning around, he told Ruth, "Stay put; they're coming behind us. Keep quiet till I say." His hand touched the pistol behind his seat under the blanket but he was praying not to have to use it. The horses were picking up speed now, running toward him. Soon they had surrounded him and brought him to a halt again.

"Hey there, boy!" the oldest man called. "You say you from Maitland's farm?"

"Yessah."

"Ain't they them ones who let their slaves go free?"

"Yessah."

"Then you're free?" the spiteful man they called Wally growled.

Bo had to strain not to look the man in the eye when he answered. "Yessah, I's free."

"A free man wandering back here near the swamp," the third man said, moving his brown stallion closer to the wagon. "How we know you really free? Could be lyin'. Might be a runaway for all we know."

"I's no runaway, boss. I got ma papers right here." Bo pulled out a folded paper from his shirt pocket. Wally snatched it from him. He read it, then handed it to the oldest man.

"Yep, says here you're free all right," the man said. He folded the paper and handed it to Bo. The fourth man backed away as if to let Bo go by, but Wally moved in closer.

"I ain't so sure this colored boy really is free."

"Why not?" the fourth man asked. He took his hat off and scratched his head.

"Wally, you don't care if he is free," the older one said, shaking his head.

"That's right, I don't. Freeing slaves ought to be against the law."

"Well, you don't make the laws so let him go on," the fourth man said, moving out of the way.

"What if I don't feel like letting him go? You plannin' to stop me?" Wally challenged.

"We're here looking for runaways. He ain't no runaway, so let him go."

"One black is good as another to me. Get down from that wagon, boy."

"Always got to be trouble with you, Wally," the third man muttered.

Bo didn't want to get down off the wagon. He looked at the oldest man, who seemed to be the leader of the posse. "I's don' wan no trouble, sir," Bo said mildly.

"Better get down, boy. When Wally gets riled it ain't wise to go against him."

Bo thought he saw a hint of sympathy in the man's eyes.

"What's got into you, Wilson, you getting soft in your old age? This here is a prime black buck. He'd be worth a fortune."

"Not to us he isn't. He ain't a runaway. We catch runaways, not free Negroes."

"So what? Roger Breckenridge in Richmond don't care if they free or not. He ships 'em off with no questions asked and pays top dollar."

"Breckenridge is a greedy, unethical slave dealer and I don't do business with him," the old man growled.

Wally got off his horse. "Get down, I said!"

Bo slowly descended from the wagon. The man stepped up close and grinned. "Now let's just take care of this little matter of you being free." He reached in Bo's pocket for the paper. With a lightning-quick reflex, Bo blocked him from pulling it out and pushed him away. The man's eyes widened with surprise that intensified quickly into fury. "You got the nerve to put your hands on me, a white man? Why, I'll teach you . . ." He rushed to his horse and grabbed his whip. He ran toward Bo with the whip slashing air.

Bo turned to shield his face as the whip came down across his shoulder and back. The force tore through his shirt and drew blood. Bo spun around and grabbed the end of the whip, snatching it out of the man's hand. "I'm a free black man! You have no right to whip me!" he yelled, forgetting to talk like a slave.

"You filthy slave!" Wally charged at Bo wildly. Bo knocked him down with two powerful punches. The fourth man pulled a musket but didn't aim at Bo because Morely held up his hand for nothing to be done. Wally sprang to his feet, coming at Bo again. He knocked Bo down with a head butt to the stomach. They wrestled on the ground until Bo was able to position himself on top. He started pounding Wally with his fists, his muscular arms delivering blow after blow, all the time growling he was free, until the man was no longer fighting back. Panting, Bo scrambled to his feet expecting to be shot or attacked by one of the other men. He pulled his opponent from the ground and held the man's limp body in front of his as a shield. He stood with his legs spread slightly apart ready to block the attack from the other three while going for his pistol. Wally's eyes were shut and he was moaning. All three had guns out but none were pointed at Bo. He didn't know what to think but he hoped to at least get to take one more down before they killed him so Ruth would have a chance if she needed to shoot another. He wanted to get to his own musket but knew he couldn't. His best move would be to take one of theirs. His mind was racing with strategies to stay alive long enough to take down as many as he could for his wife's sake.

Morely slowly trotted forward smiling. "Calm down there, boy. We ain't gonna shoot you. I've been waitin' to see someone beat the slop out of Wally for years." He laughed. "Make's it all the sweeter that you, a free black, did it." The other two men nodded and laughed in agreement.

"He won't ever live this down," the fourth man said, putting his musket back in its side holder on his horse.

"Leave him go and git before Wally rallies. He'll want to kill you dead when he does."

"Leave this swamp in a hurry, cause he's a mean rascal and he'll hunt you down if he's able."

Bo dumped Wally to the ground, picked up his hat, and got on the wagon hurriedly. "But he knows my name and where . . ."

The second man chuckled. "Don't worry. He'll forget about that after all the whiskey it'll take for him to swallow this whopping you put on him. By the time he gets over this, we'll tell him some other name. He forgets all the time when he's drunk."

"Can't even remember the name of a pretty woman after a good tie on, so he won't remember yours or where you come from—so get going." Morely glibly waved his hand.

"Yessah," Bo said, starting the horses on the way. "Much obliged!" he called as he rode off. He drove for two miles before he called to Ruth. "It's safe; you can come out now." He slowed to a stop, hopped off, and went to the buckboard. As he helped her down, he winced from pain. She stood wobbly for a moment.

"Ya hurt, ain't ya?" she said, touching his bleeding shoulder.

"Been hurt worse."

"Lemme tend ta it, but first I gotta go do my business." She scrunched her face. "I's so scared I almost went on myself."

He laughed and pointed. "Go behind that tree and hurry,

113

so we can get out of here. My wounds will keep till we get home."

As they headed home, the horses looped through the snakelike path more swiftly than Ruth was comfortable with. She held on tight as she was continually jostled around. She kept staring at Bo. Eventually he wanted to know why.

"Sorry to be driving so fast, but I don't trust those men not to change their minds and come after me. Want to hurry on down the road." He flicked her a curious look. "Something else on your mind?"

"You's a puzzle ta me. Ya fight dat white man like ya ain't care him or his friends woulda killed ya."

"I cared, but sometimes you think beyond your own safety. I had to think about you. My mind was on giving you a chance to survive if they did kill me."

"Me?"

"Yes, I had to protect you as much as possible while I could. Get rid of as many of them as I could before they did me in."

"But if ya thought they'd kill ya . . ."

"My life didn't matter the most, yours did."

Ruth was astonished. "Ya stood up ta dem men like dat fo' me?"

"Yes." He smiled. "You sound surprised."

"Well . . . maybe jes a little." She smiled back, embarrassed.

"You shouldn't be surprised; that's what a man does for the woman he loves."

Bo looked straight ahead after his declaration. He didn't try to watch her reaction, but he could feel the searing stare. It was the first time he'd told her he loved her. He'd stunned himself because he hadn't planned or even wanted to say it at this point. It just spilled out from his heart. He thought of Baby Gal for a moment, then let the thought go. Calm fell over him. He realized she would not feel betrayed because he loved another woman. Baby Gal would be pleased he was living again, because she had loved him so unselfishly. Bo silently thanked the Lord for the peace of mind and joy in this new relationship, although he still felt Ruth might leave him one day. When minutes passed with nothing but silence between them, he said, "I did it to try to protect you, but also because I was angry. I don't look for trouble. I don't want to hurt anyone. I'd like to live peaceable with everybody, but folks won't always let me."

"All dose weapons, why ya got 'em?"

"To defend myself and the people living on my land. A free Negro has more enemies than a slave ever did. Slaves aren't hated like free men are. Slaves are valued as property for labor, but free blacks are a threat to white society. Some white folks would as soon kill a freed slave as see one freed. To them it's against nature to have us around living free. The Maitlands buy guns for me, and they gave me their old muskets when they got those newfangled rifles. One day I hope to buy a nice brand-new rifle just like any white man can. I hear if you go west, a Negro can buy guns on his own. They're fighting so many Indians out there they sell to anybody . . . but Indians." He sighed. "I try not to fight, because I have to let the Lord do my battling for me. You see what just happened back there? I should be dead for sure but the Lord stepped in. That's why we're riding away alive . . . the Lord stepped in and placed His hand of protection around us. It was God who made those men not shoot me."

"Seems ta me de Lawd coulda stepped in a bit sooner."

"The Lord always does things just when He's supposed to for His purpose."

She looked at him. "Ya sho is a diffrent kinda man. I ain't never knowed no man so hard ta understan'." She hooked her arm in his and laid her head on his shoulder, smiling. "But ya ain't no coward, dat's fo' sho."

Twelve

*T*hey were both exhausted by the time they got home. Ruth cleaned and bandaged Bo's arm and back across his shoulder.

"I wanna be wit ya tonight," Ruth said timidly after nursing his wounds.

Bo was puzzled at first, but understood when he saw her expression. He shook his head. "I don't think that's wise, seeing you're not fully committed to us being married. You said you were, but I'm not sure. I don't want you to feel forced into staying as my wife."

"I's said I's committed ta bein' wit you and carin' for you. I wans to make ya happy cause ya make me happy . . . mo' den I ever knowed I could be happy."

"I told you, you don't owe me anything."

"It ain't owing ya. I cares fo' ya, das what I's tryin' ta say."

"Are you sure?"

"Don' make me stay alone in dat room tanight . . . I need ta be wit you." She couldn't stop thinking about the incident on the road and the sweet words Bo said to her on the way home. *He loved her!* No man had ever said that to her; at least no man who truly meant it. When Bo said it, she didn't have the least doubt. It wasn't just words to him; he showed his love in everything he'd done concerning her. Risking his life, thinking only of her was the defining act to his vow of love. Now she knew he truly loved her, and it warmed her all over. He'd fought to protect her. What more could he do to prove himself to her? He seemed happy that she was affectionate as he put his good arm around her. She felt tingly all over just from being close to him.

It made her happy to spend the night in his loving embrace. He kissed her with a lingering tenderness that let her know he loved her before he fell asleep. Ruth lay awake, thinking. She was experiencing happy contentment, a warmth and joy for life that until now had been unknown to her. *This must be love*, she thought. *It must be.*

When the cock crowed, Bo's eyes popped open. Ruth turned groggily and threw her arm across his chest. Daylight was just beginning to overtake the dark shadows of night. He decided not to get up at the crack of dawn as usual. He looked at his sleeping wife, thankful they'd made it home safe. He moved Ruth's arm and slid to his knees to pray. When he looked up from praying, Ruth was awake, watching him. He smiled at her as he climbed back into bed. "Aren't you cold?" he asked slyly, pulling her close to him. Love, tenderness, and harmony peaked in passionate fulfillment with their intense desire for one another.

The fire had died out during the night. She grinned, wrapped her arms around his neck, and kissed him. All the times she had suffered selfish callous men, she never dreamed making love could be so wonderful. The thought filled her eyes with tears.

"What's wrong, did I hurt you?" he asked, alarmed. She shook her head. "Are you crying?"

Ruth couldn't speak. She wanted to tell him how happy she was. That she'd never thought she would feel this way about any man. She wanted to look into his eyes and say those special words she knew he wanted to hear, but they wouldn't come. Something held her back. She turned toward him, tears streaming down her face. He looked at her sympathetically and a small degree of comprehension. "It's all right, my love, it's all right." He held her as she sobbed out her unexplainable joy.

Thirteen

Two weeks after the prophet's sermon, Ephraim was relieving his tension by chewing on straw near the door of Rooster's shack. He did not want to be there and he detested going behind Bo's back, but it was for a good cause.

It was late afternoon and Ephraim wanted to leave the Slocum farm before dark. He was indifferent toward Seymour Slocum, but he loathed Seymour's hard-driving overseer, Wes Phagan. Wes had taken to coming down to the slave quarters on Sunday nights, snooping around and tomcatting with slave women. Ever since Slocum married that on-fire-for-Jesus Mary Haverman five years ago, he gave his slaves Sundays off to rest and go to Sunday meeting. Phagan was known for chewing tabacco and jawing with the men outside Branche's Emporium. He'd brag about his sexual escapades while the other men laughed along. "Yeah, them darkies can really give a man his pleasure." Ephraim had overheard Wes's filthy remarks on several occasions and thoroughly disliked him.

Slave quarters on every farm and plantation in their

county and beyond were abuzz about the inspirational sermons of Prophet Nat Turner. Secrecy from the whites was maintained as always, but the grapevine among the slaves spread wide and fast. Word also spread that Bo Peace was but a questionable participant in the quest for freedom. Many who already disliked Bo because he was free and owned a farm let jealousy color their opinion of the situation. Sunday after church, Rooster Slocum called a gathering at his shack for that evening to discuss strategies. Bo had not attended church that Sunday morning. So Rooster thought to have a gathering and discuss Bo's and a few other people's noncommittal attitudes while organizing. Ephraim hadn't been invited either, but when he found out about it through Wiley's big mouth, he decided to go put folks in their place about the whole matter.

"What brings you to these parts, Ephraim?" Rooster asked, shooting a look at the other men convened in his little shack.

Look de guilt on every one a dese faces, Ephraim thought. "Heard der's a meetin.'"

"Heard from who?" Rooster wanted to know. Wiley Combs squirmed in his chair.

"Don't matter none 'bout how I heard. Seems ta be somethin' goin' on, so it must be right. How y'all doin'?" Ephraim waved friendly, but Rooster didn't seem too enthused to see him. "Hey der, preacha," Ephraim sang out to Preacher Jones. The other men spoke pleasantly enough as they greeted Ephraim, but the atmosphere was definitely strained. Ephraim brushed by Rooster and sat on a corner of a bench beside Jeff Littleton. Jeff lived on the Littleton farm, which was close to the Sussex County border. Ephraim knew something big must be brewing for him to be there. "Don't let me disturb ya meetin.' Go on, Rooster."

Rooster slammed the door shut and went back to the wobbly table and sat down. "We been talkin' bout de prophet Nat Turner en what he said. We needs ta organize. We needs ta organize en be ready."

"Ready fo' what?" Ephraim asked. The men looked at each other.

Rooster finally pushed back in his chair and stared at Ephraim. "We gotta be sho we kin trus ya, Ephraim. Dis here is serious and we don't rightly know where ya stand. We know we can't take no chances wit Bo, but how bout you? Fighting fo freedom or not? You's free but most us ain't and . . ."

"Ya means ta tell me ya fool enuff ta go off half-cocked wagin' war wit white folks and think ya gonna git free? Ya gonna git dead is all, shot or hung and maybe both, not to say skinned alive."

"Shoulda knowed ya think jes like Bo," Dan Boatwright grumbled.

Ephraim bound to his feet. "I thinks like me! I kin think fo' myself en I thinks y'all crazy!"

Wiley waved his hand up and down. "Settle down now. Ain't no need a nobody gittin' riled up." He looked at Rooster. "Ephraim won't betray us even if he ain't takin' part."

"I ain't no traitor ta my people but I ain't no fool either, dats fo' sho." Ephraim sat down. "Don't matter what ya say 'bout Bo neither. He ain't no traitor."

"He ain't wit us, dat's fo' sho. He too busy sittin' easy on dat fat farm a his bein' massah ta y'all free Negroes while de rest a us sweat it out working fo' de white folks," Jeff said, looking over at Ephraim.

"Ain't so, en ya know it ain't. Ain't no mo' kine, hepful man in dis county den Bo Peace. Oughta be shamed slandrin' his name like dat."

"The great en mighty Bo Peace," Fred Lockerby grumbled. He leaned back in the squeaky wooden chair twisting his mouth. Ephraim always suspected Fred didn't like Bo, but he didn't know why. Bo never said a word against Fred. Ephraim looked around at all the men gathered in the shack. He realized it was a select group indeed. They were mostly men who didn't like Bo or who he'd heard speak enviously against him. This wasn't a simple strategy meeting after all, but a deliberate character-maligning assembly.

▸ ▸ ▸ ▸ ▸ ▸

Mara sank to the ground in tears. Her broken heart just couldn't take any more. She was tired of trying to put up a brave front around people. The man she adored had spurned her love to the absolute limit. Bo was married to some unlearned plantation breeder. How could he reject her devotion so indifferently when he knew how she felt about him?

She walked from the cornfield, dazed from so much pent-up anger. Mara walked blindly, wanting never to look back, just go and not think about anything or anybody. Let Bo have his low-life breeding woman; she didn't care. What kind of godly man would want that kind of wife when he could have her, a pure, untouched woman? They were of the same cloth. Mrs. Maitland had taught her just like him. They grew up together on the Maitland farm. Mara had loved Bo since she was a little girl. Now look at her—an old maid of twenty-six, waiting for a man who didn't want her. Everybody thought Bo would marry Mara when they were young, until that Baby Gal showed up. She was only ten years old when Alfred Maitland died and his brother inherited his farm and the slaves on it. Naomi and Baby Gal were two of the dozen slaves belonging to Alfred who came to live on the larger Maitland farm after their master's death. Bo, at twelve years old, was enamored with Baby Gal from the very first. Her with her beautiful smooth brown skin and thick wavy hair like a sheep's wool. She batted her long eyelashes all the time like she was a princess. Mara had hated her even then. All the men gawked at her and Bo followed her around like a lovesick puppy. His friendly attention to Mara waned and eventually disappeared altogether. When Bo and Baby Gal jumped the broom a few years later, Mara's heart broke to pieces.

Years later when Baby Gal died after childbirth along with their newborn, it seemed things might change. Bo was alone once more, and Mara thought she had her chance at last. After all, once a man's been used to having a wife, he's not prone to living alone anymore . . . or so she thought. But the years passed and Bo remained the grieving widower. He was friendly enough to everyone, but not overly interested in Mara or any other woman it seemed.

Why the sudden change? Why did he fall for this Ruth woman when he'd ignored Mara for four years? The answer was too painful to admit. Mara refused to accept that Bo didn't care for her or want her affection in that way. What would she do at her age with no husband? She thought of Jethro, whose wife had died five years ago. He would marry her today if she'd say yes, but she didn't want Jethro. It wasn't him she loved. She loved Bo but Bo didn't love her. She was to Bo what Jethro was to her. The thought was maddening. Mara ached inside for her want of Bo in spite of her bitterness and disappointment.

She stumbled along the swamp road, tears rolling down her face, determined to leave for good and never be found. She'd go live in the swamp with the runaways and let the others think she was dead, because she was; she was dead inside. That would serve them all right . . . especially Bo. She knew he would put it all together and unrelenting guilt would nag at him. The others . . . well good riddance. They did nothing but laugh at her behind her back, call her a fool, and make light of her heartache. No one cared that she was dying inside . . . no one and especially not Bo.

After walking and crying for what seemed like forever, Mara was too tired to go on. She found a tight cluster of trees and sat down underneath a sprawling oak. Her eyes grew heavy and she dozed off.

Startled awake by a kick, Mara opened her eyes to look up into the hostile face of a white man. "What you doin' sleepin' here?" he bellowed.

Mara got to her feet and pressed herself against the tree trunk. "I's only restin'," she said clumsily, pulling out her slave talk.

"Why you restin' here?"

"I was jes walkin'."

"Walkin', eh, you by yourself back here in this place walkin'?"

"Yessah."

"You a runaway, ain't you?"

"No! I ain't no runaway! I ain't!"

"Where you from?"

"I's from Massah Maitland's farm, sir."

"Maitland?" The man's expression turned even darker. "Where's this Maitland place?"

She pointed northwest. "Dat way o'er yonda a piece."

His eyes narrowed. "Black buck be there called Bo?"

Mara was shocked by the question. "Bo?"

"You heard me! A slave called Bo, does he live on that Maitland farm?"

She stood frozen in fear having heard about the slave catchers Bo tangled with on swamp road weeks before. The man's face had marks and faded bruising. She wanted to know why he was asking for Bo. Who was this stranger? As she stared into his ice-cold eyes, her fear was overturned by the searing bitterness she felt from Bo's rejection. Her brain flashed a picture of Bo happily loving his new wife while her own heart was shattered. "Yessah, Bo lives dere," she said calmly.

The man grabbed Mara by the arm. His face changed from one kind of evil to another. His lips turned up with a lascivious smile. "You say you ain't no runaway. I don't know that, now do I? You might be lying. No sensible slave comes back here this close to the swamp for nothin', specially no gal to take a walk. I think you are a runaway."

"I ain't, I's free!"

"Free?"

"Yessah, I's free."

He swore and spit on the ground, mumbling his disgust. "Well now, Missy, we'll just see how free you really are." He grabbed at Mara's dress roughly.

She cried out, trying to break loose. "Lawd, no, please lemme go!"

"Shut up that fuss! Ain't nobody coming to help you!"

She struggled as he tore at her clothes. "Lemme go, mistah! Lemme go, I's free, I got a paper sayin' I's free!"

"Forget that paper or I'll break your neck right here and right now! Ain't no coloreds free to me, so shut up!" He threw her down on the ground.

Mara screamed, but her cries for mercy didn't penetrate her assailant's stone heart. "Oh, Lawd, mistah, don't do this! Please . . . I ain't never been wit no man!"

The agonizing ordeal seemed to last forever. Mara's screams and pleading fell on deaf ears. The man was brutal in his assault. "Slaves need to remember their place with white folks," he said, fixing himself. Mara was trying to cover herself with her torn clothing. She was hurting and humiliated.

He cracked a nasty smile. "How old are you?" he ask. She didn't answer. "I said how old are you? You answer me or get my whip next!"

"Twenty-six." She wept quietly.

"What's wrong with you? At your age you should be used to a man."

Mara broke into a loud wail thinking about what had happened. "I's not married!" she sobbed. "You ruined me!"

He grinned. "Married? Slaves can't marry, so what you talkin' bout, you ain't married?"

"I ain't never been wit no man befo'." She cried, still struggling not to speak as she normally would.

"Get hold of yourself and stop that blasted crying! What name you called by?"

"Mara," she whimpered softly.

He looked at her dispassionately. She started sobbing again, covering her face in shame. He snatched her hands from her face. "Tell me about this Bo fella, he a big black buck?" Mara gave no response. He slapped her with his open hand. "Answer me!"

She fell over. "Yessah, he big." The man snatched her up from the ground. Mara pleaded, "No, please don't hurt me no mo'!"

"Come on here, I know a man who'll pay a right good price for a good-looking wench like you."

"But I's free!"

"Not anymore you ain't."

Fourteen

*Y*anking Mara through the brush, the man came to an opening where his huge spotted horse was grazing. He took a rope from the side of the horse and tied her hands and neck. He made it tighter than it had to be so if she thrashed about to get free, it would press more tautly into her neck.

Mara had no hope of help coming or ever seeing freedom again. She was angry with God; she'd been betrayed, and it was God's fault for letting this happen. Why did Jesus let this man hurt and shame her? Why hadn't the Lord made Bo love her and marry her? She'd been God-fearing and obedient all her life, and for what? To end up alone and rejected, abused, and now dragged back into slavery. Though she was upset with Jesus, she was desperate to get away from her captor. So Mara did the only thing she knew to do. She prayed for help from the God she felt had repeatedly let her down. Her hope was that His mercy and grace she once believed in would not be witheld this time. Her heart cried out to the Lord, begging

Him to take pity on her as this devil's servant dragged her along in the darkening Sunday evening.

➤ ➤ ➤ ➤ ➤ ➤

The sky was pitch-black except for the light thrown by the full moon. On his way back, Ephraim had been delayed coming home because his horse had thrown a shoe, when he spotted the two men making a fire. His shock at seeing Mara being dragged along caused him to be extremely cautious. He followed the man and Mara to a place where another man awaited. Ephraim carefully kept watch until well into the night on purpose. He wanted to make certain of the number of men involved. He had his hatchet and knife but if there were too many, he'd have to go for more help.

When it appeared only two slave catchers were about, he decided he'd free Mara himself. He circled the campsite so as not to alert the men. His quiet stalking technique had been perfected as a young runaway in Delaware. Now he was older and slower, but his ability to soundlessly slip up on someone was as sharp as ever.

Mara looked weak and haggard. Her clothes were torn and blood was on her skirt. Ephraim considered several times going for help, but feared if he left, he would lose his bearings because he wasn't used to traveling so near the swamp. The men might pull out and then Mara would be forever lost. He had to act before it was too late.

The two men heartily ate their rabbit and drank coffee. They offered Mara some, but she refused to eat. "Better eat good while you can," the kinder of the men cautioned. "You might not get nothing tasty like this where you're going." Mara sat tied to a tree, head hung low, not speaking.

"Don't be worrying about wasting these good vittles on

her. If she won't eat, let her go hungry," the nasty one said before gnawing his rabbit to the bone. Ephraim saw something in the eyes of that particular slave catcher that disturbed him. He detected something beyond the general greed for money or disregard for human liberty like most men who made a living from this reprehensible trade. He'd seen it before in his youth, this malevolent spirit the man possessed.

Ephraim had been born and lived all of his young adult days as a slave in Delaware. The War of 1812 found many slaves willing to escape and fight on the side of the British for the promise of freedom. Ephraim was one of them. After the war, the promise was not upheld. He'd fled to the docks of Philadelphia and was captured by a vicious man who was part of the infamous Patty Cannon gang. He could sense this slave catcher he was looking at had the same evil spirit in him as those from the Cannon gang. Ephraim could identify it well. It was dark, merciless, and demanding beyond reason, spurned from the depths of an abnormally deep pool of wickedness.

People like this didn't do their dirty deeds just for money. They exacted fierce fury and violence because they could. People like this lived hating from a level of sin deep within their souls, taking pleasure in controlling and punishing. While waiting for the men to fall asleep so he could free Mara, Ephraim remembered his days as a captive of Patty Cannon. He recalled the coldhearted woman and her cruel band of kidnappers, snatching slaves and free Africans alike from the docks as far north as Philadelphia and maybe even New York. He'd been taken and held on a Delaware farm in chains with other kidnapped victims. Then he was shipped to North Carolina where an unscrupulous wealthy plantation owner bought him. Ephraim was more fortunate than most who ended up much farther south.

A year later Mister Maitland purchased Ephraim at an auction in Virginia when the North Carolina plantation was split up by greedy feuding offspring who inherited the property. It was a couple of years after that before Ephraim tasted freedom again. The thought angered him, but he was comforted by the memory of the news of Patty Cannon's death a year ago. Slave and free all along the eastern coast celebrated her imprisonment and subsequent demise. It was a small but potent blow for justice.

He thought about that and of poor Mara kidnapped by men who didn't care that she was lawfully free, men who would sell her back into slavery for profit. His blood ran hot thinking once more of the British lying to them, and all the years he spent as a slave when he should have been free.

He was resolute he would not let this thing happen to Mara, so he waited.

➤ ➤ ➤ ➤ ➤ ➤

Bo was reading his Bible when Ruth came in from the barn. She looked happy, and he felt proud that being with him contributed to this new delight for life. "Have a nice visit with the horses?" he asked, smiling.

"I sho did."

He closed the book and gaped at her.

"I knows ya think I's silly spendin' time talkin' ta horses, but I always did since I was at da Stanleys'. I like horses mo' den people. Dey make me feel good when I's wit dem. Folks mos' times don't."

"Don't I make you feel good when you're with me?" He reached his hand out for her to come to him.

She blushed. "Ya always makes me feel real good."

He wrapped his arms around her. "You know, folks here

131

aren't so bad if you give them a chance to get to know you. After a while they'll love you just like I do."

"Humph, not dat Mara. She hates me; I can feel it." Bo looked down guiltily. She stared him directly in the eyes. "Was ya sparkin' wit her 'fore I come here? Dat why she hates me so?"

"No, I never got that close to Mara. She and I grew up together on the Maitland farm, but I never saw her as someone I wanted to be with that way. She's a good friend but just a friend."

Ruth raised a brow. "She ain't figurin' it dat way."

"I never did anything to make her think I wanted to court her let alone marry her. It's the truth. Mara is a very emotional woman, that's all."

"I ain't so smart 'bout dis love business but Mara plum in love wit ya. Ain't 'bout no bein' a friend on her mine. She wanna be what I is . . . yo' wife."

"Let's not worry about Mara. She's got Jethro hankering after her, and she'll come around and marry up with him one of these days."

"Naomi say she ain't studyin' Jethro."

"Naomi told you that, huh?"

"Yep."

"What else did Naomi tell you?"

Ruth smiled. "Said she be real happy since we jump de broom."

This time Bo blushed. "I suppose she's satisfied now. She won't be nagging me about taking a wife." He nuzzled his nose against her neck.

Ruth giggled playfully. "Is ya gonna read tanight en teach me how ta talk propa?"

"Is that what you want?"

132

"Uh-huh."

"Then let's get started now."

⍩ ⍩ ⍩ ⍩ ⍩ ⍩

Ephraim had cut Mara's ropes and they were escaping when the slave catchers jumped them in the dark. The one man pounced on Ephraim while the other grabbed at Mara. "Keep running!" Ephraim yelled at her, fending off his attacker. Mara's captor stumbled to the ground taking her down with him. She crawled away, desperate to get free, and scrambled to her feet, snatching the tail of her skirt out of his grip.

When she took off, the slave catcher howled and swore, then struggled to his feet to chase after her. Though Ephraim was older than his restrainer, he was an excellent fighter and in good shape. He had managed to wrestle his man and punch him hard enough to knock him back.

By this time Mara was frantic for herself and for Ephraim. She heard the slave catcher coming behind her but was hiding behind trees, staying out of sight. Not having a good sense of direction in the dark, she ran around in a circle. Hearing the crunch of leaves, she knew someone else was nearby. Was it Ephraim or the other slave catcher? She leaned against a tree to catch her breath. Should she stay put or run? She wasn't sure. That horrid man was walking around looking for her. Mara eased farther away as he came closer in her direction. The moon's reflection was the only light to help her see where she was going.

"*You've failed me whenever I needed You most,*" she prayed silently. "*I don't know if You're real or not anymore. I used to believe in You but now I wonder if the ones who say You're not real aren't right; those who still keep the ways of our African fathers from the land they were stolen from. You*

133

always help the white man while we suffer. Why should we believe in You? Why should we worship You?" Tears ran down her cheeks but she held in her sobs. Mara's agony increased as she felt herself rejecting the Lord. She'd been taught about Him since childhood, and at one time she truly believed. She wanted to believe now, but circumstances were too hard and she felt God wasn't helping her or her people. Bitterness and fear had taken over her soul. Though her heart was pounding loudly, it wasn't so loud that she couldn't hear the quiet voice speak back to her.

My love never fails even when you turn away from Me, My child. I am with you although you don't think I am. Trust what My words have taught you. Trust Me no matter how things seem to be. . . . You must trust Me.

How can I when my very life is at risk? You let that white man capture and defile me! If You loved me You would have stopped him. You would let me and Ephraim get away, but they're after us and . . .

Trust Me through all things . . . trust Me in the face of anything happening in this fallen world . . . trust Me, your Redeemer, your God, because I loved you enough to save your soul.

Mara shook her head obstinately. Why was this coming to her when things were so dire? How could she trust . . . how? She was a ruined woman after saving herself all those years for Bo, who had heartlessly married two other women instead of her. This evil white man had had his way with her and now wanted to sell her back into slavery. How could she trust a God who allowed all this pain and degradation?

I am the Lord who set you free from slavery. The One who provided for you and cared for you even though you do not have a husband. You reject the husband I chose for you, but I

take care of you just the same. I AM the same God who blessed
you to be able to read and write and live as a free woman. You
must trust Me, for you fully well know where your deliverance
comes from.

"And we know that all things work together for good to
them that love God, to them who are the called according to
his purpose." Mara's lips moved as she recited silently,
remembering the verse Bo said was his favorite from the Good
Book. Bo . . . thinking of him made her heart ache. Oh, how
she wished he was with her now. He'd protect her from these
men. He'd save her and Ephraim.

Trust Me, not a mere man, not even My servant Bo; trust
Me, your God who is your only Savior. I AM the Source of all
things good. I AM your Protection and Provider.

Mara was spiritually torn, and in her mental wrestling
didn't hear the person coming up behind her. Someone covered her mouth and pulled her close, whispering, "Shh, don't
make a sound. It's me, Ephraim." The hand loosened and
Mara swung around, relieved to see him. He put his fingers to
his lips signaling her not to speak. They slowly crept away
from the moon's light. The woods became denser and darker
and now Mara had new fears.

"I can't see," she whispered, holding tight to Ephraim's
hand.

"We's gotta keep movin'. De dark is safer cause dey cain't
see either."

"You think they'll give up?"

"Not dat devil, no." Ephraim pulled Mara along, listening
for any indication of movement. At one point he and Mara
rested against a tree. He gave her his hatchet. "If they get hold
a ya, use this. Chop at 'em wit all ya might and don't stop till
dey dead or let loose of ya, den run fast as ya kin."

Mara took the weapon, but her spirit was still in turmoil. "Why won't the Lord Jesus help us, Ephraim?"

"He is heping," he answered. "Don'tcha know God sent me by ta hep ya?" He took her hand and they started walking again. It was a few minutes later when a musket blast pierced the quiet of night. Ephraim howled and slammed against a young poplar tree before he slid to the ground.

"Oh no, Ephraim!" Mara wailed.

"Hush. Don't stop moving! Keep going," he croaked.

She went on her knees beside him. Her hand felt the moist blood oozing from his belly. "But you're wounded! I can't just leave you!"

"Do as I say, gal, en git goin'! You wan dem ta git ya?"

"I can't leave you." Her tears fell.

"Go git hep or we's both done fo' . . . go!"

Mara rose, hearing voices drawing near. "I'll get help for you, I promise." She took off, blindly running between the trees as fast as she could. "Jesus, please, please help us!"

➤ ➤ ➤ ➤ ➤ ➤

The hues of gray gave way to the colors of the rising sun. Bo was up, dressed, and starting the fire in the big room by the time Ruth came out. "Good mornin'," she said in the best English she could muster.

"Good morning to you." He kissed her lightly, amused at her effort.

"I will make biscuits if you go get eggs." She strained to enunciate each word perfectly.

"I'd be glad to, my love."

Her heart leaped when he called her *my love*. "I'm a gonna . . . I mean . . . I am going to fix a tasty breakfast."

"Not too tasty. I have to fix a lot of fence today. I don't

want to be too satisfied in the belly." He laughed. Bo had reached the porch, opening the door after getting the eggs, when he heard the hard galloping and clatter of wagon wheels. Naomi was heading toward him in a hurry. By the time she stopped in front of the house, Ruth was at the door, relieving him of the hen's eggs.

Naomi looked worried. "Ephraim didn't come home last night! I tink somethin's happened to him."

"Where'd he go?"

"To Rooster's shack afta church, en I ain't seed him since. Ain't come home fo supper or all night."

"What did he go there for?"

Naomi's eyes darted away before she answered. "Some kind a meetin' or something," she said vaguely.

"That tree still blocking the road? I wonder if he had to come by the swamp road."

"We had ta take dat way afta Sunday meetin'. Ephraim said he tink slave catchers cut dat tree down on purpose."

"I thought so myself after I ran into those men. There weren't any storms lately to knock it down, and it wasn't rotted out to fall on its own."

"What if dem slave catchers ya tussled wit got my Ephraim!" Naomi started crying.

"Come on inside, and don't look for trouble before you have to. I'll get some of the men and we'll go look for Ephraim. His horse must have gone lame or something."

"Ya think Mara went lame too?" Naomi threw out, unconvinced.

"Mara?"

"She disappear yesterday too. Molly seen her walking up toward swamp road. Dat was de last anybody seen a her since. Jethro's crazy wit frettin' o'er her."

Bo looked uneasily at Ruth. He walked off the porch toward the wagon. "You stay here with Ruth and I'll go find Ephraim."

"And don' forget Mara," Ruth reminded with an edge.

"Somethin' awful's happen; I kin feel it." Naomi climbed down with Bo's assistance.

"Don't have ta be," Ruth consoled her. "Maybe jes like Bo say; his horse done went lame or somethin'."

"Lawd, I hope so but what bout Mara? Where she run off ta? Her and Molly had terrible words. Molly said Mara was mo' bad off den she ever seed her, carryin' on about her broke heart en givin' up." Naomi shot a look Bo's way then one of apology at Ruth but kept talking. "Say she was fed up wit us folks en dis place. Stomped off telling Molly she gonna show us all a thing a two en dat was it. Jes walk on away in a huff."

Bo dropped his head, feeling Ruth's reproachful stare. "Who knows what fool thing Mara does? She'll be all right. She's pigheaded but she's quick-witted," he said.

"Giles say three slaves is missing from Collier's since Sunday meetin' a week ago. I's scared dey's takin' folks, Bo! I know dey is." Naomi's voice was shaking.

"You help Ruth fix a good meal and I'll go find Ephraim. We'll be hungry when we get back. Don't you fret so, Naomi. Pray and have faith in the Lord to take care of this."

By the time Bo was ready on his horse, Ruth was starting to worry also. He was taking an additional horse with him for Ephraim if needed. She stood trembling by Bo's favorite brown stallion, holding on to his leg in the stirrup. "What if dey is catchin' folks?"

"What if they *are* catching folks?"

"I don't care 'bout no propa talk now. What if dey git hold a ya?"

"I'll be fine because the Lord is riding with me. All I need you and Naomi to do is pray hard for Ephraim and me."

"You got too much faith in this Lord a yourn."

"Jesus Christ is the only One I know I can have complete faith in."

Her eyes softened and the hollow look was filled with emotion. "Ya kin have faith in me. Faith that I's stayin' even when de year is up. I won't leave ya, Bo, I promise. I's ya wife fo' keeps."

Bo's smiled happily. "Do you mean what you're saying?"

"I do."

He jumped down off his horse and grabbed Ruth, lifting her in the air gleefully. "Ruth Peace, you are the most wonderful thing that has happened to me in a long, long time! Oh, how I love you!" He kissed her and squeezed her tight.

Ruth smiled and squirmed loose, glancing back at Naomi in the doorway. "You's squeezing de air outta me." She giggled.

Bo got back on his horse, grinning broadly. "Don't either of you two ladies fret! I'll bring Ephraim and Mara back for sure. Just pray to our Lord Jesus for His hand of protection!" He rode off waving his hat jubilantly in the air, galloping down the dirt road, kicking up dust.

Fifteen

The five men Bo had rallied had been cautiously making their way deeper into the swamp region for over two hours when Jethro said, "I hear something. Sounds like moaning."

"Probably jes a animal," Lem Sprocket said, moving on.

"Sound human ta me." Bo and Ned were on the western side of the road farther ahead, and Lem and Jethro were to the east with Cal Madison and Josiah Calhoun in the center. They stayed close enough to one another to help in case slave catchers attempted to capture any pair of them. They were all armed with big knives, axes, pistols, and muskets.

"I hears somethin', I tell yah," Jethro insisted. He stopped his horse and held up his arm to prohibit Lem from moving forward. A faint whimpering sound floated through the trees. He moved in the direction of the sound. Jethro was the most intimidating-looking man of the bunch, even more so than Bo. He was gigantic in height and stature with bulging muscles and a broad chest and booming voice to match. His walnut brown face was handsome in a rugged kind of way that often turned women's heads. Jethro was anxious; he wanted to find the one his heart yearned for . . . Mara.

It had been full daylight for hours and Mara was totally exhausted. Her mind was so fearful she couldn't think straight. "I can't go on . . ." Panting, she sank to the ground. "But I've got to get help for Ephraim," she told herself and sat up as best she could. "I've got to help him." Tears rolled down her dirty face. Her clothes were torn and bloody, caked with mud. Her body ached from fatigue and she had no idea where she was. All night she'd wandered, hoping to run into some of the escaped slaves whom people said lived in and near the swamp. She knew in her heart she hadn't gone deep enough into the swamp. She'd been too scared during the night.

Now that it was daylight, she'd take her chances once she rested up. If she was consumed by a patch of quicksand like folks warned about, then so be it. She had to try to save Ephraim because he'd been hurt trying to save her. She'd heard hoof steps on the road in the distance several times. The slave catchers must have gotten their horses, so they couldn't be far away. She stayed deep enough in the marshy parts where their horses couldn't get through.

Then something crackled in the distance. Mara jumped to her feet, terrified. *Jesus, help me, please, help me!* Someone was coming closer. Mara put her hands over her mouth to keep from screaming out of fright and started running. *Lord, save me!* She cried out in her head and tripped over a big tree root protruding from the ground. She fell crying into a muddy pile of leaves. She had no more strength to run, so she waited to be snatched up by the slave catchers. So help her, she'd kill one of them with Ephraim's hatchet before she'd go quietly back into bondage or let one of them violate her again. Maybe the other one would murder her in retaliation. That would be better than a future in slavery . . . death sounded better than cruel bondage.

"Mara . . . is that you, Mara? Where are you?"

The familiar voice calling her name made her raise her head. "Jethro?" She sat up with hope springing forth.

"Mara, dat you?"

The voice was undeniably his. "Jethro, it's me, Mara. I'm over here!"

Jethro came barreling out of the mossy thicket toward her. "Tank de Lawd, Mara, you's awright!" He bent down and scooped her up into his arms, holding her like a child. "I was worried sick o'er you, woman . . ." He choked on his words and his eyes watered.

Mara weakly hung her arms around his neck. "Oh, thank God! How in the world did you find me?" She laid her head against him wearily. *Oh, Jesus, You did help me. You didn't turn away from me, You sent help. Thank You, Lord, thank You!*

"We been lookin' fo' hours." He hugged her close. "Why you do such a fool thing comin' out here by yo'self?" Jethro started back toward the road carrying her.

"I was running away . . ." She answered then jerked her head up. "Ephraim!"

"Ya know bout Ephraim?"

"He's been shot! You have to help him! The slave catchers!"

Jethro picked up speed. "Slave catchers got Ephraim?"

"They had me, and Ephraim got me loose from them and they shot him." In a couple of minutes they were at the road. Jethro set Mara down by a tree. The other men gathered around after he called to them frantically. Mara didn't want to see Bo. She clung to Jethro while she babbled on about what happened. "You have to save Ephraim!" she kept repeating.

➤ ➤ ➤ ➤ ➤ ➤

Naomi snapped green beans with speed and accuracy. She wasn't as talkative or in her usual jovial disposition. Ruth was worried but tried not to show it. Both women were out of sorts but found comfort in being in each other's company, planning and preparing a good meal for the return of their men. It was early afternoon and they'd already killed the chicken, picked vegetables, made biscuits, and prepared apples for a cobbler.

"Dis here gonna be a celebration supper," Ruth said gaily. "Fresh-killed chicken and biscuits wit green beans en okra wit apple cobbler. They'll be some happy hungry folks when dey git back."

"If dey git back," Naomi mumbled. She sat on the porch in the rocker with a bowl in her lap, fingers moving nimbly.

Ruth was sitting on a stump across from the porch at the big cast-iron pot. She was boiling water, scalding feathers off the bird. "What ya mean 'if'? Deys gotta git back."

"Lawd knows I wan 'em to but I's got dis terrible, terrible feelin'."

"What kinda feelin'?"

"Terrible forbodin' kinda feeling. Horrible forseein somethin' dreadful kinda feelin." Naomi shook her head and drew up her shoulders.

"It's jes ya worryin' too much."

"I had it befo'. I knows dis dread when it comes."

Ruth held up the feet of the dead chicken and stopped her task to look at Naomi. "When befo'?"

"Firs' time when dey took my boy from me. Sole him ta a man who took him far up in Appalachia somewhere. My

143

sweet Jessup was only ten. Bout near killed me wit a broke heart. Den dey took Mack, my udda son a few years afta dat when he was only twelve. I thought I go crazy when dey took him. Each time dis dark forebodin' come jes befo' I loss 'em. Den it come again de last time when Baby Gal took sick afta she give birth. I tought afta de baby die dat was it, but she let go a life herself a week afta, poor ting."

A lump gathered in Ruth's throat. "She died givin birth?"

"A spell after. De birth was hard, real hard, and de baby died fo' de day was out when it was born. Baby Gal was so fretful over dat and weak as a kitten. She was sickly and broke hearted. It grieved her so bad dat de baby died cause it was her first chile born whole and alive . . . en her last. She loss three times befo when she was carryin'. Couldn't hold 'em. Esther, she a midwife from up yonder at the Ross farm, she said Baby Gal had ta take ta bed ta keep dat one. So she did. Bo ain't let her lift a finga while she in a motherly way. He got Mae ta come stay en do everything fo' Baby Gal. Mae is a sweet, hardworking woman en she was good to my chile en to Bo. Bo pampered my daughter de whole time. He such a wonderful husband." Naomi got a far-off look on her face. The ache of remembering began taking its toll.

Ruth observed the sorrow. "Bo a real good man, a wonderful man," she said, looking down shyly.

Naomi abandoned her memories, coming back to the present. She smiled remembering Bo's joyful farewell. She was happy her son-in-law was in high spirits again and she gave credit to Ruth for it. "Bo is special, awright. You's blessed beyond measure havin' him fo' a husband." She sighed. "But not even dat overshadow what God allows. Baby Gal carried full-time, so we all thought de worse was o'er but it weren't."

"And you still have faith in Jesus?"

"Mo' den ever. He carried me through all my hurts, chile. If it weren't fo' Him, I'd give up and lost my mind long time ago."

"What kinda help is that? Who wants ta be carried through agony? Why doesn't He stop it, help folks who believes in Him not have ta go through so much trouble?"

"De Good Book don't promise no bed a ease; jes de opposite a matter a fact. It jes says we got a Savior dat won't leave us in our troubles alone. He right der wit us, helpin' us git through it. And He does. I kin testify ta dat."

"And dat's enough fo' ya?"

"Natchly, I rather have a easy trouble-free life. Who wouldn't? But dis sin-ridden world ain't made dat way. All folks go through some rough times or other . . . white folks have der share a grief en heartache too. I's thankful ta have help in my hours a need. De Lawd kin git ya through some hard times, chile, en bring ya out de udder side witout a mess a bitterness."

"Dat's what Bo says."

"He knows, cause he sho have his share a heartache."

Ruth looked at Naomi with a serious expression. "Think I kin make him happy?"

"Ya already done made him happy. Keep doing what ya doin'."

"All I's ever done since I become a woman is make men 'happy.'" Ruth snatched a handful of feathers.

Naomi rocked her chair. "I knows how ya feel. It 'pears ta be a woman's lot in life."

"Some mo' den others," Ruth grumbled. "Puttin' up wit a man is what I wan no parts of no mo' . . . till I comes cross Bo."

"And now?"

"I reckon it ain't all bad when ya got a good man. I ain't never knowed no man like him befo'."

145

"And you ain't gonna ever again," Naomi said, smiling at her. "Ain't many men God fashion like Bo Peace."

"Ya think it's God why he so special?"

"I know it is. De Lawd is all over dat man. Bo walks wit Jesus in a way most people can't or jes plain won't. He got a stronger closeness wit de Lawd den most us, real strong. I think he a prophet."

"Like Prophet Nat Turner?"

"He different from Nat Turner."

"What do ya think about Prophet Turner?"

"Don' rightly know. He a smart man, all right, and he knows de Word a God real good, but what Jesus taught en what dat man saying don't all quite come together fer me. I knows dat much."

"He speak from the Good Book like Bo. Why ain't it de same?"

"Folks sometimes turn de Good Book round ta satisfy what dey wan. People sees what dey wanna see and dat can be mo' den what de Lawd is really sayin'."

"Ya sound awful lot like Bo."

"Tell me chile, where yo' babies at?"

Ruth froze as her body went numb. She didn't look at Naomi. "Why ya ask me dat?"

"Jes curious."

Her head dropped shamefully. "Dey only let me keep my babies two years and . . . and dey give em ta Mammy Salome ta raise on up." Her voice trailed down.

"Oh, I's so sorry ta hear dat. How many ya have?"

Ruth's face paled. "Three."

"I reckon it breaks yo' heart not bein' round ta raise ya own younguns."

"I don' wanna talk 'bout it . . ." Ruth mumbled.

"Course, sweetie, pardon my meddlin'."

"Ders some quail and turkey down yonder a piece, Bo said. Maybe he and Ephraim will catch some fo' de harves' party." Ruth forced herself to smile and sound cheerful.

"Quail would be right tasty, en Bo jes loves himself some turkey wit my corn bread stuffing."

"Dat's what we'll have den. Some quail en turkey fo' de Harves' Celebration." She looked at Naomi silently rocking away, snapping beans. She wished Bo would hurry back home and her mind could be at peace.

Sixteen

$\mathcal{E}$phraim looked up through his blurriness to see Bo bending over him. He thought he was hallucinating at first until Bo spoke. Bo gave him water to drink. He was so thirsty, his mouth was like cotton.

Ephraim could faintly hear other voices talking back and forth. Bo was not alone; he was relieved to know that. The men carried the injured Ephraim to a clearing, then began to work on his wound. Bo was praying a lot, asking for healing grace and safety to return home.

"You're going to be all right," his friend assured him, but Ephraim had been lying there a long time waiting to die. He had resigned himself, accepting it most likely would be his time to go to the Lord, and he wasn't afraid if death called for him now. He'd made peace with his Maker years ago and did so again as he lay bleeding just to make sure. He didn't want to die and leave his beloved Naomi, but he knew it wasn't in his hands. "Mara's out there," Ephraim whispered. "Ya gotta go fine her and hep her fo' dey catch her again."

"Mara's safe. We found her and she told us to look for you. Jethro's taking her back to the farm and bringing a wagon to fetch you home. It's going to be fine, just you rest."

"Slave catchers . . ." Ephraim wheezed.

"Mara said there's only two of them. There are six of us so we can take care of them if we have to. Don't you worry. We came prepared." Bo stroked Ephraim's head. He knew the injury was bad. Ephraim had lost a lot of blood. Blood had soaked his clothes and the ground.

"Yeah, we's jes waitin' fo' some ole slave catchers ta come at us. We'll revenge dem good fer shootin' ya," Lem said.

➤ ➤ ➤ ➤ ➤ ➤

Ruth poked at the roasting bird in the cast-iron pot in the fireplace. It was almost tender enough to take out. The green beans and okra were done and sitting on the side. Corn boiled outside in the big black pot. It should have been an unusually festive meal with good eating to be had, but Ruth couldn't begin to enjoy it until Bo and Ephraim were home safe. Keeping busy all day helped, but it was early evening and they still hadn't returned.

Naomi paced in circles on the porch, back and forth to the field and to and from barn to barn. She kept busy slopping hogs and feeding chickens and horses, and even the dogs got extra eatings as she exerted nervous energy. Anxiety and dread hung heavy in the air. She'd just settled back on the porch with a burlap sack of sweet potatoes she'd dug up when little Malcolm Brewster came running up the road toward the house. "Miz Naomi! Miz Naomi!" he was yelling. He ran and collapsed on the porch. He was gasping. "Mistah Jethro brought Miz Mara back! Dey foun' her and she say Mistah Ephraim shot!"

"Shot! Oh, Lawd, no!" Naomi sprang to her feet, sweet potatoes tumbling to the floor.

Malcolm jumped up catching the rolling sweet potatoes. "Mistah Jethro gone back wit a wagon ta fine 'em. Dey went ta git Mistah Ephraim. He gonna brang Mistah Ephraim here," he recited breathlessly, putting sweet potatoes back in the sack.

Ruth heard the excited conversation and came to the door. Naomi was flapping her apron, pacing in circles. "I's goin to meet up wit Jethro. I gotta git ta my Ephraim. He needs me!"

"Mistah Jethro's gone awready," Malcolm said. "He sent me ta tell ya. He way up by Swamp Road by now."

Naomi lifted her arms in the air. "Dear Jesus, save my man! Bring him home alive! Don't let him die out dere all alone in de swamp!"

Ruth stepped out the door. "Jethro say anything 'bout Bo?" she asked the boy.

"No ma'am, only dat he en de others went lookin' fer Mistah Ephraim. I had ta stop at Miz Lila's to git her to come here fo' Mistah Ephraim when dey brings him." Malcolm had finished retrieving the sweet potatoes and was sitting on the porch floor rubbing his bare feet that ached from running so hard.

"You must be exhausted. Come git a cool drink a water. Are ya hungry? We got a big supper here. You's welcome ta eat if ya wan' . . . roasted chicken, biscuits, beans en okra, en corn and cobbler."

Malcolm's eyes popped. "Yes ma'am! I's hungry like a bear!"

"Go round by the well en wash de dirt off ya en come inside," Ruth told him.

Naomi fell on her knees in prayer. Ruth wondered if praying would do any good. For Naomi's sake she wanted to

150

believe it would but she had doubts. She was worried about Bo and the slave catchers. She knew if Bo ran into that slave catcher he'd beaten, it would mean his life for sure. There was nothing she knew to do that would help. At least Naomi had something she could do that she believed would help. Ruth admitted to herself for the first time that she had nothing to soothe the horrible blows of life without faith in this Christ Jesus.

It was well into the evening and dark outside when the wagon pulled up to the house. Naomi bolted through the door with Ruth on her heels. Bo, Ned, Lem, and Jethro carried Ephraim to the small room in Bo's farmhouse. Preacher Jones had been summoned along with Lila Lightfoot, the closest thing to a doctor the blacks had. Lila was forty-five years old with a tall lean frame and dark-brown skin. She was wise about all things concerning healing, from being born on the plantation of Doctor Norris Cutler who for years was one of the only two physicians in the county till Doctor Murdock moved to the area. Doctor Cutler taught Lila's mother to assist him with the health care needs of the slaves on his plantation, and she taught Lila to assist her in the slave quarters if she wasn't available.

Lila married Johnny Lightfoot, a half African, half Sioux, who bought her freedom from Doctor Cutler. Through Johnny and his Sioux relatives, Lila had learned the medicinal cures of the Indians and combined them with African remedies her mother and grandmother had taught her. Both cultures were added to what she'd learned from her mother's teachings from the doctor. The three disciplines made her highly reputed as a proficient healer throughout the area. Her skills, capped with a strong faith in Christ, were often more effective than anyone else's in the county. Even some white patients called for Lila when the professional medical men fell short on solutions.

People were coming to the farmhouse and adding their prayers to the already fervent ones being sent up. When the men arrived with Ephraim, Lila went right to work on him. Jethro rushed off to be by Mara's side. Women brought more food, and the men ate and strategized about what to do concerning the slave catcher problem. Lila Lightfoot, Naomi, and Preacher Jones kept vigil over Ephraim. Lila told Naomi and Ruth that Mara was in a state of partial shock from the ordeal but that was all she would say, purposely omitting what Mara had gone through. She would never speak of it, bound by the ethics her mother taught her.

The crowd died down as the night went on. Ruth was glad; she was worn out but didn't dare complain. Bo looked tired too, but she knew he would fight his fatigue. She kept busy feeding folks and washing dishes. When a group went into a prayer circle, she watched but didn't participate. Finally it was just Naomi and Ephraim, the preacher and Lila Lightfoot and her husband, Johnny, left inside the farmhouse.

"Sit down, Ruth, you look tired," Bo suggested. He and Johnny had been discussing the events of the day. Johnny went to check on Ephraim.

Ruth sat on the bench by the door, happy to get off her feet. "Do ya think he's gonna make it?" she asked softly.

"It's in the Lord's hands. Ephraim's strong, but he lost so much blood . . . it's up to God is all I know."

"Po' Naomi, she worried all day. She knew somethin' terrible happened."

"I know you were a comfort to her."

"Not much a one."

"She told me you were."

Ruth's face lit up. "She did?"

Bo nodded, then motioned for her to come sit on his lap. Ruth looked toward the sickroom door. "Not wit folks in de house," she whispered.

"You're my wife, it's fine."

"It ain't decent wit folks about." She got up and sat on the floor at his feet, which was one of her favorite places to be. "This ain't so brazen." She smiled. Johnny Lightfoot came from the room looking solemn.

"How's he holding up?" Bo asked.

"Well as can be expected but it don't look good. Lila says she's done all she knows to do. It's up to the Lord. Says if he makes it through the night, he might stand a good chance."

Bo nodded and said, "It's in God's hands." Ruth flinched, thinking how tired she was of hearing people say that. What had God done so far but let all this trouble happen in the first place?

It was almost two hours later when they heard Naomi's bone-chilling shriek. Ruth was still on the floor half asleep with her head against Bo's leg. Her heart raced when she heard Naomi. Bo jumped up from his groggy state and rushed to the room. Johnny Lightfoot was startled while praying as he sat in the thatched chair. He got up and helped Ruth to her feet. The door to the sickroom remained ajar. They knew from the emanating sounds what had happened. Naomi's wailing was so deep and desperate it broke the hearts of those who heard it. Johnny and Ruth could hear Naomi pleading, "Don't leave me, Ephraim! No, Lawd, don't take my man from me! Not him too, Lawd . . . no, nooo!" Her pitiful pleas filled the house with the heaviest of sorrow.

Ruth turned away as her own tears came flooding. Johnny patted her sympathetically, struggling to be strong against his own manly emotion. Ruth dropped her head into his arms and sobbed. "Why?" She looked up at Johnny, demanding an answer. "All of ya prayed so hard, why did he die?"

"Ephraim's with the Lord now, in a better place."

Ruth moved back abruptly. "How ya know dat? Ya don't know fo' sho where he at."

"The Bible says when Jesus' people are absent from our bodies we are present with the Lord. Ephraim is with the Lord now." Lila came into the big room hanging her head and looking exhausted. She slowly made it to the thatched chair and sat down. Johnny went to her and rubbed her shoulders.

Sorrowfully she said, "I couldn't save him."

"You did the best you knew how," he told her. "It wasn't your failure but God's will that prevailed."

Ruth was angry with this God everyone adored so much. She stared at the sickroom awhile before going in to try and comfort Naomi. When she stepped in the room, she saw Naomi draped across Ephraim's lifeless body on the bed. Her crying by then was in low-volume bursts. Bo stood over her. Preacher Jones was standing by the window, mumbling what sounded to Ruth like more worthless prayers.

She walked up to Bo and he immediately took her hand. It was comforting to connect with him. Ruth's free hand went slowly on Naomi's back. "Naomi, I's so sorry . . ." She could barely get the sentence out when Naomi jerked up and grabbed hold of Ruth.

"He gone, Ruth! My Ephraim done gone!" Her crying pitched high again. "I's all alone now. I ain't got nobody!"

Ruth looked at Bo. "Ya have us, Naomi. Ya ain't alone, cause ya have us."

"That's right, you'll always be family to us," Bo joined in. "You're the closest thing I have to a mother. You are my mother and we both love you."

154

"Ya got a wife now. Ya don't need no mother no mo'." Naomi sniffled.

"I need you," Ruth said from the bottom of her heart. "I need ya to be a mother ta me . . . en a friend."

"No ya don't, ya got a husband. Ya got each udda en dats how it should be. I ain't got nobody, no sons, no daughter, en now no husband. I's all alone. God done left me by myself wit nobody."

"Ruth is your daughter now and Bo is your son," Preacher Jones said. "God has provided for you, Naomi."

Naomi looked at the preacher, then at Bo and Ruth who were both embracing her. Ruth smiled and hugged Naomi affectionately. "I was sold from my momma years ago. I be yo' daughter if ya have me." Naomi hugged Ruth back and cried harder.

Bo had his arms around both women. "God has taken what life has torn apart and made it whole again. We're still a family till death do us part. Thank You, Jesus."

Seventeen

*F*armers all over the area were in financial distress. Crops were wholesaling for less and merchandise was more expensive than ever. The drought that lasted most of the spring and into the first part of the summer made farmers come up short for harvest.

Not so on Bo's farm. His harvest was noticeably more bountiful than others'. The sharecroppers and all his community were bursting at the markets with healthy fruits and vegetables. The piglets and chickens were fat and lively. Branche's Mercantile Emporium took much of Bo's produce, which cut out some of the white farmers. Ill will began to rear up on account of it.

By the time a month passed since Ephraim's death, harvest gathering occupied people's minds and helped the sorrowful memory dull. But not for Naomi. She kept busy, but her countenance had noticeably changed.

Bo and Ruth grew closer during these weeks. Ruth learned to help more around the farm, taking every new task to heart.

Naomi was showing Ruth how to be a farmer's wife and was pleased by her willingness and quick ability to learn. Bo worked hard as did the others on the farm. Spirits were starting to revive as it neared time for the Harvest Dance.

"I hope I kin have dis dress ready in time fo de dance," Ruth said. She was sewing by candlelight while Bo pored over the financial book figuring out the winter's budget.

"I hope we can have enough left over after I get seed and feed to buy you a pretty store-bought dress."

Ruth's eyes widened. "Ya sayin' I kin get a sto'-bought dress fo' me?"

"Yes, a store-bought dress for you," Bo corrected.

"I beg ya pardon, a store-bought dress for me."

"Once I get everything we need for winter, we'll see."

"I thought dis yard goods was somethin' but a sto' . . . I mean store-bought dress . . . dat's even better."

"Nothing's too good for my hardworking wife." He closed the ledger and rubbed his eyes. "How is Naomi doing, you think?"

"She's tryin' ta be brave but she's missin' Ephraim somethin' terrible."

"It'll hurt for a long time, but Naomi's a strong woman. She made it through losing her children. That's one of the hardest things a woman can go through, they say." Ruth looked away. Bo felt the wall come up again. He had held his questions until now. He wanted to know so he would have to ask, since Ruth wasn't volunteering any information. "Ruth, I'd like to know . . . where are your children?"

"On Stanley's plantation bein' raised by old Mammy Salome, a slave." She didn't look at him. Her head stayed dropped as she sewed with more concentration.

"How many did you have?"

"Three," Ruth said shortly.

"What are their names?"

"I don wanna talk 'bout my babies. It's too hurtful."

"I don't want to upset you but I was wondering if we could buy their freedom from . . ."

"I said I cain't talk 'bout 'em now!" Ruth looked at Bo's startled expression. "I's sorry I jes cain't talk bout it, not now. I jes cain't."

"All right, don't upset yourself. We'll talk about it another time."

➤ ➤ ➤ ➤ ➤ ➤

The flaxen-colored mare was one of the most beautiful horses Ruth ever saw. She brushed the animal, awed that it was now hers. The long off-white tail and mane were striking. "She de mos' wonerful horse I ever seed. How kin ya part wit her?"

"Golden Gal was Ephraim's horse, his favorite one, en seein' her keeps up too much memories. Ya love horses en well . . . I thought ya like havin one a ya' own. I's too old ta be tending ta mo' den I need. Two ta ride or pull the wagon is plenty fo' me. I think Ephraim would be happy fo' ya ta have his Golden Gal."

"I promise, I take real good care of her."

"I know you will, jes like ya takes good care a Bo." Ruth looked at Naomi sideways, then dropped her head. "Somethin' wrong 'tween you and Bo?" Naomi asked.

Ruth sighed and stopped brushing. "I ain't deservin' a such a good man like Bo. I knows I ain't."

"Ya talkin' foolish. Course ya deserve him. He chose ya, didn't he?"

"He didn't know who he was choosin' when he did."

"I think he did. He married who de Lawd tol' him ta pick . . . you."

"I doubt de Lawd would pick me for anything."

"Bo tol' me God tol' him ya be his wife."

"I ain't the right woman for Bo. Maybe . . . maybe he shoulda married Mara instead."

"Mara? What brought all dis bout?"

"I's not who he thinks I is. I done things, wicked things en . . ."

"We all got a pass, chile—all a us—en we all needs forgiveness. Dat's why Jesus come en die so we kin be forgiven fo' our sins."

"Dis got nuttin' ta do wit Jesus." Ruth rolled her eyes.

"But ya wrong. Everything got somethin' ta do wit de Lawd." Naomi took Ruth's trembling hands. "Whatever ya think makes ya unfit, give it ta de Lawd. He kin forgive ya. Den take it to Bo en he kin forgive ya too."

Tears welled in Ruth's eyes. "Nobody kin fo'give what I did . . . nobody."

"Jesus kin."

Ruth began to weep on Naomi's shoulder. "Not even yo Jesus, not de evil I did."

"Now ya jes calm down en tell me what ya talkin' bout."

"I cain't . . . you would hate me en never fo'give me. I cain't talk bout it cause I cain't fo'give myself. Dats why I don't deserve ta be so happy."

"Tell it ta de Lawd. Ya gotta learn to unload yo' burdens on de Lawd. If ya don't, ya won't never have no peace." Naomi gently raised Ruth's face up. "Tell it ta Jesus. Ask Him ta be Lawd of ya life, chile."

"But I'm not sure I believe in yo' Jesus."

"Pray fo' faith enough ta believe."

"Is it dat easy?"

"It kin be."

"How kin ya keep believin' after Ephraim?"

"It broke my heart ta pieces ta lose my man like dat but I still believes in de Lawd. If it weren't fer de Lawd, I never git o'er it . . . never. Jesus give me strength nuff ta go on. He gives me calm in de worse a times."

"But He let Ephraim die."

"He took Ephraim to His bosom. Ephraim's wit de Lawd now. Death for God's chillun is jes passage to be wit de Savior forever."

"You say dat like ya knows fo' sho'."

"I do, de Good Book say so."

"Ya base everythin' on dat Book?"

"It de Word a God. Him tellin' us what ta do en why en how." Naomi smiled peacefully.

"It gives ya calm, ya say?"

"Yeah, peace when ya need it mos'."

Ruth stared brushing Golden Girl again. "Bo says de same thing."

"Ya wan peace in yo' heart?"

"Uh-huh."

"Den give ya heart ta de Lawd."

Eighteen

ara sat on the ground looking up at Jethro. His
brawny build made her feel safe every time she
looked at him and thought of how he came to her rescue. She
pushed the basket of apples to the side, making room for him
to sit next to her. Jethro sat and stretched his long, muscular
legs out comfortably. As chilly as the oncoming winter
weather was, he was feeling warm all over. "Mara, you look
real purty today."

"You say that every day, Jethro."

"Cause ya look purty every day." He put his broad arm
around her shoulder. Mara pulled away instinctively. Jethro
took his arm from around her. "Why don't ya let me touch ya,
Mara?"

"What do you mean? You touch me."

"Ya pull away whenever I touch ya."

"That's silly, of course I don't."

"Yeah ya do, ya jes did. When I try ta take ya hand, ya all
time pullin' it back."

"Well . . . well, I don't mean to."

"Ya pull back when he touch ya?"

"Who?"

"Bo, dat's who. Don't act like ya don't know who I's talkin' 'bout."

Mara rolled her eyes. "Bo Peace is a man spoken for."

"En dats what got ya in such a dither ya almost got yo'self killed or took o'er."

"You're just repeating foolish gossip, is all. I never told you I . . ."

"Ya don't have ta tell me. I ain't blind. Don't ya think I kin see how ya look at him when he's 'round. I knows ya got a powerful hankerin' fo' Bo en had it fo' a long time. Everybody knows."

Mara looked toward the field of mums to her right, avoiding his gaze. "Not anymore, I don't."

"Ya sho bout dat?"

She turned and looked Jethro in the eyes. "Yes, I'm sure."

There was sadness in her eyes and voice that Jethro couldn't interpret. "I's do all I kin ta make ya happy, Mara. Why don't ya give me a chance?" He slid his arm around her shoulder again. "Ya needs a man . . . a husband. Ya oughtn't be on ya own like ya is all by yo'self."

"I do all right for myself. I can take care of me just fine."

"I'd take care of ya and ya wouldn't have ta fend fo yo'self." He moved in closer. "I'd protect ya en provide fer ya. I'd be good to ya . . . jes as good as Bo Peace any day."

She snatched away. "Why you keep bringing him up?"

"Don't git mad, sugar."

"Then don't mention his name."

Cause I'm not fit to be Bo's wife anymore. I'm as low as

162

*that breeding woman he married. I'm not fit to be any man's
wife now.*

"Ya really is put out wit him, ain't ya?"

"Bo Peace is of no never mind to me." Her chin jutted up.
Jethro grinned at the good news and slid his other hand around
her waist and pulled her in for a kiss. Mara's stiff resistance
weakened as their lips met. Holding and kissing her went to
Jethro's head as he tightened his grip. Mara began to struggle
as his kiss became slightly more aggressive. His hold tightened even more, and memories flooded in of the horrible rape.

She pulled back. "Stop it!" she screamed and slapped his
face. Fear was wild in her eyes as she moved away from him.

"What's wrong? Why ya always fight agin' me when I try
ta get close ta ya?" He reached for her but she jumped away,
terrified. "Mara, I'm not gonna hurt ya. All I wan is to love ya
and . . ."

"And have your way with me," she snapped.

"Is dat what ya think a me after all dis time?"

"That's what all men want . . . all of you beasts!" She got
up and started running toward the creek. Jethro got up running
after her.

He caught her but she struggled to get loose. "What I do
wrong? What's de matter wit ya?"

Her eyes were bulging uncontrollably as she struggled to
get loose from his hold. "Let me go! Let go of me!" She
scratched at him wildly. "Take your filthy hands off me! You
won't hurt me anymore!"

"Mara, stop dis!" he yelled. She froze and looked at him
in confusion before she burst into tears, falling into his arms.
"What wrong wit ya? I never hurt ya. Don't ya know dat?"

"He forced himself on me!" she blurted out. "That slave
catcher, he ruined me and after I saved myself for marriage

all these years! He hurt me so bad, Jethro."

Her sobs made Jethro's heart ache with pity and rage. "Ya mean, he hurt you . . . like dat?"

"Yes, yes, yes, I'm ruined! I'm not fit to be your woman or anybody's!" She wept and would not be consoled.

He held her close. "Don't cry, Mara. It don't make no difference what dat devil did. It weren't yo' fault." He whispered, repeating his comforting words.

"It was my fault! If I weren't so fool and didn't run off . . ."

"Don't matter none ta me. I still loves ya en wants ya to be my wife. You is still pure en good in your heart. Dat's all dat counts."

Mara looked hard at Jethro. His sincerity began to overcome her apprehension. "How can you want me after what you just found out about me?"

"You mean dat yo' heart is pining fer another man?"

"I told you, not anymore. I don't pine for Bo Peace no more and never will."

"Den dere's no cause fer me ta worry is dere? If Bo Peace can't steal yo' heart away, I know ya kin someday gro' ta love me. Be my wife, Mara."

Mara thought of all the time and effort Jethro expended trying to get her attention and court her. *He is the one God sent to rescue me . . . and to be my husband. The one the Lord said I rejected.* It was Jethro who heard her cry in the marshy woods. It was him who brought her home and hurried to sit by her side, not Bo. It was Jethro who had been there for her all along. He was kind to her, and regardless of her off-putting responses, he never gave up.

"He won't steal my heart away, Jethro. If you still want me, I'll marry you come spring."

➤ ➤ ➤ ➤ ➤ ➤

When the two men entered Branche's, the half dozen patrons fell silent. The proprietor looked up at the strangers walking in with their dark countenances. People watched because they were strangers, but more so because it felt as though they were shrouded with a mysteriously oppressive spirit.

One man was tall and wiry with frizzy brownish-blond hair and beard. The second man was big-boned and muscular. He was medium height with dark hair and beard. More noticeable than their grimy appearance was the ominous air they ushered in with them.

Penelope Carpenter was at the ladies apparel counter waiting for Cheasley's wife to fetch her package from the back storage room. She stared at the newcomers curiously. Jack Dudley stopped fumbling over the cigars to check out the strangers. Henry and Fannie Lucas were bickering over Fannie getting more yard goods for yet another dress for this year's Harvest Ball. Fannie snuck the pretty pumpkin-colored material in with their other purchases while her husband's head was turned toward the newcomers.

Strangers always got a lot of attention, but these two received more than usual. It was well known by now that slave catchers were near the swamp. They were capturing free blacks as well as stealing other people's slaves. These two men fit the profile perfectly. Ephraim's death and Mara's capture along with several slaves gone missing prompted farmers to call a town meeting.

One of the other incidences was when Emory Littlejohn's slave Big Bubba went missing. Bubba went to see his woman, Suzy, over in Sussex County on the Fisher farm like he always did. He'd left Fisher's place heading home to the Littlejohn farm and was never spotted again, neither he nor his master's old retired plow horse. That was two weeks ago. Several men got their slaves to chop up the gigantic fallen tree that blocked the road, but by then Ephraim was dead and several slaves had vanished. That meant lost money and labor, so the slave owners were as upset as the slaves themselves. They didn't care about the free blacks, but they did care about their property being stolen.

Cheasley was taking gumdrops out the glass canister for young Oberlin Howard and his little sister, Aggie. Every day they came to the Emporium to buy candy. Their mother was a close friend of Cheasley's wife so he was expected to slip them extra for their penny. Cheasley was tightfisted, so he seldom did so unless his wife was nearby watching. She was in the back rummaging through packages for Penelope, so he gave the children exactly what they paid for and was shooing them away from the licorice whip jar when the strangers walked in.

The atmosphere was immediately charged with curiosity and something more. Cheasley instantly disliked the ill-kempt men, not because they were filthy but because he knew instinctively what they were. "Now get on home, you two," he told Oberlin and Aggie. They were drooling over the other candy jars. "Too many sweets will make you sick and spoil your supper."

"We never get sick," Oberlin said, eyeing the peppermint sticks. "Sure would like one of those," he added, pointing.

"I should tell your father you're in here begging. He'd not take kindly to that, I bet. He'll tan your little hides if he found out. You got your candy, now get." The children's faces sank

166

and they slowly walked away from the counter toward the door.

Cheasley directed his attention to the strangers who were walking around taking stock of various items. "May I help you gentlemen?" He was courteous but cool.

The dark-haired man said, "We need some thick rope and gunpowder."

"Is there a place a fella can git a room and take a bath round here?" the wiry man asked.

"Saddlebrook Mansion is the only place like that in these parts."

"Where's that at?"

"Right in back of here is Saddlebrook Road; follow it out for ten miles or so." Cheasley reached down and came up with some rope. "You fellas new round here?"

"Just traveling through," Dark Hair answered.

"You round these parts hunting for game?" Cheasley asked, trying to sound casual.

The stranger looked at Cheasley warily. "You might say that."

"What kind of game you hunting? We got plenty deer, quail, and rabbit around these parts."

"Need some chewing tobacco too," the man said, ignoring the question.

Jack and Henry shot questioning looks at each other. Cheasley narrowed his eyes impatiently. He put the tobacco on the counter. "Where you fellas say you're from?"

"You's mighty nosy for a shopkeep," Dark Hair growled.

"Just being friendly," Cheasley muttered.

"We don't need friendly. We need two new shirts iffin ya don't mind."

Cheasley walked them to the men's apparel. "Shirts are over here."

Henry went to the window and glanced at the horses the men rode in on. They fit the sketchy descriptions of the slave catchers' horses. There was a large gray splotchy stallion and a huge black-and-white painted mare. He motioned for Jack to join him at the window. They stood there whispering while Cheasley sold the strangers two shirts.

Penelope was an attractive woman dressed in dainty, stylish attire. She was trying on an overembellished hat, looking at herself in the mirror. The dark-haired man kept eyeing her. She rolled her eyes and turned away, but that didn't daunt his efforts.

He walked up to her, grinning. "You don't need that thing on yo' head," he told her. "What you need is a man like me to let that pretty red hair of yo's down."

"I beg your pardon!" Penelope huffed and smacked the hat down on the counter.

"Ya married?"

"I am not, but I will not stand here and be spoken to in this crude manner by the likes of you, sir!"

His face soured. "What you mean by the likes of me? I ain't good enuff for ya?"

"Come on over here, Wally, and leave the lady be," the taller man said.

Wally looked Penelope up and down spitefully. "You may be all fancied up, but you ain't no better than me and you better remember that."

She turned away with her nose up in the air. "Humph, you disgusting smelly creature."

"So I'm a disgusting smelly creature? I'd like to get you by yourself and I'd show you who's boss. I don't care if you is some snotty highfalutin old maid."

"See here, mister, what gives you cause to come in here

insulting my customer?" Cheasley demanded. "Leave her be, ya hear?" His hand went under the counter and rested on his pistol. Henry and Jack took their stances side by side in front the window, feet spread wide, hands balled into fists and faces looking like they were ready for trouble.

Dark Hair looked around and realized he had called too much attention to himself.

"Beg pardon, ma'am," Taller Man said sheepishly, trying to ease the situation Wally had caused. He turned to his companion. "Let's just pay for our gear and get out of here, Wally. We don't want no trouble."

Nineteen

The shadows of her past had chased her long enough, Ruth told herself. She knew Bo had questions and he deserved answers. The answers would probably change everything between them, but she knew she couldn't keep avoiding it. Her chest tightened from fear. She'd never been so happy, and contentment clung to her. She didn't want to lose it. She'd never known the kind of love and gentleness Bo demonstrated every day they were together.

How could she have known her life would change so drastically? The horrible truth that lurked in the corner all the time and engulfed her mind when she was alone had to be spoken or she would never have peace. It would break Bo's heart but at least he would know. He had a right to know. Ruth cringed, thinking it would destroy their happiness, but she had one small glimmer of hope. Bo talked often of forgiveness and the grace of God. He was different than other men . . . maybe, just maybe his forgiveness would extend to this too. Perhaps Bo could find it in himself to forgive her even though no one else ever had and she never could herself.

The supper dishes were washed, and Ruth sat at the table for her nightly lesson. Her first inclination was to sit at her husband's feet as she sometimes did, but tonight she wanted to be able to look directly in his eyes for this important confession. She'd been quiet all day, and Bo knew something was bothering her and had been for a while. Today she didn't chatter on about the Harvest Dance, which had been a topic of great expectation for weeks. Her mood was somber, edged with trepidation. Bo didn't push for an explanation. He prayed about it and waited for her to come to him when she was ready. After he read the Fifty-first Psalm aloud, he closed his Bible. "This psalm was written by King David," he told her.

"It sounds so sad. Like he was guilty of doing something terrible," she remarked.

"That's it exactly. He was ashamed and fearful because of the sin he'd committed."

"What he do?" Ruth wanted to know.

"What did he do? He committed adultery with Bathsheba, another man's wife and she was with child, David's child not her husband's. Then to make matters worse, he misused his position as king to have the husband killed in battle to cover up his dirty deed. God sent a prophet to confront David. He broke down in guilt and repented. This psalm comes from his acknowledgment and repentence of his sin against God."

"What God did ta him? I mean, what did God do to him?"

"He forgave him."

"Fo'gave him?"

"Yes, don't forget God is full of mercy and grace and forgiveness."

171

Ruth looked out the window. "Folks ain't so fo'givin'."

"That's true, but you will find Jesus can even make a difference with that."

"I wonder . . ."

"Wonder what?"

"If it's so easy as ya think."

"It's not easy necessarily. There were consequences David paid for his sin. The child Bathsheba carried died. David had to confront betrayal from within his family. His daughter was shamed by her own half brother, who was also his son. One brother had the other brother killed for what he did to the sister. Then his son challenged David for the throne. The king had to flee from being murdered, and his son had to be killed to stop him."

"So God ain't truly fo'give him since He made all dose terrible things happen."

"I don't think it was punishment but the natural and spiritual consequences of his actions."

"How is dat different?"

"How is that different?"

"Yeah, how is that different?"

"God didn't cause those things to happen, but David did by sinning and allowing the Devil's spirit to come into his family. David opened up the door of evil into his own life and his offspring's life. He courted the demons of lust, murder, misuse of power, and evil intent through his sinful behavior. Once you embrace sin, you can make a way for its influence for generations to come. That's what God warns us about."

"If dat's . . . I mean, if that's how it works, what's the good of fo'givin' . . . um, forgiving?"

"God kept His hand on David and his reign as king. His son's attempt failed and David remained a victorious king until death. God's mercy and protection was still there because David repented and still loved the Lord in spite of his sin. He was a faithful servant to God, only with faults. We aren't expected to be sinless or perfect, Ruth. God knows our nature won't be able to live up to it. That's why Jesus Christ was sent to do what we aren't able to do. David lived before Jesus came, but his relationship with God was strong although he was far from perfect. Our blessing now is if we open that kind of destructive door, we can get Jesus to close it for us."

"Ya saying God will fo'give anything?"

"Yes."

"No matter how bad?"

"That's right, if you ask for forgiveness and truly repent in your heart."

"What means dis ree-pent?"

"What does repent mean? Repent means to resolve not to do a thing anymore. Have a strong desire to turn away from it."

Ruth looked at Bo, searching for strength to say what was on her mind. "Is ya . . . I mean are you able to fo'give anythin?"

"I don't know, but I need to because I've been forgiven much."

"I hope ya kin fo'give me for what I's gonna . . . I'm going to tell you."

He took her hands in his. "You're my wife and I love you. It's my prayer to have a forgiving spirit toward you more than any other person on this earth. I don't know what you've done or think you've done, but I want you to be able to tell me anything that weighs on your mind. But if you can't tell me, tell Jesus."

"Naomi tol me ta tell it to de Lawd and I tried. I tol de Lawd but I's not so sure He was listenin' to de likes of me."

Ruth frowned, knowing she failed correcting her speech.

"I'm sure He listened."

Her gaze moved away from his. "Ya asked me about my chillun."

"Children."

"My children, then, but let me git dis out de best I kin. Dis ain't no time fo' improving my speech."

"I'm sorry; by all means, go on."

"I ain't tell ya de whole story befo'." She looked nervously at his stolid expression. "Dere's somethin' I think ya should know." Bo said nothing, just sat and lovingly watched her. "I gave birth to livin' babies but . . ." His eyes gazed into hers with a gentleness that gave her the courage to go on. "Only one of my babies is livin' now." She breathed out loudly as if relieved to have finally said it, but she wasn't.

"You told me your last baby was born dead. Are you saying your other two children died at birth?"

Ruth's eyes watered. "Yeah, they dead."

"I'm sorry. I know this must be hurtful . . ."

"Dere's mo' to it den ya think."

"More?"

"When I was younger I lose two babies fo' time but dat ain't what I's talkin' bout. I gave birth ta three live babies afta dat. My babies . . . ya see, I was so miserable bein' a slave. What's worse I hated bein' a breedin' slave."

"Of course you did."

"Let me say what I has ta say." Her face turned away. "I hated livin' like I had ta live en I didn't want no chillun of mine ta have ta live in such misery. It's no kinda life. You know dat and so did I. But I didn't seem ta have no choice. I wanted freedom fo' my baby boy."

"You have a son?"

"His name Willie Boy. He's five years old and Mammy Salome is raisin' him on the Stanley plantation."

Bo smiled. "Nice name."

"After Willie Boy was born I was mad I give birth knowin' what kinda life he had head a him. I wanted freedom fo' my baby but dat wasn't ta be. When he was two dey took him from me. I couldn't even raise my own chile. I was carryin' another baby den. They lied ta me and said dey took Willie Boy jes till I give birth and rested, then dey was gonna give him back ta me. Lizzy told me de truth befo' I gave birth again. She was the Missus' personal slave en she knew everything that happened on de plantation. She tol me I weren't never gonna raise my son no mo' and dat's how it gonna always be wit my chillun. Massah say I was too stubborn en hardheaded. He didn't want me teaching dem hardheaded ways ta my chilluns." Ruth stopped to slow her breathing. Her heart was racing from fear but she had to go on. "Lizzy tol' me Massah ain't wan me getting' so tached to em cause he was fixin' ta sell my babies when they got old enough. So he decided it best I not keep 'em too long. I'd be allowed to see my boy en he'd know I was his momma, but dat was all. Visit him en watch him from afar while dat old wretch Salome trained him ta Massah's likin'."

"Stanley must be an ungodly cruel man. Decent God-fearing men wouldn't force procreation in the first place, but to take him from you at such a young age . . ."

"Massah Stanley said he a businessman and nothin' else matters but de business of makin' money. He was heartless ta most, including his own family en specially ta his slaves."

Bo sighed. "He'll answer to God for what he did."

"Bo, I went crazy when I learn how de rest a my life en my chilluns' lives gonna be. Den I give birth ta my second living baby. I couldn't stand de thought a my baby bein' taken from me en brought up in dis slave life . . . I couldn't stand it . . ." Ruth's vision was blurred from her tears. "I wanted to die en I wished so much I was never born." She choked up on her next thought.

"Go on," Bo urged.

Everything in Ruth's countenance sagged. "So when I give birth . . . it was a girl dis time. A girl like me who be made ta let men have dere way en make her a . . . I couldn't stand thinkin' bout it. I had a little girl that would be treated like I was, made to let men use her. Working all day en taking orders from white folks who had no right to give ya orders ceptin' dey pay money fo' ya. Living all ya life workin' fo other folks en having nothing ta call yo own . . . not even ya children. Being a feared all de time en not havin' no freedom . . . I kept thinkin' death had ta be better. It had to be. I was havin' pains in de middle of de night when time fo' de baby ta come. Lizzy went ta get Rosemary in de slave quarters. Rosemary was mid-wife fo' us slaves. Lizzy en me was house slaves en we live in back a de big house on the hill. By de time Rosemary and Lizzy got back ta me, I awready give birth en de baby was dead."

"The child was stillborn?"

"No."

"What happened?"

Ruth froze for a moment. Her voice got low and raspy. "I killed my baby so she wouldn't have ta live a life of misery in slavery." She broke down into sobs.

Bo looked shocked. "You killed your own baby?"

"It was fo' mercy's sake," she wailed.

Bo didn't know how to respond. He ran his hand across his head trying to absorb what she just told him. "What happened after that? Did they find out what you did?"

"No, not den cause dey thought de cord wrapped round her neck en she born dead from chokin'."

"How did you . . ." Bo could barely bring himself to ask. "How did you . . . end the baby's life?"

"Smother her, den put the cord round her neck."

Bo shut his eye from the sheer horror of the vision. "The other live birth?"

"He was a boy en I did de same, but Rosemary figured out what I did dis time en tol' de overseer."

"What happened then?"

"He beat me somethin' terrible after he tol' Massah."

"The lash marks on your back?"

"Uh-huh." She wasn't looking at him anymore. She couldn't stand the disappointment when their eyes met. "I ain't care bout no lashin'. I deserve it fo' what I did. I deserve worse. He beat me so bad right after givin' birth, I almost die. Don't know why I didn't, cause I wanted to die."

"The Lord had other plans," Bo said calmly.

"I was with chile again and I ran away de next time. I couldn't stand killin' no mo' a my babies. So I tried to reach freedom somehow. I was in de woods trying to survive en make my way north. I got caught en brought back ta de plantation. Somethin' was wrong inside me though; I could tell nearin' time to give birth. It was a hard birthin' dis time en de baby died soon afta it was born witout me touchin' it. Somebody was made ta stay wit me de whole time ta watch me. I was glad it died on its own. It was a boy too. I was all messed up inside en de doctor tol' Massah I most likely never have any more healthy babies. Dat's when Massah say he fed up wit me en gonna git rid a me."

There was a lengthy uncomfortable silence. Bo finally

looked at her. "I don't understand how you could kill your own babies."

"I did it fo' mercy's sake. I did it so they ain't suffer through life like me."

"I suppose that's how you saw it."

"I know it was a wicked evil thing ta do. I know I deserve ta burn in hell fo' what I did." She cried more, but Bo didn't try to comfort her this time. She needed his comforting embrace more than ever before and it was not given. He looked at her as if she were a stranger. He was shocked and at odds with his feelings and his faith. He prayed silently. Ruth took the silence as rejection. She pulled herself together and standing up announced, "I know ya hates me afta what I tol' ya so I go back ta sleepin' in de little room."

"Ruth, I don't hate you," he countered.

"Ya don't feel lovin' toward me, do ya?"

Bo didn't respond. She went to the small bedroom and shut the door. He could hear her weeping but made no attempt to go console her. It bothered him that he wasn't being more sympathetic but he couldn't . . . not at the moment. "Jesus, help me to see this the right way, as You would. Give me a heart to forgive."

The next morning, things were strained. Bo got up early and Ruth did too, but there was no happy exchange between them. He was polite to her. She was quiet and spoke only when necessary. After eating his oatmeal, Bo went to the north pasture. He kissed Ruth good-bye on the cheek, which took her by surprise. She wasn't expecting any affection whatsoever. She'd made up her mind the night she confessed, that forgiveness didn't stretch far enough for her sins. "I'll be mending fences till evening," he told her.

He heard a wagon pulling up in front of the house and went

to the door to see who it was. Joshua and Rebecca Greene sat in front of the house in their big covered wagon. Bo looked back at Ruth before he stepped outside the door. "Would you heat up some coffee again? We got company calling."

This was the first time Ruth met the Greenes. They were a lively older couple who seemed to be good friends with Bo. This was the first time since she'd been with Bo that white people actually came inside the farmhouse to visit. When Ephraim had died, two of the Maitland women came to pay their respects to Naomi and bring food, but they did not enter the house, just stayed outside talking to Bo and Naomi on the porch.

This pair was awfully friendly with their funny accents and charming ways. Ruth was nervous at first, but they were so kind she quickly warmed up to them. Joshua was thin, medium height with gray hair and a short beard. He wore glasses that made his dark eyes look bigger than they were. Rebecca was a plump, short woman with thick, pinned-up hair that was dark with a sprinkling of gray. Her figure was shapely in spite of her round physique. She had beautiful dark eyes that sparkled when she smiled.

She hugged Ruth, happy to finally meet her. "I told Joshua if he didn't bring me here to meet Bo's new wife, I was coming on my own." She smiled vibrantly.

"Do you live far away?" Ruth asked, dislodging herself from the stranger's genial squeeze.

"We live smack on the border of Sussex and Southhampton," Joshua replied.

Rebecca grinned. "Bo, you must bring Ruth for a visit." She turned to her husband. "Poppa, go get the soup and bread I made for Bo and his bride." Joshua stood up, and Rebecca turned back to Ruth. "Bo just loves matzo soup and challah. Hope you like it too."

"We heard the dreadful news about Ephraim," Joshua lamented.

"My heart went out so for poor Naomi." Rebecca turned to Bo. "We're going to visit her when we leave here."

"What happened with those devil slave catchers?" Joshua asked, moving toward the door.

Bo answered, "They say two of them might be staying at Miss Emily's, but it's not certain they're the same ones or that these two are even slave catchers for that matter."

"What's the law doing to find those murdering scoundrels?"

"Nothing," Ruth said dryly. "Dey don't care bout no slave catchers lessen de farmers git ta complainin' bout dey property gone missin'."

"I won't be satisfied until this inhumane practice of slavery is outlawed altogether." Joshua sighed and went out the door.

"God has got to put an end to this soon; He has to." Rebecca spoke emotionally. "If not, something horrible is going to happen in this country. I just know it. God is not pleased."

"God don't seem ta be studyin' bout helpin' no slaves." Ruth folded her arms across her chest.

"I know it may seem that way but He is. Our people were many years thinking the same."

"Who's yo' people?" Ruth asked.

"The Jews, or at that time we were known as Hebrews. We were enslaved in Egypt for hundreds of years."

"You's a Hebrew?" Ruth's mouth dropped open.

Rebecca smiled sweetly. "We're called Jews now, my dear, but my ancestors in ancient times were referred to as Hebrews, covenant descendants of Abraham."

"I've been teaching Ruth from the Old Testament," Bo told Rebecca.

"Ah, excellent."

Ruth stared at Rebecca. "They say Jews killed Jesus."

"Ruth, shush, don't be rude," Bo admonished.

Rebecca chuckled. "No, that's quite all right, don't shush her. She's right, that's exactly what Jew-haters love to say about us."

"I's sorry fo' bein' rude."

"You were honest, my dear, about what you heard. That's not being rude. You see, Ruth, it was my people who served Jesus Christ up to the Romans. It was the Romans who crucified Him, but the Jewish religious leaders were behind it. It was Jewish people who were the catalysts, but in all truth, Jesus came to give His life, so the crucifixion was ordained by God to happen. It was destined for the sake of humanity."

"I's confused cause Bo tol' me Jesus was a Jew."

"By birth and culture He was, but He made enemies among some of the Jewish religious faction when He taught things above and beyond what they practiced. He also exposed their hypocrisy and ungodliness. Jesus—Messiah—spoke against man-made traditions and prejudices. The final straw was that He claimed to be the Son of God. He was too much of a threat to the religious system of that time and they wanted Him gone for those reasons. They did not believe He was the long-awaited Messiah. Most Jews did not believe, but some did. Even today most do not believe He was the Messiah, but some do."

"Do you believe He was?"

"Yes, I do. I know Yeshua was the prophesied Messiah and He will return again to prove it. Joshua and I are Jewish believers in Him. There are few of us in existence. Jews are not well received in most places. Our people were scattered all over the world. There are very few of us in these parts, I'm afraid, so we stay to ourselves because we have to. We are not wanted. At best we're tolerated. They call us Jesus killers like you said. What's worse, Jews who believe in Yeshua are rejected by Jews who do not." She snickered. "We are the rejected of the rejects."

"How can ya laugh bout such a thing?"

"We've learned to live with the minds of men. Christ is in our hearts, so we find joy among the people who love the Lord as we do; people like Bo. This is a rare pleasure because many Christians distrust us." Joshua reentered the house, carrying two containers. "My people may be hated and my Savior denied by many, but knowing Christ as I do, it cannot take away my peace or joy. I know the Lord loves and takes care of us. We are under the Abrahamic covenant and no one can change that. The hand of God rests on my people and especially those of us who believe Yeshua is Son of the Most High God and our Messiah. I know this regardless of what people say about me or do to me."

"Who is Yeshua?"

"That's Jesus in our Hebrew dialect." Joshua set the containers down. "Have you ever tasted matzo soup?" he asked Ruth.

"No, sir."

"It's really good. You're in for a treat," Bo said.

"I made you a fat loaf of challah to go with it," Rebecca said, grinning.

Bo nodded appreciatively.

"Are you farmers?"

"Yes, to a degree. We have a small farm we work, but mostly we make our living selling wares. We travel to all the small towns and farms selling household goods and things people need on a regular basis," Joshua explained.

"Things like knives?" Ruth's face brightened. "We could use some better knives around here."

Rebecca stood. "Yes, we have excellent cutlery. Joshua sharpens them mercilessly; come see. We just purchased some lovely oil lamps from Richmond and some new pans and oven pots."

"I could use a bigger fryin' pan and a new Dutch oven," Ruth murmured, casting Bo a hopeful look.

"Go on out to the wagon," Bo said. "Get what you need and I'll settle up with Joshua after."

"I wouldn't mind some more of that coffee," Joshua said, sitting down. Bo got up to get the coffee as Ruth and Rebecca scrambled out the door. "Mighty pretty wife you got there."

"Thank you."

Joshua noticed Bo's response was lacking enthusiasm. "I have to tell you, I was surprised when I heard you took a wife."

"It kind of caught me by surprise too."

"Becca's taken a liking to her, I notice. Seems like she's a nice woman. Lovely as she is, I can see why you hurried and swooped her up."

Bo brought the piping hot pot to the table and poured into Joshua's cup. "It wasn't like you think," he told Joshua who gave him a curious glance. "Well, not exactly."

"Are you happy with your decision in making her your wife?"

"I was . . . I mean, I am, I suppose."

"What's bothering you? Obviously something's weighing heavy on your mind."

Bo sat down after pouring himself a cup. "I know she's the one God wanted me to marry, but things aren't like I thought they would be. Not like it was with Baby Gal and me, I mean. Ruth's a woman with a lot of troubles. She's a good woman, don't get me wrong, and I care very much for her but she's . . . she's complicated I guess is the word."

Joshua smiled. "First of all, this woman is not Baby Gal, so you need to let go of that thought. It's not fair for Ruth to constantly be compared to her. Next, what woman do you know who isn't complicated?"

"Baby Gal wasn't and Rebecca doesn't seem all that complicated."

"To you maybe, but you aren't married to Becca. That woman and I used to make each other crazy. As we matured, we learned how to get along with each other, like all married couples have to."

"Tell me, what if Rebecca had done some terrible thing before you met her. Would it change how you felt about her when you found out?"

"Depends on what it was and why . . . and what kind of person she was since I knew her. People can change." Joshua looked searchingly at Bo. "We all have pasts and we all need to be forgiven. What human do you know hasn't made mistakes?"

"What if it was a really, really bad thing?"

"Is there anything Yeshua hasn't forgiven you or me for?"

"All right, what if you can forgive but your view of her will never be the same?"

"Is she repentant?"

"I think so but . . . I'm not sure what's in her heart."

"Maybe it's not *her* heart you need to search," Joshua suggested.

184

Rebecca didn't want to go until Ruth tasted the soup and bread, so the Greenes didn't leave until after sharing a hearty lunch.

Once they were gone, the atmosphere thickened again between Bo and Ruth. She was disheartened at his quiet attitude and refusal to talk about her confession. She was afraid to bring it up herself. She knew his opinion of her had been sorely damaged. Still, she longed for his capacity of forgiveness to reach her. How could he be so forgiving of everything else and deny her the same kindheartedness? He even forgave white slave owners, so why couldn't he forgive her?

Bo was courteous and distantly kind, but the warmth was gone. There was no affectionate play or caressing, no lingering kisses or whispers of her name close to her ear. He didn't look at her with longing as he had before. Ruth was terribly disturbed by this change.

"It's late in the day to be starting, but I'll get a little work done before sundown." Bo slid on his jacket.

"Awright." Ruth was putting a pot of vegetables on for stew.

Bo walked over to her and gave her a quick peck on the cheek. She looked at him, aching for a real kiss, wanting to feel him against her holding her tight and pressing his mouth into hers. She refused to show the hunger she had for him. Her eyes were cold. They had that hollow stare again that Bo had almost forgotten. "I'll be back later," he said and left. When she heard his horse trotting away, Ruth sank into the wooden chair at the table and cried, wishing she had never told him the horrible truth.

Twenty

George Maitland was a tall, willowy gentleman. He was educated, socially polished, and kindhearted. His features were much like his father's except for his sizeable nose and a dark mole on his lower right jaw, which had been passed to him from his mother's side of the family. The Maitland farm was another of the standout prosperous places among the struggling farms in the Tidewater region. George was grateful his yield was so favorable when his neighbors were barely breaking even.

"I hear you did well this year too," he said to Bo.

"Yes, sir."

"The Lord has been gracious to us indeed."

"That He has."

"My fruit trees yielded smaller sized fruit this year, I suppose from the drought, but all the rest were bumper crops. Even the tobacco was thick. How was your fruit?"

"My trees were popping with fat fruit, sir. Plenty of peaches this summer, and the apples and pears are plentiful even now. The plums were a bit shy at first but they came out pretty good before summer's end."

"Hmm, I shouldn't have let that Craig Cassidy tend my orchard this year. He's such an ornery ole cuss. His foul spirit probably hindered the fruit's growth. I felt sorry for him and his ailing wife, so I gave in to his pleading for work, but from what I hear he's nasty to the workers, so I won't be keeping him on. I hate to let him go for his wife's sake, but I think he brings a bad spirit to the orchards and that hurts the trees."

George had been shuffling papers on a huge wooden desk. "Ah, here they are. I made several copies in case one gets lost. As always I'll keep one here just in case you ever need my verification, and I'll file them with the county clerk. The seal is right there. I imagine your wife will be glad to get these in her hand. Especially with slave catchers on the prowl."

"Ruth will be happy for these, I know, but slave catchers don't always care about manumission papers."

"Those unethical cretins should be jailed," George growled. He looked at Bo closely. The beaming happiness he once saw in his friend was not there. "How are things on the farm?"

"God has blessed me, sir, beyond what I ever expected. Harvest was bountiful all around and Branche was willing to take most of what I offered. There's plenty for everybody and money to reseed and feed the stock all winter. I got another goat and some more chickens. Getting a cow come spring. I was even able to help a few other farmers this year who are having a hard time. Saving a little toward getting another slave to set free too. The Lord has been so favorable to the land and to me."

"Glad to hear it. The Lord blesses you because you bless others, Bo. You're a good man with a disciple's heart." George noticed Bo's countenance. "Is something bothering you?"

"I try to do what Jesus taught, but I don't always fare so well. It's hard to be like Jesus all the time."

"Indeed it is. You're only human, and Jesus was both human and divine. We aren't able to always be perfect or He wouldn't have had to come down to be our Savior. Don't be so hard on yourself."

"It's not myself I'm being hard on," Bo mumbled.

"You're one of the most understanding and forgiving men I know. I'm sure you're just in all things."

"I always tried to be."

"Do you want to talk about it?"

"No, sir, it's real private."

George shifted his eyes. "I see, well, in that case I advise you to keep it in prayer. As my father always said, we have a friend in Jesus to whom we can tell anything."

"Yes, sir, we sure do."

"A friend who will forgive."

"Jesus forgives . . ." A pang of guilt stabbed at Bo.

Ruth stared at her precious paper and was speechless for several moments. "I's really free now." She sighed.

"You've been free since you came here. This doesn't change anything, it's just a legal statement of what already was."

She looked at him wide-eyed. "I never thought this day would ever really come."

"We've been neglecting your lessons for over a week. Do you want to continue tonight?"

"Ya don't have ta put yo'self out."

"It's not putting me out. I want you to learn. You're a very keen woman and you have a good memory. You were doing well."

188

Ruth frowned. "Ya mean I's embarrassin' bein' so ignant." Her eyes rolled.

"That's not what I said . . ." He took a deep breath and exhaled slowly. "Why would you say that? You know better. I'm not ashamed of you at all."

"Oh, ya ain't?" The eyes rolled again. "I knows I's a disgrace and unworthy to be yo' wife. I ain't educated like ya friend Mara. Don't know how ta be a good farmer's wife like Naomi. En worse of all, I'm a wicked woman who killed her own babies. Dat's why ya can't stand ta be wit me no more. Don't ya think I know dat?" Ruth eyes welled up with tears until they fell down her face.

"I never said I didn't want to be with you," he protested.

"You ain't got nerve nuff ta tell me to my face, but I know. Ya never ask me back into yo' bed. You don' treat me like ya use ta either. Ya barely talks ta me since I tol' ya 'bout my shame. You don't wan me here no more, I see it. Dat's why ya brung me dis here paper—ya hopin' I leave."

"You're wrong." Bo reached for her hand, but she moved away. "I don't want you to leave, but you're free to do as you please. I've told you all along, you are free. You can stay and be my wife or leave and start a new life somewhere else. The decision is yours."

Regretting her outburst, Ruth fell into the chair at the table. "I know ya been good ta me en ya mean ta give me my freedom. I thank ya fo' dat, but I see ya don't feel de same bout me no mo'."

"Give me time to take it in. That's all I need, is a little time."

"Ya can't fo'give me. Nobody kin, I's knowed it all along but I kept wishing cause ya fo'gives everybody else so I thought maybe . . ."

189

"I have forgiven you, Ruth, but I admit not fully. It doesn't happen quickly all the time. Sometimes it takes awhile and a lot of prayer to get to a place of Jesus' kind of forgiveness. I don't hate you and I don't want you to leave, but I need time to sort through my feelings."

"So where dat leave me? Waitin' en wonderin' how it's all gonna end. Bidin' my time hopin' ya kin git over what I did. Wit ya lookin' at me wit those questions in yo' head. I's seen how ya look at me when ya think I ain't lookin'."

Bo looked down. "I'm sorry if I've made you feel uncomfortable or unwelcome."

"Unwelcome? Ya ain't touched me like a husband since I tol' ya . . . dat says it all right dere."

"I thought we both needed time to simmer. You left our marriage bed of your own accord. I didn't demand it or necessarily want it."

"Ya didn't try ta stop me neither. Ya ain't ask me ta come back, have ya? Ya won't admit it but I think ya glad I'm gone. You's jes too kind en polite ta say so."

"I don't know what to say."

"Say what's in ya heart like ya used ta."

"I love you, Ruth."

She closed her eyes with gladness when he spoke the words she'd longed to hear. "After what ya know 'bout me, you kin still say ya loves me?" she whispered. Then she opened her eyes and saw the pools of tears in his. "Ya loves me but . . ."

"But I don't understand. I can't bring myself to figure out how you took the lives of innocent little babies that you just gave birth to. Baby Gal and I wanted children so bad and she could never give birth full-term. The third time we thought was good, but that child died too after being born. It broke

190

Baby Gal's heart so bad I think that's why she gave up and died. Then at least she's with our babies in heaven. We were happy together, and all we lacked were children to fill up our home but we never could have them. God blessed you with healthy babies and you took their lives . . . smothered the life out of them. I don't understand how you could do that. That was murder and so very wrong."

His stark words chilled Ruth. "I knows now what I did was horrible wrong but den I thought I's doing de best fo' dem babies. I did it out of lovin' dem too much to want dem living all der life as slaves. Cain't ya see dat?"

"The choice was not yours to make."

"Why not; I's der mother! Who else gonna save 'em if I don'?"

"Jesus would have saved them, and the truth is you didn't save them, you took their lives."

"Try ta see it like I seed it den. I hated dat my mother give birth ta me. I wished she never let me live. I didn't wan my chillun feelin' dat way 'bout me. I didn't want dem ta live workin' like animals en havin' no freedom. I couldn't stand de thought a it. At least dead deys free, ain't dey?"

Bo was wearied from the emotion. "But your momma did have you and she let you live. Now you're free. Free like she never was, but you are, and what if she'd done you in at birth?"

"I didn't think dere was no hope fo' freedom . . . ever," Ruth cried.

"You would have if you believed in the Lord. Then you would have had hope."

"You believe in Jesus but ya never could have chillun. Now ya got another wife who can't have no mo' babies. Is dat why ya can't stand me? Ya resent dat wit ya first wife ya didn't have a family en now I'm barren too?"

"No, of course not."

"I don't believe ya, and I don't think ya believe yo'self. I guess it's easier ta blame me than yo' so holy Jesus."

"What do you mean by that?"

"Who is ya really mad at—me or de Lawd you hold so much store in? De Lawd who didn't give ya any chillun; de Lawd who took ya precious Baby Gal away and now stuck ya wit me. De same Lawd dat let Ephraim die and Africans be slaves all these years. Who is ya rightly mad at, Bo?"

"Certainly not God; I'm not mad at God."

"I think ya is but you cain't bring yo'self to say it."

"You're wrong! Besides, what do you know about how I feel about the Lord?"

"I figure if it's Him when things go right, then it's Him when things go wrong."

"That's not true. That's how the world thinks but—" Bo's voice wavered. "I love Jesus . . . I do."

"Ya says ya love me too but ya sho ain't pleased wit me. Maybe ya ain't pleased wit de Lawd either."

"What are you saying?"

"I said it befo'. I think ya mad at God but ya too scared ta say so."

"That's nonsense."

"I know you's a smart man believin' in the Lawd an' all but—"

"I'm not mad at God!"

"Whatever ya say. I's done wit it. Ya don't have ta worry. Come spring I be gone outta ya way."

"Why? You're my wife and I don't want you to leave. You said you were here to stay."

"Things done changed now. Ain't like ya feel de same 'bout me."

"I still care for you, Ruth. I still want you as my wife and I still love you. That hasn't changed."

"Ya foolin' yo'self if ya think it ain't." Her lips trembled. "I know ya feelin's done changed toward me. What ya sayin' is one thing but how ya actin' is another."

Bo felt trapped. "I'm human, what do you expect from me? You tell me something like that and expect me to not react, just take it and say . . . what? It's all right? I have no issue with it? Is that what you want?"

"I want ya to be honest and understandin' like ya is about everythin' else. That's all I want . . . is yo' fo'giveness." Her tears came unchecked.

"I do forgive you as much as I'm able right now." He reached for her again. She didn't move out of his way this time. Bo embraced her tenderly while he prayed for answers to his own confusion. Was she possibly right in saying he was angry with God and deflecting it to her?

Being in his arms again felt amazing to Ruth. Her head reeled with sensation. She'd long for this moment when she could feel like he wanted her again. She could feel Bo trembling as he held her. Burying her face in his chest, she wondered what he was thinking. Then he said, "I'm sorry if I made you feel you weren't wanted. I never meant to do that. We can make it through this rough patch. Just give me time."

Ruth blinked and pushed out of his hold and looked at him. "What ya need time fo'? Time ta wanna be my husband?"

"I am your husband. What are you talking about?"

"Ta be my husband in bed. Ya need time fo' ya kin touch me again, is dat what ya need time fo'?"

"Is that why you're upset?" He stepped back. "You think I don't want you because I haven't been with you?"

"When a man loves a woman, don't he wanna be wit her?"

Bo was shocked. "Yes, but there's more to us being wed than just sleeping together. I want a wife for more than just that. You're not a breedin' slave anymore, Ruth. Get that through your head. I want companionship, someone to share my thoughts with. Someone I can talk to and be happy with and work together with to build a good life. That's the most important part of being together. The rest is just an extra gift from God."

"I don't know 'bout all dat. All I know is if a man ain't havin' his own way wit me or I ain't havin' babies, I ain't worth nothin'."

Lord, Jesus, help me show Ruth that her value is more than that to You . . . and to me.

"You're wrong. You are a worthwhile woman in many ways beyond that. Jesus loves you for reasons that have nothing to do with your womanhood or breeding, and so do I."

"I don't believe ya loves me. You did but not now. As fo' Jesus . . . it don't matter 'bout Him, He ain't studyin' me nohow, not a wicked woman like me."

"The kind of forgiveness you want from me, that's how Jesus forgives . . . right away without question or tussling with the matter. People take longer and we have to work things out in our heads and heart. Submit your life to the Lord, Ruth, and you will get forgiveness right away. Then you'll begin to see more worth in yourself. The Lord can clear away the hurtful things slavery put in your head. The Bible says we need to renew our minds when we come to Christ, and we do. I changed a lot of what I was taught to think through Jesus' love, and you can too."

"It's always about Jesus wit you. I'm talkin' 'bout you and me."

"There would be no you and me if it hadn't been for the

Lord. God brought us together and God had us unite as man and wife. It's been God all along, and it will be God keeping us together. Matrimony is what God created for our benefit. Don't you see? We have to keep Jesus in the midst of everything concerning our life together."

"Them's mighty fancy Bible words fo' a man who don't wanna touch his woman no mo'."

"You're not just a piece of female flesh, Ruth. Stop seeing yourself that way. I told you when you first came here I would not take advantage of you, and I meant it. Our bed should be like our relationship as a whole, blessed by God. I didn't ask you to leave it. That was your choice and it will be your choice to return."

➤ ➤ ➤ ➤ ➤ ➤

Bo thrashed for hours on the straw-packed mattress, worrying about Ruth's accusations. He felt guilty for his inability to see her as before. He'd always thought of Ruth as a victim, but now he kept thinking of her as an executioner, a destroyer of innocent life. He felt like a hypocrite talking about forgiveness when he couldn't fully forgive his own wife. Then there was that *mad at God* business. That really vexed his spirit. It was a couple of hours after he'd gone to bed when he heard the door creak as Ruth slowly opened it. Bo pretended to be asleep. Ruth shut the door and went to the fireplace, poking at the remaining burning embers. He heard the clunks of two more pieces of wood being thrown into the fireplace, but he didn't move a muscle. Minutes passed before he realized she was beside him. Fortunately his back was to her. She put her arms around him and waited for him to respond. Bo silently prayed that he would be of some help to his wife as they both struggled through this difficult time.

Lord, help me show her that true love is not just satisfying our desires. He turned facing her and kissed her forehead gently.

"You say I left dis bed on my own and I's ta come back on my own. Well, I's back. Ya love me or don't ya?" she asked softly.

"I do love you," he told her. Bo silently asked for strength not to give in to his thoughts. *I'm only human, Lord. How much can I stand of this beautiful woman, my wife in my bed like this, and not touch her?*

"If ya truly loves me, show me dat ya wan me," Ruth whispered, hoping for the right response. *Why was he hesitating?* To her there was only one answer that made sense.

Bo wrapped his arms around her and kissed her nose sweetly. "Go to sleep, my love." Although tension was high, he eventually fell asleep holding her. Ruth remained awake, fighting tears. The pain of his rejection was too much to bear, so she slid out of bed and went back to the small room where she cried herself to sleep.

Twenty-One

Saddlebrook Mansion

Emily Saddlebrook was an energetic sixty-year-old woman. As the widow of General Lawrence Albemarle Saddlebrook, she enjoyed a comfortable lifestyle due to his substantial financial provision. She reveled in the distinction of his esteemed military service and benefited from his family's privileged name.

Born and raised in the Tidewater, Emily came from humble beginnings. She was the daughter of a farmer who never made much in the way of a fortune but managed to hang on to his land and keep his family fed and clothed. The general was from a prominent Georgia family of political influence and monetary wealth. He built his lovely bride a sizeable manor in her home region just to make her happy.

Emily and the Saddlebrook matriarch had not gotten along. Prudence Saddlebrook did not approve of her son's marriage to a farmer's unsophisticated daughter. Lawrence and Emily, who could never live up to her mother-in-law's rigidly superior standards, left Georgia and moved into their new Virginia home as soon as construction allowed. Emily no longer cared about gaining Prudence Saddlebrook's approval. Her husband was handsome, young, and moving up the military ranks. They lived happily on their 250 acres in Virginia, away from Mother Prudence's persnickety ways.

Later in life and after years of taking it relatively easy in semiretirement, war broke out in 1812, becoming another opportunity for the general to exhibit his cunning campaign strategies, fearless fighting mentality, and masterful leadership ability against the British. He returned home again a hero, but during this particular war was stricken with Swamp Tick Fever from which he never fully recovered. Five years after the War of 1812 was over, he died, losing the battle with the debilitating illnesses that plagued him.

Three of the Saddlebrooks' five adult children were married and living elsewhere when the deceased general's home became a popular boardinghouse.

Only the second oldest son, Albemarle Franklin Saddlebrook, his wife, and four children, along with his unmarried sister, Sadie Lynn, still lived in the house with their mother. Albemarle farmed two-thirds of the property and owned ten slaves. Emily had her own two slaves and two indentured servants.

Theirs was a comfortable life, so when Emily decided she wanted to open the mansion for boarding, Albemarle objected. "Mother, this idea is idiotic."

"No more idiotic than your father's sending you to military school and having you end up a farmer," Emily rejoined.

"That was different. I never wanted to go to military

school or be in the military at all. That was Father's idea, not mine. No one asked me what I was suited for. You just shipped me off to West Point."

"Yes, yes, I've heard it all before. Nevertheless, you could have told your father before he wasted all that money."

"I tried, but I couldn't. Each time I tried to tell him, he made such a fuss over my good grades and honors. Told me how proud he was of me for keeping with a new family tradition. Everybody at West Point made a fuss over my being his son. I was trapped."

"You could have told me."

"And you'd go running right to Father like you always did. You told him everything you knew or thought you knew."

"If you will remember, I took your side when you said you wanted to work the land instead of choosing a military career. It was I who calmed your father down when he was up in arms against it. I talked him into letting you do what you wanted. I supported your desire to farm and it's fitting you support me now. And furthermore, I don't apologize for confiding in the general. He was my husband, after all."

"Your husband would be appalled at this latest idea of yours. Father would never allow it. He valued his privacy. Why would you compromise our privacy by allowing strangers to roam around our home?"

"No one will roam around our home. Boarders—let's call them guests—will have their own rooms, use of the downstairs parlor, and will join the family for meals in the dining room," Emily delared.

"Why are you so fixed on this anyhow? We don't need the money," Albemarle argued.

"It's not about money."

"Then what is this all about?"

"It's about my being tired of the same faces day in and day out. I want to meet new people and hear about what's happening in the world outside of this place. I want to let some of the world into my life . . . and my home. At least I'll be able to meet a few folks this way. You may think I'm getting older and past all that, but I still crave some degree of socializing."

"There are better ways to ease your boredom and need to socialize than making your home a public accommodation for . . . well, who knows who will turn up? If you are so discontent with your life, then why not go visit Allison in England?"

"Why would you think your sister has time to entertain me?"

"I know you two write each other and you miss her. And it would do you good to travel. Get this foolish business of running a boardinghouse out of your head. What are you going to do? Let anybody who knocks on the door spend the night here?"

"I can afford to be selective about whom I allow to stay here," Emily assured him.

Albemarle's wife, Libby, spoke up. "But Momma, who's going to do all the extra cooking and cleaning around here, tending to strangers?"

"Did I ask you to do anything?"

"Morley and Sally have enough to do already, and I don't think Clara and Bessie are willing to take on any extra work."

"I've already talked it over with Clara and Bessie, and I've told Morley and Sally what will be expected of them. It's all settled. Any more problems you want to bring up?" With hand on her hip, Emily stared her son and daughter-in-law down.

"I don't like it, dang it. I just don't like it. What did Reverend Norris have to say about this boardinghouse business?"

"Not that it's any of his concern, but he's sending me my

first guests. Three ministers from South Carolina coming to stay the week during camp meeting. The church fund is paying up front too."

Albemarle smacked his forehead. "I bet they'll be three loudmouthed, hellfire-and-damnation-hollering preachers . . . and for a whole week?"

"Stop blaspheming and listen here. This is my house, and if you don't like what I'm doing with it, you can build yourself your own house for you and your family."

Albemarle frowned and grabbed Libby's elbow, propelling her toward the door. "I just might do that. This place is going to get too crowded for my family and me. I'll build my own house where we can have privacy."

Various guests came and went in the mansion, and the grand establishment became known as Saddlebrook Mansion. People from all walks of life stayed there, and Emily's two indentured servants, Clara and Bessie, moved in permanently after their time of obligatory service was over. They took jobs working at the boardinghouse for small salaries, plus room and board.

Emily was having the time of her life. She was meeting the most interesting people, and dinnertime conversation sparkled. However, not every guest was a paragon of sophistication.

Emily didn't like the looks of the two unsavory strangers when they first came to her door that autumn. The one named Wally made sure she saw he had a wad of money, a most vulgar display to her way of thinking. She hoped their stay would be brief since they said they were only passing through, but several days came and went and they were still there.

For the first two days the men stayed in their rooms and had their food brought up to them. Though they had cleaned up and shaved and in general were more presentable than when they'd first arrived, Emily still wasn't thrilled having them around. They had hearty appetites and too much of a liking for her peach-and-apple brandy.

Even when they started taking their meals at the table, the two men, Wally and Bud, kept to themselves, rather than trying to be sociable. Emily wondered why they were so secretive. She caught Wally eyeing Sadie Lynn, Sally, Clara, and Bessie. *Indecent*, she thought.

Before these two strangers arrived, she'd heard that slave catchers were in the area. One day a neighbor dropped by to inform her that her guests were rumored to be part of the gang of slave catchers near the swamp, capturing Negroes regardless of their legal status or ownership. She was relieved knowing Morley and Sally lived on her property and didn't go near the swamp. She'd owned those two for more than ten years. She would be inconsolable if they were stolen from her.

Emily thought there was getting to be too much controversy over the ownership of slaves. She was convinced it was because of politicians blowing hot air for recognition and religious fanatics trying to win a way into heaven with their determination to interfere in Southern lifestyle. Slavery had always existed since way before she was born and always would, she was sure. Although she didn't cotton to whipping and being excessively abusive, the general always said they had to make slaves understand their role and know who was in charge.

The Saddlebrooks never split up families or exacted cruel punishment. That fact satisfied Emily that the practice of enslaving another human being was acceptable, even necessary to the Southern economy and their way of life. To her and many like her, uncompensated servitude was the proper place for these inferior creatures. The general had said so many times. They needed someone to look after them and and find productive work.

The table was full with the family and boarding guests for the Sunday midday meal after church service. Emily sat quietly watching the two unbecoming strangers while a cheerful Professor McKinley talked on about the peculiar properties of the red dirt in that region.

Emily was also observing her newest guest, Caroline Cane, a New York actress who claimed to be in her midthirties. She was on holiday with her younger companion/manager. He had to rush home to see his dying grandmother in Isle of Wight County, Virginia. The unmarried couple had to separate as not to offend the man's family. So he planted his ladylove at Saddlebrook in the neighboring county with the promise to return for her soon.

"Miss Cane, you aren't eating much. Don't you like our food?" Emily asked her.

"Oh, certainly. I mean, it's fine." The woman sounded irritated at being singled out.

"Fine?" The professor snorted. "Why, Miss Emily's Sally is a fine cook if there ever was one. She makes the best biscuits and gravy in the whole county. Her ham is splendid, and her roast turkey and stuffing absolutely delectable." He kissed his finger to show his appreciation.

"Yes, it's certainly a change from New York. Have you tasted beef Wellington with béarnaise sauce over portobellos? Delicate champagne crepes filled with fresh fruit, sprinkled ever so lightly with sugar?" Caroline's hand waved about expressively as she spoke. But her sparkle dimmed when she looked down at her plate of ham, string beans, white potatoes, and honey-glazed carrots. "This is tasty enough—very good, really—but I can't help missing my fabulous meals at the New York City restaurants when I'm away traveling."

"It sounds so exotic," Sadie Lynn gushed.

"It's wonderful," Carolyn assured her. "And I also enjoy a brand-new café in Manhattan opened up by two brothers from Switzerland—they call it Del's after their last name, Delmonico. They're hoping to expand into a larger place someday."

"I bet it's so exciting. All those people and fancy places to go," Libby chimed in.

"New York City is a whirlwind of activity, but even *it* pales compared to Paris."

"You've been to Paris?" Sadie Lynn asked, impressed.

"Three times," the actress said proudly. "Paris is more *magnifique* than anyplace in this country. Every day is like an adventure there. And the food is simply exquisite."

Emily smiled faintly. "Where were you headed . . . before you had to . . . ahem, change your plans?"

"We were on our way to Savannah to get a ship to Europe."

"Europe?" Albemarle asked, as he gobbled up his biscuit.

"Don't talk with your mouth full," Libby admonished him.

"There's a very wealthy American in England who has a fancy for the theater and saw me perform in New York. This gentleman has commissioned me to perform in London with some other Americans."

Albemarle's mouth twisted a bit. "What kind of perform-ance? Dancing?"

"I am an actress, a serious performer of plays, soliloquies, and song."

Sadie Lynn asked, "Did you perform in Paris?"

"Indeed I did. I was onstage at the Maristraux."

"What's that?" the professor asked as he reached for the bowl of honey-glazed carrots as it was passed.

"Only one of the most coveted places to perform in Paris. Theatre De Maristraux is where the toast of Parisian nobility go to be entertained. Those who appreciate the finer forms of entertainment, that is."

"Paris must be an awfully exciting place to visit." From her place at the head of the table, Emily's eyes scanned her guests. "Professor, you must try Sally's pumpkin pudding. It's delicious." She smiled coolly at Caroline, but her intent was to snub the actress for the degrading comment about dinner.

Emily had had her fill of snobbery during her interactions with her in-laws and wasn't about to put up with it from some stage performer. How dare this creature come into her establishment, turning her nose up at the food . . . high and mighty restaurants indeed!

"I have a daughter who lives in London," Emily mentioned casually as she sliced her meat.

Caroline fluttered her eyelids. "London is quite nice, of course, but nothing is as exciting as Paris."

"You've already been to London?" Sadie Lynn dropped her fork from excitement.

"I was an actress in a Shakespearean troupe that traveled all over Europe for four years. I was fortunate enough to see places most people only dream about. We played London, Paris, Barcelona . . . We toured large cities and as well as small villages in Scotland, Ireland, and Greece and also throughout Austria, Hanover, Bavaria. Europeans are thirsty for quality entertainment regardless of their financial status. It was a marvelous time in my life."

"Oh, how wonderful it must have been!" Sadie Lynn gushed. Albemarle was irritated, but his wife was impressed. The professor was curious but more interested in the food and getting back to his discussion of red dirt.

Of the two men, the blond wiry one was enjoying his meal and catching bits and pieces of the conversation without much interest. He was on his second biscuit and third slice of ham, having polished off a good portion of turkey and stuffing. His companion, however, ate slowly, keeping a close eye on the boastful actress. He tried to be discreet about his interest, but Emily didn't miss a thing. Occasionally he shifted his gaze to Sadie Lynn or one of the servant women, but mostly he watched Caroline with her flamboyant airs.

"Honestly, sometimes I think the whole world consists of this dull place." Sadie Lynn was wistful. "There's a big ole world out there and all I've ever seen was what's between here and Atlanta."

Caroline picked at the food on her plate. "You should travel, my dear. It will open your eyes and mind to so much more."

"Her mind is opened up well enough," Albemarle grumbled. "Maybe too well."

"How would you know?" Libby countered, rolling her eyes. "You could stand some culture yourself."

"I don't see you have much to complain about," Albemarle retorted. He held his annoyance in check, aware of his children listening.

"Like Sadie Lynn says, life is more than just farms and Tidewater. There are wonders we can only dream about out there."

"That's enough, now," Albemarle ordered. Libby lowered her head and didn't say anything else. Emily noticed Wally smirk a little at Libby's being put in her place.

"There's no need to be testy at the dinner table, brother." Sadie Lynn dabbed the corner of her mouth with her napkin, intent on her family making a good impression before guests.

"Libby was only expressing her desire to expand her horizons," she added mildly.

"That's enough," Emily interjected. "Carrying on like this on the Lord's Day. And at the table." She gave an embarrassed laugh.

"Albee started it," Sadie Lynn muttered.

"I don't care who started it. It ends now, do you understand? I will not abide this ill-mannered carrying on at the table while people are trying to enjoy their meal." The room went dead quiet. Sally was bringing in more food and cautiously froze in her tracks. Emily sternly scowled at her relatives. "No more bickering." Then she looked over to the boarders. "I extend my deepest apology to our guests for this most undignified outburst."

After an uncomfortable silent spell, Emily looked at Caroline. "Miss Cane . . . "

"Please call me Caroline. Miss Cane sounds so formal."

"Very well, Caroline it will be. We have a bit of excitement going on ourselves right here. We're having our annual Harvest Ball this coming Saturday."

"A Harvest Ball?"

"To celebrate the good fortune of profits brought in from the farmers' harvests."

"Fancy big-city folk might call it a hoedown," Albemarle muttered.

"A dance; how nice," Caroline said politely.

Libby said, "This isn't just any ole backwater hoedown, honey. The Harvest Ball is the biggest event in the entire county. We dress up in our absolute best and everyone is on their grandest behavior."

"It does sound delightful. I've been to parties and dances in small towns and large cities, but I've never been to a Southern

Harvest Ball." The thought of a party piqued her interest if for no other reason than relieving her boredom until Preston returned.

"You will come, won't you?" Sadie Lynn asked anxiously. "It will be such a coup to bring a world-traveled actress to the ball as our guest. Mary Dickerson will be green with envy." Sadie Lynn's face was flushed from the thought of it. Albemarle started to speak, then glanced at his mother and stopped.

"Oh yes, you must attend the Harvest Ball," Libby said. "You'll get to meet everybody who's anybody around here. It's held in the biggest mansion in the county. Major Guthrie will be there and Allen Smith of the Kentucky Smiths . . ."

"The Kentucky Smiths?" Caroline repeated, confused at having several names to keep straight.

"Why, the Smith clan of Kentucky owns the largest horse breeding farm in that state. Their youngest brother, Brock, lives right here in Southampton. He owns the stable."

"I see."

"She's not interested in any horse breeders or farmers or balls. Can't you tell?"

"Of course, she is," Sadie Lynn rejoined. "You'll get to meet Butler Mason."

"Don't bother. Butler Mason is an irresponsible scoundrel. He has no direction in life and thinks his father's money will always buy him out of his atrocious behavior," Emily declared.

"And you say he's very rich?" Caroline asked, looking more interested.

"He's very rich and extremely handsome. Or at least his poppa is rich," Sadie Lynn said, grinning.

"Butler's father has money, so he gets anything he wants." Libby sighed.

Albemarle frowned. "You hurry up and finish your dinner.

208

You need to lie down. I think you're sick with fever talking like this."

"I don't have a fever."

Sadie Lynn leaned over to her sister-in-law and whispered, "At least not the kind he's talking about." They both snickered.

"What's so amusing?" Emily asked, eyeing the pair suspiciously. "Sadie Lynn, you seem unusually rambunctious this evening. What in the world has gotten into you? All this talk of fancy faraway places has gone to your head; or is it the thought of that rapscallion, Butler Mason?"

Sadie looked at her mother, insulted, lips curled in a defiant smile. "Both. I'm simply giddy thinking of all the places I've never been . . . and how I might change that one day."

A silence fell over the room as everyone finished the meal. The professor sighed with contentment; he seemed to have said all he needed to about red dirt and was glad to sit quietly and wait for dessert to be served.

Sally quietly came to clear the table. When she left, Caroline said, "Your . . . um . . . staff seems very competent."

"We're happy with them," Emily replied. "We picked up Sally and Morley ten years ago. They're worth all we paid for them and more."

"That's something I can't understand about the South," Caroline admitted. "Some people"—she looked pointedly at Albemarle—"look down on me because of my profession. But buying and selling other human beings . . ."

"What about it?"

"Slavery is a disgrace and against human decency, not to mention against the law."

"For your information, it's not against the law in these parts."

"It ought to be. It's horrible and cruel."

209

"We aren't cruel to our slaves," Emily assured her.

"Ownership of another human being from monetary procurement is an atrocity, no exceptions."

The two strangers looked at each other and back at Caroline. All eyes were on the actress. The professor had slowed down eating and spoke up after wiping his mouth. He was finally ready to expound on a subject other than soil. "It is a historical fact, dear lady, that slavery has existed for centuries and in many cultures. Why, as far back as ancient times long before Jesus' birth, there have always been slaves. In the annals of humankind and beasts alike, the strongest always makes use of the weakest. Those who do not have always serve those who do have. I'd not be so quick to offend if I were you, madam. Like an actor taking a bow onstage or audience applause is to a performer, slavery in the South is a way of life."

"It's a wrong way of life. No offense intended."

"Some could say a single lady traveling unchaperoned with a man is wrong," Emily suggested icily.

"Miss Emily, I am highly regarded among my peers. I *am* a woman of quality and I'm decent. Ask anyone in New York theater about Caroline Cane and you will not hear a word of reproach." Caroline's arms flew out dramatically. "Preston and I are not hurting anyone. *We're* not taking away people's liberty and using them like work animals."

"We do no such thing; besides our slaves are happy," Libby defensively interjected.

"I beg to differ. How can an imprisoned subservient man or woman possibly be happy under such conditions? Would you be happy as a slave? The idea is absurd. You people tell yourselves that to justify what you're doing, but you should know better."

210

"Many slaves have good lives—a place to live and food to eat. And not all darkies around here are slaves anyway. Take Bo Peace. He was freed and now he has a nice producin' farm and lives happy and peaceable right here in this county." The two strangers glanced at each other. Wally paid close attention to what was said next.

Sadie Lynn chimed in. "That's right, Bo Peace is one of the happiest Negro men alive. He's polite and very religious too. Never says a bad word about a soul and is always ready to help folks."

"This here Bo fella, he lives on that Maitland farm?" Wally asked.

"Why yes, sort of. It used to be Maitland land. How did you know?" Emily was puzzled by his interest.

"Thought I heard some folks at the Emporium talkin' 'bout him."

"He doesn't live on the Maitland plantation, actually. His land used to be part of it, but it belongs to Bo now. It's right next to Maitland's place though," Sadie Lynn explained.

"This slave owns property?"

Sadie Lynn nodded. "Bo was a slave; he's been freed and he owns that farm." Sadie Lynn smiled sweetly, but the expression on Wally's face gave Emily a feeling of unease.

Caroline was not finished making her point. "You say he's free now. Then that's why he's happy. No more bondage to a master who is no better than he. All slaves should be freed." Caroline noticed Wally narrowing his eyes at her, but she didn't care.

Albemarle's anger simmered. "Slavery is not against the law, so it doesn't matter what you think."

"One day it will be when people down here become more civilized in your thinking." Caroline's eyes sparkled with satisfaction at the shocked expressions around the table.

"Are you an abolitionist?" Sadie Lynn wanted to know.

"Oh no, I have no political loyalties whatsoever. Mine are strictly humanitarian beliefs. I simply do not approve of people owning other people for free labor. I think it's a throwback to barbaric times."

Caroline was startled by the gasps around her. She had gone too far. The children were suddenly taking an avid interest in the adult conversation. "I didn't mean you were barbarians," she amended. "I was speaking about the practice of slavery."

After an uncomfortable slience, Emily turned to her guest. "Miss Cane, it would behoove you to keep your opinions to yourself while you're staying in my home. We Southerners are very proud of how we live. Our customs are not at the mercy of scrutiny from people from up North." The hostess looked around and cleared her throat before continuing, "My home welcomes guests, but we do not expect to be maligned. The Saddlebrook Mansion is a notable establishment in this community and all guests are expected to respect me, my family, and the hired help as well as other guests. But also . . . and this is not open to discussion . . . you *will* respect our way of life and what we stand for if you wish to remain under this roof."

Caroline looked up, defeated, tears filling her eyes. "I sincerely apologize, Miss Emily. I did not mean to insult anyone. I really did not . . . and the food is very tasty." Her voice trailed off.

Emily looked across the room at the portrait of her beloved late husband, the general. He would have known exactly what to do in such conflict. She sighed, weary of the entire matter. "We graciously accept your apology, my dear, as we Southerners are gracious people. And I'll be certain to tell *my slave* Sally that you approve of her cooking."

Caroline stared blankly at Emily. She couldn't think how to respond, so she said nothing.

The rest of the mealtime passed quietly, with strained energy in the air. The professor, however, was undaunted by any of the emotions of the previous conversation. He continued to eat voraciously and shower compliments galore about the food. Sadie Lynn was apparently peeved . . . at whom, it was uncertain. Albemarle was fuming and kept cutting nasty looks at his wife and the actress. Libby worked hard to appear aloof about any of the argument and ignored her husband's unpleasant stares. The two strangers finished their dessert quietly with a few more rude whispers between them. Caroline was the first to excuse herself from the table and retreated quickly to her room.

➤ ➤ ➤ ➤ ➤ ➤

Southampton County had two harvest affairs per year. The Harvest Ball was for the white citizens, and slaves and free blacks enjoyed their own event, the Harvest Dance.

The ball took place with its usual elaborate formality at the Willoughby Mansion. The beautiful white-columned home was lighted up, and strains of music from the hired string quartet drifted outside as guests arrived. Ladies were led on the spiral staircase to rooms upstairs where they could leave their wraps and check their hair. Many of the guests would stay for a few days, since they had traveled a long way for the occasion. The Willoughbys had plenty of house slaves dressed up and working hard who added to the glamour of the evening.

When Caroline Cane arrived, heads turned at her chic garb and exaggerated mannerisms. She flitted and fluttered like a butterfly throughout the ball as if she were star of the event.

She outshone every lovely debutante and pretty women of notice.

The men in the room seemed especially fascinated.

Quite a few noticed that Butler Mason seemed particularly taken with the exotic beauty from New York City and her with him. Even Cyrus Willoughby, the powerful patriarch of one of Southampton's founding families and host of the grand affair, was enamored.

To her surprise and pleasure, the meal of ham, boiled mutton, beef à la mode, vegetables, and scalloped oysters rivaled entrees she'd enjoyed in New York and abroad. After a dessert of plum pudding and stewed apples in cream, the women excused themselves to go upstairs and freshen up while the men enjoyed their cigars.

Then the dancing began. Carolyn whirled with several partners in a cotillion and other country dances, and even taught her new friends a waltz she'd learned in Paris.

She was giddy with all the attention. She was angry at Preston for dropping her off at the boardinghouse and not returning yet, and was determined to enjoy herself. Too bad for him, feeling she was not suitable to meet his family; she would make him regret his thoughtlessness. She danced gaily, never short of partners. Laughing coyishly and flirting shamelessly, she danced the night away until she was near exhaustion. To her surprise a few impressively wealthy men lived in or near this backwater place. Becoming more impressed with the region's citizens and longing less for Preston, the pretentious actress was entreated with company by several available gentlemen, including Butler Mason, the prize of the lot.

❧ ❧ ❧ ❧ ❧ ❧

"This is a disgrace!" Albemarle hissed after yet another gentleman caller had visited Caroline in Saddlebrook's downstairs parlor.

"There is nothing improper going on in this house and you know it!" Emily was so exasperated with her son she nearly stamped her foot.

"Men are visiting her in the parlor, acting like mindless imbeciles. What if this Preston fella comes back and finds her with other suitors about? We don't want our family name connected with a scandal."

Emily Anne looked out the door and saw Wally and Bud, her least-favorite guests, coming in from where she didn't know. For days now they'd been leaving very early in the morning and stayed gone till after dusk. She turned to Albemarle. "There are other things more important to keep an eye on than the romantic whimsy of some silly actress," she told him.

"Such as?" Albemarle wanted to know.

"Like those two."

Albemarle looked bemused. "Them? What have they done?"

"I don't know for certain if they've done anything, but as you know it's suspected they may be slave catchers."

"Idle gossip if you ask me. Nobody's proved it or even tried to from what I see."

"There's something about them . . . that Wally in particular."

"They pay regular, they're quiet, and mind their own business. I have no fault with them."

Sadie Lynn pressed her forefinger to her cheek. "I thought they were just passing through. It's been ten days and they're still here . . . why?"

"Why not? They might like it here. What's the problem with that?"

Emily ruffled her completed flower arrangement staring at it thoughtfully. "Just keep an eye on those two and stop obsessing over Caroline. Something's not right with them."

Twenty-Two

The time came for the blacks' harvest celebration at the Old Meetinghouse barn. It was not the formal affair like the Harvest Ball, but it was a good time to be had for all the hardworking slaves and free blacks. The event began with a prayer meeting thanking God for His blessings, getting slaves through all the hard work of harvesting and blessing free Negroes with a bounty. The prayer meeting was followed by music, dancing, games, and plenty of food.

The Harvest Dance brought Negroes together, something especially needed now. It was a time of gratitude and celebration, not a time for political debate. Since Prophet Nat Turner had come, there was division in the church among those who wanted violent revolution and those who opposed it. This difference in philosophies resulted in cool retreat from the once familiar friendliness among some of the black population. Little was openly spoken. There were no outright confrontations over the matter but a subtle attitude of suspicion, distrust, and disagreement swelled through slave quarters all around.

Bo was scarcely aware folks considered him the central figure in the antirevolt group. He could tell there was an invisible dividing line forming and vowed not to take sides. Actively involved or not, he was indirectly thrust into the matter to his dislike. Bo was not looking forward to the dance as he had in past years. The loss of Ephraim's happy presence making everyone laugh at his tomfoolery and out-of-sync dancing would be deeply missed. Things were still strained between him and Ruth.

On the morning of the dance, Bo was dressed and sitting at the table as he waited for Ruth to come out. He noticed her excitement about the festivities had waned, but he was hoping the merriment would cheer her up. He gazed out the window, thinking hard about his part in their problems. Ruth finally came out the small room, interrupting his self-admonishment. He turned to see her in her new frock. Her hair was made up with the pretty green ribbon woven through it. The dress was a perfect fit, and the pale green color made her skin look radiant. Everything was wonderful—except the hollow look in her eyes.

"You look beautiful," he said sincerely.

"Thank you," was her dull response.

"Are you ready to go? Don't want to miss too much of the prayer meeting."

"I come later. I don' wanna sit through no prayin. I wanna wait fo' de party ta start."

Bo was disappointed. "We had a truly blessed harvest this year. It's only fitting we thank the Lord for His favor."

"You thank Him," she said brusquely.

Bo believed it was his fault Ruth was unwilling to go, but he could only leave the matter in God's hands. "Very well, if that's what you want. I'll come back and fetch you."

"You don' have ta, I kin ride Golden Gal."

"In your new dress?"

"Sho', I ain't so fussy. I kin ride in anything. You take de wagon wit de food and I ride Golden Gal to de party later on."

"Most women don't ride horseback in their Sunday-go-to-meeting clothes. Why are you—never mind. If this is want you want to do, it's fine with me, although I was looking forward to showing up with my beautiful wife by my side."

Ruth made a frustrated expression and turned away. Bo walked over to her and took her in his arms. He wanted to say so much but couldn't find the right words and decided it was not the right time anyway. He didn't want to stir up any more emotions before the dance. He'd tell her later when they got home. She looked so beautiful he wanted to kiss her but didn't think such an endearment would be welcomed. His eyes searched hers for some sign of life, but there was none. They were as coldly empty as they were the first time he ever looked into them.

He'd done this to her; sent her back inside her vacant self. He had to make it right. God had cleared up some very important matters with Bo in his spirit. He'd wrestled with them for a long time during the night, but morning came and he knew the truth about his faith, himself, and his love for his wife.

Ruth was thinking hard about Bo, hoping his tenderness would encircle her again. She wanted to feel his love surround her like before. She couldn't feel it anymore. All she felt or thought she saw in his face was disapproval just like from everyone else. She winced as the thoughts stabbed at her heart. His feelings may have changed for her, but her feelings were the same toward him. She was in love with Bo and couldn't let go of it no matter how much she wanted or tried. This sweet sentimentality was an emotion she had never experienced before. It would not be controlled by anything she could harness. It was untamed and powerful, and it frightened Ruth to realize how much it took over her mind and life. She needed to be free from this bondage. That's what it was, another kind of slavery that brought her unhappiness.

Bo pressed her gently to him. "You are so precious to me, Ruth," he said, his voice shaky with emotion.

Ruth thought she almost felt love encompass her but she shook it off as wishful thinking. "Ya better git goin' fo' ya miss out on prayer meetin'." She was hoping he would release her before she collapsed from fighting to keep from begging for his forgiveness.

Bo let her go, feeling the tension in her body. The Spirit urged him to make it right at that very moment. He felt the strong push but put it off for later. "Yes, you're right. I better get going." He pulled Ruth's hand with him, walking to the door. She stood at the door confused by the mixed signals she was getting. Baffled and distressed, she watched him climb onto the wagon. Bo waved good-bye as he started off. "You be careful on your way to the dance, my love," he called.

"I will." She waved back briefly. Her eyes watered as she closed the door. He had called her his love. Oh, how she wanted to really be his love again.

When Bo arrived, he stopped at the big barn where some of the women were setting up tables with food. Unloading what he brought didn't take long. Mae and Naomi were among those helping. "Where's Ruth?" Naomi asked.

"She didn't ride in with me."

"Why not? She said she was coming."

"She'll be here for the dance. She wanted to ride Golden Gal in," he said and walked off back to the wagon to avoid further questions.

The worship service was already going on when he reached the meetinghouse. The congregation was singing, and there were many more in attendance than usual.

Bo nodded at Mr. and Mrs. Abernathy, who sat in the rear near the door. Their white presence was conspicuous, but no one was surprised to see them. The Abernathys often came to the church services of the slaves. When he didn't see the Purdys in the crowd, he assumed they were still out of town with Mrs. Purdy's sick relatives. The meetinghouse was on their property and closer than the white church. They were Christians who'd spent their youth converting slaves to Jesus. They hated the slave system and freely socialized amicably among the slave population.

When the singing stopped and everyone was seated, Preacher Jones stood at the simple wooden podium ready to speak to his congregation. His hand grasped the lapel of his too-tight suit jacket and he began.

"Well now, this has been a hard year for many in this county. Things are as dismal as the swamp, they say, but I say God has kept us in this hard time while upholdin' us with His mercy!"

Murmurs of agreement circled the sanctuary. "A lot of farmers are hurting, but we know what the mighty hand of the Lord can do! No matter what happens to other folks, God will provide for His children. Our Lord can take the worst of things and change them into blessings like He did with Joseph in Egypt. As it is, we have a Joseph among us who provides the pharaoh's grain to those in need. Praise Jesus, the Lord set him up and he is faithful to his calling."

Many people glanced at Bo. They knew he was the Joseph the preacher was talking about. Bo felt uncomfortable being included in the topic of a sermon. Rooster turned and frowned at him. Bo was disappointed, because he'd never done anything against Rooster. He knew why his old friend was annoyed with him but he didn't think it was fair. Bo never asked to be involved in any revolution and resented being singled out and then blackballed for not participating.

He cleared his mind of the matter, hoping it was all just talk from Prophet Turner and would never come to fruition. He turned his thoughts back to the sermon. The preacher was now speaking on forgiveness and how Joseph forgave his brothers. The words pricked hard at Bo. He had not been that example to his wife as he should have been. He vowed he would correct his erroroneous behavior. He didn't understand what she did or how she could have done it, but he did want to fully forgive her. He knew she was sorry and that her mind had been in a desperate place when she performed those dreadful deeds. If he could show her Christ's love through himself, then maybe, just maybe she would believe. He'd shown her caring, tolerance, and courtesy, but not real forgiveness.

"Joseph was used of God to feed His chosen children. Only because Joseph bowed to the will of God over and over in the worst situations could he have been used so thoroughly." Bo froze at the confirmation of the minister's words. They were eerily similar to what the Lord said in his spirit the very night before.

Bow your will to Mine and open your heart to the woman you are joined to. If you do not forgive her in earnest, I cannot use you.

➤ ➤ ➤ ➤ ➤ ➤

Ruth went to the barn to get Golden Gal ready for the ride to the dance. She wasn't in the mood for frivolity or party

222

games but she'd said she would go, so she would.

Golden Gal was a striking animal, huge and perfectly built, an odd golden color that attracted attention. She whinnied more than usual and restlessly pulled her head up repeatedly. "What's the matter, girl? You's mighty fidgety today." Ruth hoped a brisk ride on her beautiful mare would calm the horse and help her feel better by the time she got to the dance. She kept thinking about things Bo had said to her; how precious she was to him and his calling her "my love." Was it possible that he did still love her? Was she being foolish to think he could care for her after what she confessed? She couldn't keep her mind on anything but him. Somberly she led Golden Gal toward the house and tied her to the tree in front.

Going inside the house to get her new bonnet, she crossed the threshold. A hand went across her mouth from behind. She heard the door kicked shut and felt a tight grip on her waist. She could see someone else, a dark-haired man standing nervously by the fireplace.

"Don't bother to scream when I move my hand. Keep your mouth shut," came a deep-throated command from hot breath reeking of liquor. He loosened his hand from her mouth and spun her around facing him. Ruth was breathless and too frightened to speak. "Ah, a really fine-looking wench we have here," the man said crudely, his eyes scanning her body. He had that look she'd seen before in the eyes of men who were up to no good. He grabbed her arm and slung her into a chair. "What do you think, Bud? She'd bring a mighty good price, won't she?"

"Whaddya wan . . ." Ruth managed to ask. The man who grabbed her was evil-looking, with dark hair. His voice was familiar.

"That black buck, Bo Peace, is what we want! Is he here?"

"N–no."

"Where is he?" the man demanded. Ruth said nothing. Wally grabbed her up roughly, looking directly into her eyes. "You either answer me before or after I beat the living daylights outta you. The choice is yours."

"Take it easy, Wally," his companion cautioned.

Wally looked at Bud, annoyed, then back at Ruth. "Now I'll ask you one mo' time. This where that Bo Peace live?" Ruth nodded affirmatively. "He ain't here but do you know where he's at?" She didn't move except for her eyes widening with fear. Wally's slap was forceful enough to knock her to the floor. "I see you're willing to take a lot of punishment fo' this fella."

"Hold up, let me try," Bud said, wanting to minimize the brutality he knew Wally was capable of inflicting on the frightened female. Bud was a milder man, and Wally's rage always uneased him. The man would lose control far too quickly, especially after he'd been drinking. Bud knew Wally was full of hatred for slaves. That's what made him a much sought-after slave catcher, and previously an overseer who ruled slaves with a whip and the same hateful spirit. Wally was originally from Mississippi, Bud from Georgia. They had been paired together after other men refused to ride with Wally anymore since he was so violent and he drank too much. He quickly earned a reputation of being nearly impossible to get along with.

Bud remembered being told by an acquaintance of Wally's that his own mild manner should balance Wally's volatile inclinations. Unfortunately Bud soon learned that Wally wasn't standing for any balancing. Things had to be done his way, all the time.

Bud helped Ruth up into a chair. He kneeled in front of her, trying to give her time to collect herself. He saw she wasn't crying or pleading for mercy like most females would. He admired her toughness. "We're looking for the slave, Bo Peace. You his woman?" Bud asked gently. Ruth nodded yes. "We won't do you no harm. Just tell us where he is."

"Wha . . . what ya wan' wit him?"

"I'm gonna break his black neck!" Wally bellowed.

Bud looked back at Wally, frowning. He was getting tired of the brashness. "If you don't say where he is, I won't be able to control him," Bud said quietly to Ruth.

She pointed to Wally. "I ain't tellin', 'cause he wanna kill my Bo."

"Aw, get out of the way. I'll make her talk."

Bud waved his hand. "Leave it to me! I've seen your ways of making people talk."

Bud's unexpected backbone took Wally by surprise. "We don't have all day to fool with this black wench."

"Look, this is where he lives, right? Then he's bound to come home and we'll be here waiting when he does. Why should we go riding around all over tarnation looking for him? Let him come to us."

Ruth wondered why she hadn't seen or heard their horses approach the house. Wally was pacing around the room. "I guess you're right. We can wait here; it's comfortable enough."

Her stomach lurched, knowing what was on his mind. Without thinking she blurted out, "No need waitin' 'round here 'cause he be gone all day, maybe to tomorrow."

"Is that so?" Wally grinned, showing the gap where the tooth Bo had knocked out had been.

"He at the harves' dance. It go on forever."

"So that's why you all gussied up. Going to the dance, was you?"

"She may be telling the truth, Wally. I heard them slaves of Miss Emily's talking about going to some big party today."

"They just had that dad-blasted harvest thing last week, didn't they?"

"Dat was de white folk ball. Dis is fo' us," Ruth informed him.

Wally sat down on the bench by the door. He opened the door, looking out. "How you get such fancy clothes and a nice horse?"

"De horse was given ta me."

"I bet." Wally sneered. "You probably stole it off some white man you murdered." He stood up looking out on the land. "How a slave get all this? A cozy farmhouse and plenty a land . . . fat chickens, cows and goats and ground fertile more than most, so I hear."

Ruth heard barking in the distance and knew Brody and Chance were headed home from their daily romp in the woods. She figured they might attack the two men if she could get them inside or the men outside. The barking got closer and more intimidating.

"You got a pack of wild dogs?"

"Only two."

"They mean?"

"Not ta me, but they don't take much ta strangers."

Wally slammed the door shut. "You don't make it to the dance, your slave man should come back looking for you."

"He ain't no slave. He free and he my husband."

"Free and havin' all this. Ain't right when white folks scratching dry dirt to make a livin' and some so-called freed slave living all comfy."

226

"Bo work hard as any man livin'. He deserve everythin' he got." Ruth was beyond scared now. She was angry.

"He wouldn't have a thing if a white man hadn't given it to him," Wally countered.

"Massah Maitland give dis here land fo' Bo's family's hard work en getting nothing all dem years. Dey earn it en Bo earn it too, workin' like dogs all der life fo' dem Maitlands."

"Slaves supposed to work! That's all they're good for. He ain't earned nothin'. It's sacrilege to set 'em free and give 'em land!"

"Massah Maitland ain't think so."

"And what's this nonsense 'bout he's your husband? Africans can't marry. It's against the law for slaves to marry. He ain't none a your husband."

"Preacha say words o'er us en we jumped de broom, so we's wed good and propa."

"Preacher said words over you? Since when does a preacher fool with your kind?"

"Preacha use ta be a slave hissef."

"You mean the preacher is African too?"

"That's right, en we's married cause we jump de broom en had ceremony en Preacha say Holy Words o'er us. Sides, we ain't slaves no mo'. We's free and free folks kin marry."

"Bah, nonsense! You were born a slave and far as I care you'll always be a slave! Whoever heard of slaves getting married with African preachers performing ceremonies of all things? It's sacrilege! You people gettin' carried away thinkin' you as good as white folks!"

Bud saw his companion's face redden. "Let's get something to eat while we wait, Wally. I bet she's a real good cook." He wanted to defuse the heated debate. "What ya got here to eat?" he asked Ruth.

"Nothin' much, cause I sent all I cooked on de wagon fo' de party."

"You ain't got nothing tasty you can whip up?"

"Some sweet potatoes and maybe some eggs in the hen-house."

Bud was thinking how he was missing a hearty meal of fried chicken and cornmeal dumplings in collard greens at Miss Emily's. He heard Sally and Emily talking before breakfast about what Sally had prepared before she left for the slaves' celebration dance. He had smelled the delectable aromas of her cooking all morning. Now since they'd left the boardinghouse, he'd miss out on the midday meal.

He regretted knowing the comfort and home cooking of the boardinghouse was a thing of the past. Once Wally got his hands on Bo, they would have to leave Virginia for good and in a hurry. Bud tried to talk his stubborn companion out of his vengeful quest. Wally was not willing to forgo retaliation after suffering a beating from a Negro. He wanted Bo's blood.

Ruth moved slowly around the room, starting a cook fire. Wally watched her intently. Bud noticed Wally's lascivious staring. He knew what was on his mind, and was sickened by it. One thing he had learned being with this man was that Wally did not respect the fairer sex, white or black. Bud had decided early in their association he would never let Wally, with his harsh language and brutal nature, near his wife or two children back in Georgia.

Ruth grabbed up a basket and opened the door. Wally jumped up to stop her. "Where you think you going?"

"To de henhouse ta git eggs."

"Never you mind no eggs. One of us will take care of that." He snatched the empty basket from her hand.

"Awright," she said, hoping he would go out so the dogs would maul him.

"I ain't goin' out there by myself with them dogs prowling round," Bud threw out.

"You think she'll come back if one of us don't go with her? She'll be on that horse riding away in a flash."

Bud got irritated. "Then just forget the dang eggs. Fix something else. We already had eggs this morning."

Hope dashed, Ruth's smile faded. "I kin fix some sweet potato biscuits. Got molasses ta go wit it."

"Go on then and do it," Wally growled.

Bud had doubts about eating food prepared by a woman whose husband they meant to harm. Wally was just arrogant enough not to think twice about it. "Why don't we just go back to the boardinghouse and—"

"Stop trying to talk me outta what I'm fixin' to do! If you ain't got the stomach for it, leave, but I'm settlin' the score with that black dog if it's the last thing I do!"

"Don't get riled. I just thought it'd make more sense to eat at the boardinghouse."

"What are you sayin'? Leave her here to go runnin' off to warn him? That's a fool thing if ever I heard."

"No more fool than this," Bud muttered.

"Fix the sweet potato biscuits," Wally ordered Ruth. She kept glancing at the pistol shoved down the side of his belt. She was desperate to get away and warn Bo. He was safe as long as he stayed at the dance, but what if he came back for her? She had to do something to save his life. She loved Bo no matter what hard times they were going through. He was the only man in her life who ever showed her kindness and demanded nothing in return. She was determined not to let him be murdered by these evil people.

Ruth vowed she would do whatever it took to save Bo's life even if it cost her own.

➤ ➤ ➤ ➤ ➤ ➤

Prayer meeting was over and people had gone to the big barn to dance, eat, and make merry. Bo was anxious for Ruth to arrive. A few of the unattached females had already cornered him for dances as was customary with single men, but he was no longer available and he wanted it to be clear he wasn't.

Pete Nolan and his fellow musicians were picking their banjos and playing their instruments vivaciously. The festive mood reached the highest rafters of the barn. Bo was hoping the happy atmosphere would infect Ruth. Momma Maybelle even got up and danced with Herman Dorsey, a man she always said got on her nerves. Momma lifted her checkered skirt and hopped around the floor like a young girl. Flossy Laws was eyeing Bo, but he ducked between Naomi and Mae. Harriet, the youngest daughter of Harry Spraggs, was making a beeline for Bo when Mae intercepted, insisting he dance with her. He was relieved to dance with sweet ole Mae. "Where's Ruth?" Mae asked when she saw Harriet's frustrated expression as she retreated and walked away toward Duke Emory.

"She'll be here soon, I reckon."

"She better hurry up. I's too old ta be tryin' to keep these fast-tail women off ya much longer." Mae smiled as she dipped and swirled around Bo in a lively dance step. By the end of the musical number, she was holding her chest, breathing hard. Bo escorted her to the table where the apple cider and pear punch sat. Mae plopped down on a bale of hay to recuperate. "I declare. I don' know how dat Maybelle do it. She be up swingin' dem hips like she a youngun en she way ol'er den me."

Naomi looked over at Momma Maybelle and grinned. "She got extra spring in her step cause she in heat, dat's how."

Mae's eyes bugged. "In heat? Who, Maybelle?"

Naomi chuckled. "Dat's right. Maybelle's ain't dancin' ta be dancin'. She's doing a matin' call. Can't ya see? She calling on Herman wit dem swinging hips."

"Time fo' Virginny Reel!" Pete shouted. The dancers cheerfully lined up. One line had the young folks and children. The next line was for the younger adults, and the third was the mature adults. Those who didn't participate were ready to keep foot-stomping time. Bo nudged Naomi but she shook her head. Mae was still winded from the previous dance.

He saw Mara watching him from the line where she and Jethro stood across from one another. He smiled faintly and nodded. He hadn't seen Mara since he heard about her agreeing to couple up with her valiant rescuer. He thought it was long overdue that they marry. Jethro looked deeply in love and happy as could be about it. Mara looked more wistful than a woman should with having such a doting beau, but she'd always been melancholy even as a child. Bo remembered her mother saying Mara was her most trying baby. She cried all the time, and was stubborn and fussy. Nothin' done made the infant happy and gurgly like other babies. At best she stopped crying and went to sleep or just looked around curiously.

Her poor disposition followed her through childhood, but not toward Bo. She'd always adored him, hanging on his every word and following him around like a puppy. Growing up, Bo liked Mara as a companion and got used to her constant presence. As they got older, Mara wanted an amorous relationship, something more than climbing trees, catching frogs, and fishing at White Lily Pond.

Bo did not share her romantic yearnings, so things remained as they were until Baby Gal won his heart. He'd always felt a little guilty because he knew how Mara really felt about him, though he didn't return her affection. He took special care not to take advantage of her feelings, and decided that pulling back on their friendship was the kindest thing to do. That was more rejection than Mara could tolerate. She became bitter and more miserable than ever. Bo understood Jethro loved her with the same devotion she had for him. At long last their union was coming to fruition.

While Bo was thinking about all this, he was suddenly grabbed by Flossy and pulled to the dance line. He tried to protest, but the crowd pushed him along. The music started and it was too late to bow out. The band started with a snappy rendition of "Boil Them Cabbage Down" followed by "Turkey in the Straw" and ending with "Cotton-Eyed Joe." By the end of the dancing, Bo was more anxious than ever for his wife to come rescue him.

Rooster and his crew were at a long table eating. They hadn't danced much or socialized with many. They were too busy talking about more important matters. The harvest dance was a perfect venue because most of the slaves were allowed to attend.

Bo wanted to talk to Rooster but the man was clearly avoiding him, so he asked Naomi to fix him a plate, hurried to the table, and sat right across from Rooster. Rooster knew this was a strategic move on Bo's part, so he bit into his chicken leg and concentrated on his chewing, ignoring Bo. Young Tommy Sledge was sitting next to Rooster. He idolized his mentor and fancied himself an adopted son under Rooster's tutelage. Tommy was a young slave at the same plantation. Rooster liked the boy and enjoyed teaching the eager lad important lessons of life as a slave. Tommy was eating his okra, corn, and tomatoes hungrily. "Boy, I tell ya, nobody makes okry like my gran'ma Peggy."

"Yeah, yo' gran'ma's cookin' hits de spot," Rooster agreed, trying to ignore Bo's stare.

"Chugging that apple brandy makes me mighty hungry," Mississippi Mel said.

Naomi brought Bo a plate of fried chicken, okra, corn, tomatoes, and potato salad. "Here ya is, sugar. Enjoy." She glanced at Rooster and rolled her eyes. Then she smiled at Tommy and winked at Mississippi Mel who was stuffing his face with her chicken and dumplings. "You boys want anything else?"

"You make dat tadda salad, Miss Naomi?" Tommy asked, eyeing Bo's.

"I sho did."

"Den I be obliged fo' a taste of it if ya don't mind. I 'member from last year, ya make mighty good tastin' tadda salad."

"En de best chicken 'n dumplin's I ever et," Mississippi added.

"Why, thank you. I bring ya some tadda salad right back." Naomi left, smiling with pride.

"How have things been going for you?" Bo asked Rooster casually, trying to initiate conversation.

"Bout same as usual . . . bein' a slave en all."

Bo wasn't for biting his tongue on the heels of that stinging reply. "What's wrong, Rooster; you got a bone to pick with me?"

"What you mean?" Rooster acted disinterested in Bo's concern.

"Why does it seem like we are at odds with one another?"

233

Rooster cocked an eye. "Cause we is."

"Since when?"

"Since ya decide ya too good ta be wit Prophet Nat Turner en de rest of us."

"The rest of who? I didn't decide anything. I said I didn't want to involve myself in something I don't understand or necessarily approve of."

Tommy stopped eating and looked at Bo. "Ya don't approve a freeing slaves?"

"I don't approve of murdering folks to do it and waging a war we would lose in the first place."

"Ain't no udda way it gonna come 'bout fo' most a us. Everybody ain't lucky nuff ta git it like you did." The envious edge in Rooster's remark was evident.

"There has got to be a better way to get freedom for everybody. God's hand will show us the right way like He did the Hebrews, but not by killing white folks."

"White folks ain't got no problem killing us," Mississippi Mel said. "They ain't gonna just up en give us freedom lessin' we do fight fo' it. Dat mean some of them gots ta die."

"That's not God's way. The battle is not ours but the Lord's."

Rooster shot Bo a nasty look. "You's real good at quoting de Good Book, ain't ya? All dem fancy words ya use all da time. Don't know 'bout what you read cause I can't, but I heard where God did a lot of killing in dat dere Book—even tol' other folks to kill up some folks."

Bo didn't want to debate Scripture. "Do you believe God is behind what the prophet said?" he asked.

"Yeah, I sho do."

"Well, I don't and I can't take part in it. If you want to hold that against me, so be it."

"I ain't holdin' nuthin' agin ya."

"Is that so? Well, I heard some mighty strong statements you made about me. Don't know for sure if you said it all but I'll say this to your face; if you got something to say about me . . . good or bad, I'd be obliged if you were man enough to say it to me first." Mississippi Mel looked up from his plate.

Rooster put his piece of chicken down, furrowed his brows, and stared menacingly at Bo. "I's man nuff ta repeat whatever I say in or out a yo' company." Tommy put his fork down and watched Rooster carefully. Mississippi Mel kept his attention on Bo.

"You're set on making us enemies and it doesn't have to be this way, but if that's how you want it, then I'll handle it. I won't be shamed because you don't like my stand on this slave uprising talk. I won't be made to feel bad either because the Lord blessed me with freedom. That doesn't mean I don't want all my people free, 'cause I do, and anyone who knows me knows I do. I just don't think this Nat Turner—"

"Prophet Nat Turner, he's a man of God," Rooster interrupted.

Bo ignored the correction. "His way isn't how slaves are going to be freed. I know it in my heart. It will cause more harm than good in the end, just you wait and see."

"We's got ta be willin' ta die fo' de cause," Tommy declared.

Mississippi Mel nodded. "Yeah, death ta git freedom or death from workin' yo'self in a early grave fo' massah. Dat's what it boils down ta."

Rooster cracked a half grin, picked up his chicken leg, and pointed it at Bo. "You fo'git, Bo's already free. He ain't willin' ta die fo' nobody else ta git free."

Bo balled up his fist and banged it hard on the table. "You don't talk for me, Rooster! You don't know what I'm willing to die for! Just because I don't get carried away about your almighty prophet doesn't mean I don't want all slaves freed!" People in the vicinity started staring at them.

Naomi hurried over with Tommy's potato salad and looked at Bo's angry expression. She stood behind him and put her hands on his shoulders. Looking Rooster in the face, she said, "Dis here a party, if you please. No time fo' arguin' 'bout uprisin's, ya understand?"

"He started it," Rooster said, pointing his chicken leg at Bo.

"Don' care who started what." She lowered her voice when she saw people staring at her. "Cut it out fo' trouble gits ta brewin'. Dis ain't de time or de place. Dis a happy celebration, a time ta be thankful."

"Yes, ma'am," Tommy answered, lowering his head.

Mississippi Mel mumbled, "Beg pardon, Miss Naomi."

Bo sighed and shook his head. "You're right, I'm sorry. I shouldn't have said anything in the first place. It was my doing."

Naomi took her hands off Bo's shoulders. "Awright, dat's better; now you boys play nice en forget all dat nonsense 'bout revoltin'. At least fo de res a de day." She looked to the end of the table where three young girls were eyeing Tommy. They were whispering and giggling, trying to get his attention. With his mind solely on Rooster and Bo, he was oblivious to their flirtations. "All dese purty gals in here hankerin' ta dance . . . dis ain't no time fo' young strappin' menfolk ta be bickerin'." Having said her piece, she walked away.

Twenty-Three

Saddlebrook Mansion

*C*aroline heard the knocking on the door before she was consciously aware of her surroundings and could respond. Sadie Lynn nudged the door open, and seeing Caroline, went right in, singing a cheery good afternoon. She walked toward the bed in the darkened room.

"You didn't come down for breakfast or lunch, so I thought you might not be feeling well." She moved in next to the bed straining to see Caroline. She choked down her gasp at a closer sight of the actress. Then she leaned over the bed linen to make sure she was seeing correctly. "Oh, my word! What in the world happened?"

Sadie Lynn had her hand to her mouth as she stared at the woman's swollen, bruised face. After the shock passed, she ran to the window and opened the curtains. "What happened?" she asked again, seeing more clearly the battered female.

"He did this to me," Caroline gasped, turning away to

avoid the sunlight and straining to sit up.

Sadie Lynn threw open the other window's curtain. "Who, who did this to you? Was it that man of yours? Did he come here last night and do this? Albee said this would happen if he caught you with one of your admirers."

Shaking her head, she said, "No, of course it wasn't Preston." Caroline finally pushed herself up in the bed into a sitting position.

Sadie Lynn stared at the bruised shoulder and ripped sleeping gown in disbelief. "Who then, who would do such a horrible thing to you?"

"That man with the dark hair and evil eyes who's staying here. The one called Wally. He beat me and he . . . Why, oh why did he hurt me like this! I feel filthy." Caroline broke down sobbing, hiding her face.

Sadie Lynn rushed to the door, screaming, "Momma, Momma! Come quick, Momma!"

"No, don't—" Caroline feebly protested. "I can't bear for anyone else to see me like this."

"Momma has to know. She has to tell the authorities. That man is evil, Caroline. He can't get away with what he's done to you. He's a madman and ought to be put away from decent people."

"No, it's too humiliating. I can't . . ."

Emily stepped into the room. "What in the world are you screaming about, Sadie Lynn?" She glanced at Caroline and froze. "My gracious, what happened?"

"She was attacked by that despicable Wally. No wonder they checked out this morning. He knew what he'd done. He's an evil brute, an absolute animal!"

"Attacked?" Emily moved closer to Caroline. "Oh, you poor dear . . ." Caroline's crying heightened. Emily sat on the

238

bed and embraced the distraught woman. "Now, now, dear, it's going to be all right. I knew there was something wicked about that man. It's not your fault; don't cry so."

"He said it *was* my fault!" Caroline wailed. "He said women like me needed to be taught a lesson! He covered my mouth and hit me and kept hitting me over and over! Then he . . . he . . . he pinned me down and . . . and he forced himself on me!"

Sadie Lynn gasped in horror, nervously and quickly shut the bedroom door. Caroline held tight to Emily's arm. "I tried to fight him off . . . I tried to get away, but he punched me harder and said vile things to me. He was too strong . . . too strong for me to get away!" The sobs increased as Caroline fell sideways on the bed.

"When did this happen?" Emily head whirled with the thought of such brutality occurring right under her roof.

"Sometime during the night or very early this morning. I'm not sure, I can't think clearly, but it was still dark outside when he came into my room like a madman. I was asleep and he woke me up when he put his hands over my mouth. He said it was people like me making trouble over slavery that caused the South to look bad. We white trash from the North need to mind our business and keep our mouths shut about how Southern people live. He said he was going to beat all that freeing-slaves talk out of me once and for all. And he did . . . I must have passed out. The last thing I remember was him saying he reckoned that would change my fancy abolition talk." She stopped and looked around in a trancelike manner. "He said that to me after . . . after . . . standing over me . . . after . . . after he'd violated me," she whispered.

"Oh no, this couldn't happen right here in our home. How utterly awful . . . what a terrible thing to have to endure." Sadie

239

Lynn was wringing her hands and pacing in circles.

"It's going to be all right," Emily repeated, trying to comfort Caroline. "Be still, Sadie, you're getting on my nerves with that pacing. Get some fresh bed linen and a basin of hot water and some towels. Then get some iodine and salve from the hall cupboard. Young Jimmy Crawford is here, since Morley's at the Harvest Dance. Send him to get the doctor first and then the sheriff." Emily put her fingers to her temples. "I wish Sally and Morely were here. Lord knows I wish they were."

"Should I go fetch Albee?"

"No!" Emily Anne snapped. Sadie looked at her mother questioningly. Checking her vigorous response, Emily spoke more calmly. "No, don't tell him yet. We need to help Caroline first and make her presentable before she has to face people's questions. Get him later after we tend to her."

➤ ➤ ➤ ➤ ➤ ➤

Bo was not enjoying the festivities after the confrontation with Rooster or in the absence of Ruth. He wanted to leave but stayed, pretending to have a good time until the effort took its toll. After a while he decided to go outside and distance himself from the noise, crowd and gaiety. Sitting on the wagon he prayed. *Lord, looks like everyone's mad at me. I haven't done right by anybody, have I?*

An amorous young couple flirted on the side of the barn and seeing them made Bo even more needful of his wife. *I must make things right with her as soon as she gets here. I want us to be like we were before I found out what she did. I know she wants that too. I forgive her even if I don't understand what she did. I know she's a good woman who's had too many bad things happen to her. You forgave me, Jesus, so I can forgive her no matter how horrible what she did seems right now. It's the past and not how she is anymore, so I can let it go.*

He sat listening to the music in the background, thinking of his past but mostly focusing on his future. There was something pulling at him he couldn't make out, some vision he couldn't quite distinguish, but he saw it in haziness, a vague shadow of things to come. *Lord, what is it?* Naomi interrupted his thoughts when she came out of the big barn, calling for him.

Climbing on the wagon, she began to chatter, "Whew, dey's all done gone dance crazy in dere en eatin' like dey's plum starved. It's getting' up in de day. When Ruth comin'?"

"Anytime now, I hope." Bo looked at Naomi trying to suppress her own downheartedness. "Why aren't you dancing? You love to dance."

"Not witout my Ephraim I don't." Her feigned smile faded.

"You two were always the liveliest pair out there, dancing like young folks. I really miss Ephraim."

Naomi looked up at Bo, tears brimming. "Daytime I kin make it . . . kin make pretend iffin I have ta, but at night . . . at night I ain't so brave. Ain't no pretendin' my man next ta me in a empty bed. I miss Ephraim somethin' fierce. I don't think der ever stop bein' a big empty hole in my heart." She leaned on Bo, tears rolling down her cheeks.

He put his arm around her. "I know, I know exactly how you feel. I thought I'd never get over Baby Gal . . . never . . . but—"

"But Ruth come along?" Naomi wiped her wet cheeks with her hands.

"Yeah." He glanced at her. "You always knew, didn't you?"

241

"De Lord tol' me ya been on ya own too long. Was time fo' ya ta stop grievin'. Was His doin' got ya together, not mine." Naomi sighed. "I thought nothin' could hurt so much as losin' my chilluns, havin dem snatched way from me. Den when Baby Gal died, I thought my heart was shattered to pieces en weren't never to be fixed but I was wrong. Losin' Ephraim like losin' part a me en it hurt jes as bad if not mo'."

Bo hugged Naomi close to him. Forgetting his troubles, his heart ached for her. "Ephraim was a good man, a very brave man."

"Too brave en it git him killed."

"At least he's with the Lord now."

"I knows but I wan him here wit me. I still miss him even if I knows he's wit de Lawd." The barn door opened and Mara stepped out, looking around. She spotted Naomi and Bo and made her way to the wagon.

Mara stopped beside Naomi, taking her hand. "How are you doing through all of this?" she asked tenderly, patting her hand.

"I's makin' it," Naomi said slowly, sliding her hand away.

Mara pretended she didn't notice. "Well, how do, Bo."

"Mara, you look well this fine afternoon."

"Thank you, kindly. Where's your wife?"

"She'll be along soon."

Mara's attention moved back to Naomi. "Is there anything I can do for you?"

"No, honey and I tol' ya, ya don't have ta fuss o'er me no mo'."

Mara looked disappointed. "I just wanted to make sure you were all right."

"I may never be awright again in my life, but it ain't yo' problem or yo' fault. Ephraim's dead en gone en I's gotta come

242

ta grips wit it on my own in de good Lawd's time."

Mara's head dropped. "He's dead because of me."

"He's dead cause de Lawd chose not ta let him live no mo'. He wit Jesus now in a better place."

"He'd be alive with you if he hadn't helped me."

"But he did help ya, en I don't fault ya none fo' dat. I's glad ya awright."

"Maybe you don't fault me but some of the others do and I blame myself. If I hadn't been so foolish . . ."

"It's not your fault, Mara. Let go of the guilt," Bo said.

"I would if I could, but what if other folks don't let it go?"

He thought of Ruth. "I can't speak for other people, but I think they will in time. Naomi does and the Lord does; that should be all that really counts. You have to get free of this guilt or it will take you over."

Mara looked at Naomi sadly. Placing her hand on Naomi's arm, she said, "Ephraim was a brave man of God. I know he's with Jesus. For that I'm glad, but for your hurt, I am so very sorry."

Naomi patted Mara's hand that was resting on her arm. "Me too chile, me too."

"I promise it won't be for nothing. He gave his life for my freedom and I won't ever forget it and I won't shame his sacrifice . . . or you."

"Now you need freedom from feelin' guilty and I need freedom from grievin'. We both oughtta straighten up en make Ephraim proud."

"I hear you're pairing up with Jethro," Bo said, purposely steering the conversation to a happier note.

Mara looked away, embarrassed. "Yes, I am."

"He's a good, hardworking man. Jethro will make you a fine husband."

"I know he will," Mara said softly, still not looking at Bo.

"And you're a fine woman, Mara. You will make him a good wife. I wish you both the best of everything."

"That's very kind, thank you."

"'Bout time ya put dat lovesick man outta his misery." Naomi chuckled.

Mara looked up at Bo, and for one moment she felt the love she had always felt for him. Garnering her new emotional strength, she didn't drown in its overpowering presence. She let it go and put her mind on the man she knew loved her. Loving Bo was too costly, too painful with no beneficial return. It wasted too many years, cost Ephraim's life and almost her freedom. Bo was not the man the Lord meant for her to be with, so at that moment she deliberately released him to be happy with the wife he chose. She finally accepted it wasn't nor would ever be her. She would be content with Jethro. Mara was determined to learn to be happy with that good man who loved her and the Lord had put in her life. The Lord who answered her prayers . . . yes, He was there for her and He saved her. He forgave her turning away, her doubts, and anger. She was at last renewed in her faith. She looked at Bo's searching stare, remembering the hurt she felt from his rejection. Pushing those feelings down, she forced a smile. "It took me a long time but I know what's best for me now. Jethro's a loving, patient man and he's always been that way toward me. God put us together; I know that now." Saying the words out loud was a big step toward putting painful memories down for good.

Bo nodded. "I agree and I'm real happy for you."

"If there's nothing I can do for you, Naomi, I'll get back inside before Jethro comes looking to see what's taking me so long. I told him I was coming out to check on you."

"Thank ya, dear, but dere's no need ta worry 'bout me. De Lord keeping me strong." Naomi placed her hand lovingly on Mara's cheek.

Mara turned and walked away with her head held high. Bo watched as she went back into the barn. He could tell she was different in some profound way. One positive outcome of the tragedy was Mara's gaining wisdom and finally finding happiness being freed from unrequited love.

Bo was worried about Ruth. He cut the turn on the road too short, and the wagon almost tilted from the speed he was driving. Why hadn't Ruth come to the Harvest Dance? He drove up to the wooden gate, which was open wide. He could see the farmhouse in the distance, almost a mile away. The chickens, geese, ducks, and guineas scattered as he speedily drove through. When he got there he barely stopped before jumping off the wagon, running inside calling her name. Ruth was not there.

The empty farmhouse worried him more. She might have had an accident on her way to the dance, but he'd have spotted her on his way home. He hurried to the barn. Golden Gal was gone. Bo went back to the farmhouse. It was getting dark and he imagined the worst . . . she had left him for good. Ruth had run away from their life together because she was disappointed in love, in him, and decided to go for her freedom. If he couldn't forgive her, then why should she stay? She didn't need more condemnation.

His guilt swelled as his heart broke, thinking of life without her. The old loneliness crept in on him in his solitary misery. Bo broke down and wept. He was ashamed of his lack of compassion toward Ruth when she bore her soul so bravely to him. She believed what he said about forgiveness and redemption but he didn't rightly apply it to her. He failed with the one person closest to him. Viewing his future without her was gloomy but just punishment for his hypocrisy. He wished she were there so he could make it right, but it was too late for that now.

➤ ➤ ➤ ➤ ➤ ➤

The two men rode silently for miles with a harnessed Ruth and Golden Gal in tow. Wally and Bud were at odds ever since Bud stopped Wally from taking liberties with Ruth at the farmhouse. Wally was steaming mad because Bud was standing up to him. "I'm still gonna kill that black slave Bo after we sell his missus and them others we got stashed away." He looked at Ruth grudgingly. "Don't think he's gettin' away, 'cause we left with you. I specially want him to know I took his wife before he dies."

Ruth's head snapped around. "Ya promise if ya could get a good price fo' me, ya let Bo live. Ya promised!"

Wally sneered broadly, showing his raggedy mouth with its brown tabacco stains, rotted spots, and missing tooth. "Guess I lied." He chuckled, then looked at Ruth. "You think you can outsmart a white man, offerin' yourself up for exchange for his sorry life? I'm gonna sell you *and* kill him." He cut a nasty look at Bud. "And gonna have my pleasure with you before I do."

Ruth's heart raced with fear for Bo, not herself. "Ya say ya leave him be if I—"

"Shut up 'bout what I said! That man of yours is dead. Period!"

Ruth looked at Bud, who rode on stone-faced. He waited a minute and said to Wally, "He might disappear once he knows you're after him."

"Nah, not that one. Ain't got enough sense to run. He'll

figure out I got his woman. He's coming for her and after me and when he does, I'll be waitin'." Wally winked at Ruth. "See, you played right well into my plans, you pretty little gal."

Bud didn't like the idea of Bo coming after them. "If he comes, he won't come alone or unarmed."

"The more the merrier. I'm in a darkie-killing mood now." He looked at Ruth and grinned. Ruth looked at him with hatred in every fiber of her being. She would surely kill this man the first chance she got. He saw the furious resolve in her eyes. "Ain't no need a you getting' any stupid ideas 'bout doing me in either. I'd a soon cut your throat as your man's."

➤ ➤ ➤ ➤ ➤ ➤

Bo didn't sleep that night. He doubled back to the dance and looked for Ruth. When it became widely known she was missing by the next morning, people began gossiping about the beautiful but ungrateful breeding slave he had no business jumping the broom with in the first place. She'd up and left him after all he'd done for her.

"Them light-skin women think dey bettering de res a us anyway," Lisbeth told Maggie when Dilly, a freed slave share-cropping on Maitland land, spread the news. Dilly always carried news first and fast. She thrived on trouble and gossip. Bo had admonished her several times about causing problems with her tale-carrying ways, but it did no good because she never stopped. Dilly's husband, Otis, was a great farmer and the prize worker of the Maitland plantation.

Dilly made Bo angry when she stirred up trouble, but Otis was a good man, a quiet God-fearing man who could grow crops out of dry dust if he had to; he was almost as blessed as Bo with agricultural productivity. He was a decent man who unfortunately admitted he couldn't control his wife's "flapping jaws," as he put it. Bo knew Dilly was probably making her rounds to spread the news of Ruth's departure.

All the next day he prayed for his wife's return as he busied himself on the farm. Any sound of horses sent him running to check. By late afternoon he heard several horse hooves coming toward the south barn. He looked out at a small posse of white men led by Sheriff Crowder. Sheriff Thomas Crowder was a short, sunburnt stumpy man who chewed tobacco and seemed to spit continuously. He thought too highly of himself and his position, wielding his power to suit his ego. He had a truly mean temperament when crossed, and it was rumored he'd unlawfully disposed of a few troublesome types in a permanent way. People feared Sheriff Crowder and with good reason.

Bo came out of the barn and stood holding his pitchfork when the sheriff rode up to him. Crowder didn't like any of this freeing slaves business, but it was lawful so he held his peace about it most of the time. As long as the free Africans obeyed the law and didn't cause any trouble, he'd put up with them.

"What brings you out this way, Sheriff?" Bo asked, dreading that he might have bad news about Ruth.

"We's looking for two white men, slave catchers, we think. See any strangers 'round?"

"Can't say as I have. You know the Harvest Dance was yesterday. Everybody was at the old meetinghouse."

"I know, but I was told you were coming and going from the dance so I figured you might a seen them on your travels."

"No sir, didn't see any strangers."

"Where's your missus? I'd like to ask her."

"She's not here . . . she left."

248

"Left?"

"She moved on, I guess." Bo's face twisted, indicating he didn't want to explain.

Crowder cocked an eye. He knew Bo wasn't one for talking about his personal business, and he wasn't much interested in the love life of coloreds, so he didn't press. "Those men we're looking for, one of them attacked a woman at Miss Emily's. We're warning folks just in case he's still around."

"You said they were slave catchers?"

"That's what we think, but they were crafty enough not to admit it. We came out here because Miss Emily mentioned they once showed a odd interest in you and this farm."

"In me? Why me?"

"Don't know. But didn't you have a problem with some slave catchers near the swamp? Cheasley Branche told me."

"Yeah, but that was before they killed Ephraim."

"In my opinion, it's all connected. Those slave catchers are behind all the troubles going on around here lately. They stayed at Emily's boardinghouse. I guess they got tired of swamp filth and had to take a break. We want them, and we're gonna find those dirty scoundrels. They defiled a white woman and that's going too far."

"That's right, we ought to hang em high!" Elsley Drew growled. Elsley had a wife and six daughters and a mother-in-law in his home. No man would lay hands on any one of them and get away with it, not while he was alive and kicking.

Bo looked at the four men on horseback: Sheriff Crowder and his unassuming Deputy Louis Farmer, Elsley Drew, and another man Bo didn't know. This man was younger than the others and fashionably attired. Bo observed the rigid manner in which he sat on his horse. The firearm he carried looked expensive and new. The young man's face was darkly serious, intent on his purpose for joining the posse. Bo wondered who he was, but decided it would be unwise to inquire. He wasn't a local man, certainly.

Listening to Crowder talk about the fugitives stoked memories of the man he had fought near the swamp. "What do these men look like, Sheriff?"

"The main one is a dark-hair fella with a scraggly beard. He's got a nasty look about him, they say, and he's got bad teeth and one missing in the front. His companion is a lean lanky man with frizzy yellow-brown hair. The dark-haired one is the one who violated Miss Emily's guest. His name's Wally." Bo's eyes popped in recognition.

"You know this man?" Crowder asked.

"That was the name of the slave catcher who tried to capture me. Mara said he was one of the ones who shot Ephraim too."

"All the more reason to hang 'em," Elsley growled. "Old Ephraim was a good ole black soul. Never hurt nobody."

Crowder cut in. "Keep quiet about hanging folks, Elsley. I'm the law 'round here or did you forget?"

Bo wasn't fooled. He knew Crowder's reputation, and he knew if Wally put up the least resistance to being arrested, he would swing from the nearest tall tree.

Crowder eyed Bo as if reading his mind. "You keep a lookout. We're headed down Swamp Road. After we look there we'll meet up with the rest of the posse. Them men might have gotten out of this county by now if they're riding hard, but if we ride harder, we'll catch them lowlifes near the swamp."

The sheriff turned his horse around. The others followed. Bo watched the men leave before he went back into the barn. His mind was racing. He wondered if Ruth had encountered the slave catchers. Could she have been captured? She shouldn't have gone near the swamp since the tree was removed, but who knows where these men were.

Before he knew it, Bo was on his horse riding fast toward the swamp by way of a back road. He didn't want Crowder to know he was looking for Ruth near the swamp. He rode out prepared for the worst, with a gun and two knives, whip, axe, and rope. He thought of Ephraim's fatal lone attempt rescuing Mara but the fear wasn't strong enough to stop him from saving his wife.

Ruth had no idea where she was or how far they had traveled since they left the farmhouse. Wally seemed to get more agitated as the journey went on. He spit and cursed and threw her around violently the first night. They just stopped for the second night earlier in the evening to hunt food. She was tied to a tree while Wally went in search of possible supper. Bud gathered kindling to make a fire.

Ruth took advantage of Wally's absence. "You cain't let him kill Bo," she said. She hoped to tap into his kinder disposition.

"I can't stop him if that's what he's a mind to do."

"Den lemme go so I kin warn him. At least he have a fightin' chance."

Bud shook his head. "You think I'd risk my neck to save some free Negro I don't know?"

Ruth futilely struggled against the ropes. "He promise ta let him live!"

"From a man like Wally, a promise ain't worth much."

"Why's ya wit such a evil creature like him?"

"I need the money bad 'cause my crops didn't bring in much. A fella I knew back home made a passel of money catching runaways, and next thing I knew I got hooked up with Wally. I was told he's the best when it comes to catching slaves. They said Wally would make lots of money for me. I didn't know what kind of man he was. I didn't know he kidnapped free Negroes too, and I sure didn't know he was so out-of-control mean."

"He's wicked, pure evil."

"I won't argue that, but like I said, I need the money. We're splitting the profits fifty-fifty. I got a wife and kids to take care of."

"You not like him. If ya let me go, ya kin say I 'scaped."

"He'd most likely not believe me and then he'd kill me. I ain't getting on Wally's bad side no more than I have to. The best I can try to do is keep him off you, at least in my presence."

"And how long ya think ya kin do that?"

"Don't know, but I'll keep tryin'."

Something rustled the leaves near the camp. Bud put his fingers to his lips for silence. Ruth looked around but couldn't turn enough to see anything. "Might be a fat rabbit. Some tasty rabbit would hit the spot tonight or some squirrel. I'm gonna check my traps and see what they've turned up." He made sure her ropes were tight and went off on foot in the direction of the rustling sound.

She was tired from struggling with the ropes to no avail. Sitting on the cold ground thinking of Bo and his faith in God, she felt a tug on her soul. *Lord Jesus, I ain't all that sure You's what he thinks Ya is, but Bo believes in Ya wit all his heart. He tries ta live like he thinks Ya want and do what's right. Please, not fo' me but for Bo, save him from dese men. Help me ta get away from dem so I kin warn him. Or do some miracle thing and send dem back where dey come from. Bo reads 'bout all dem miracles You's suppose ta done in olden time. Do one now fo' his sake. I ain't askin' fo' me cause I knows Ya ain't studyin' me. But if Ya help Bo stay safe, I might believe, really believe like he do.*

After her prayer Ruth wondered about Bo's reaction to her disappearance. What did he do when he found her gone? Was he glad? Was he worried? Did he look for her? Would he survive an attack from Wally? Her heart still ached with love for him although she felt he'd rejected her. His forgiveness may not have extended to her sins but she cared deeply for the man all the same. She had to think of a way to stop Wally. She knew killing him was the only sure thing. She heard someone coming, and Wally appeared from between two weeping pines. He looked around. "Where's Bud?"

"Checkin' dem traps," she muttered. Ruth saw the sinister grin move across his face as he looked down at her. She knew what he was thinking.

"Got you to myself now," he said, and bending down in front of her, loosened the rope. "You do as I say and I might not make your man suffer too much before he dies." Ruth turned her head and closed her eyes. She couldn't stand the thought of him touching her that way. Wally didn't waste any time with his intentions. She shouted for him to leave her be and he hissed back at her, "Keep quiet!"

She had hoped she would never have to endure another unwanted encounter of this kind ever again in her life. "Keep away from me," she said, her voice viciously tight. He was impressed she didn't blubber in fear like most women. There was a hardness about her he admired but was determined to break. She stopped struggling and lay still, trying to wait until she could grab his knife from its holder.

Ruth cringed inside every second as she had many times

before in her young life. She kept her attention on the knife and its position. Memories of the brutal Jasper came to her and the demanding overseer who made her do despicable things. In an equally swift flash without much forethought, Ruth grabbed the knife out of its sheath and plunged it into Wally's side as she screamed, "No more! I won't let no man hurt me no more!"

Wally's yelp was from surprise and pain. He fell over and grabbed the protruding blade, pulling it out of his side. Ruth tried to scramble away from his reach, but he recovered quickly enough to grasp one of her ankles with his bloody hand. "I'll kill you dead for this!" Her frantic kicking didn't shake him off from pulling her back toward his onslaught of blows and foul language.

"Do what you will with me but don't hurt Bo," she pleaded. When Ruth's mind rallied back, she could hazily make him out. He leaned over her on his knees, holding his wounded side. "I'm gonna make you pay for this. You're a tough one, huh?"

Ruth dropped her face down toward the dirt and dug her nails in hard, trying to brace herself for his abusive violation when someone yelled, "You black-hearted swine!"

The gunshot caused her to lift her head and turn away quickly. It was so loud she knew it was close. She saw the look of horror in Wally's eyes as his body shivered and rocked on its knees. She looked past him and saw a young white man on horseback, holding a smoking pistol. Wally had strength enough to hold on to a low-hanging tree branch and pull himself up. He slowly turned around. Blood oozed from the wound to his lower back. Ruth covered her eyes at the horrible sight.

"Who are you?" Wally wobbily demanded of his assailant.

"Preston Purcival Henderson is my name, you dog! I'm

the intended of Miss Caroline Cane, the woman you attacked at the boardinghouse." Other horses were approaching fast.

Bud appeared between two thick trunk trees that had lost their leaves. He was running and out of breath, but stopped when he saw the stranger with the gun. "Wally, what's goin' on?" he asked. Then he saw the other posse members riding in. He looked at Wally's back and dropped the small animal he had in his hands whose blood he'd just drained before he heard the gunshot.

"He shot me! Shot me in the back . . ." Wally managed to choke out before he staggered and fell to his knees.

Bud looked at Ruth on the ground, trembling, holding the torn portion of her dress sleeve. Blood was visible all around. Bud couldn't make sense of anything he saw. He looked up at the stranger. "Why?" he asked the man.

"Help me, I'm dying . . ." Wally croaked in a weak angry voice looking at Bud.

"I'd advise you not to move," Preston warned, gripping his whip while dismounting his horse. "This man was committing a heinous act right here with this woman and I stopped him. Undoubtedly he's the one who assaulted my fiancée at Saddlebrook Mansion. Did you join in or have knowledge of his crime?"

"No . . . no I didn't know nothin' 'bout no crime. I can't believe he'd do such a thing to a lady. I don't take to no hurtin' womenfolk." He looked at Ruth's battered face and dropped his head, ashamed.

"I find it hard to believe you didn't know of your traveling companion's vile character." The rest of the posse had reached them and were dismounting.

"I swear I ain't had nothin' to do with no dishonoring nobody!"

"I doubt you're as innocent as you claim, but Caroline did say he was alone so I have to accept your word for now." Preston stood dressed in his fine clothes with his legs braced in a battle stance, looking foreboding. Wally fell face-first on the ground, swearing and trying to crawl.

"These here the two slave catchers I gather?" Sheriff Crowder said, walking toward Bud.

"Catching runaways ain't against the law," Bud said, noticing the sheriff's badge.

"Yeah, but snatching free Negroes is." Crowder looked over at Ruth. She was sitting up, fastening her jacket for cover. "What's your name, gal?" he asked.

"Ruth . . . Ruth Peace."

Crowder turned around. "Peace? You Bo Peace's woman?"

"I'm Bo Peace's wife," Ruth answered with confidence. Preston walked over to Ruth and helped her to her feet.

"You a slave?"

"No sir, I's free. Got papers to prove it."

Crowder turned to Bud. "You've been capturing free coloreds and slaves belonging to farmers 'round here. That *is* against the law. You're under arrest."

"But I didn't . . ."

"Let's hang 'em both, the no-goods." Elsley moved to find a rope.

Sheriff Crowder looked over at Wally convulsing in the dirt. "Don't need no rope for that one. He'll be dead in a spell." He spit on the ground nonchalantly.

Bud yelped, "You can't hang a man for catching runaways!"

"We ain't hanging nobody, so hold your horses. But you's going to jail and answer for kidnapping free coloreds and them missing slaves from 'round here."

"I just took up with him not long ago. He's been here

256

before, he told me. He keeps his captures in an abandoned farm northwest of here."

"Northwest, how far? In what county?"

"Charles City."

"Them your horses?" Crowder asked, looking at Golden Gal enviously.

"Ours and hers," Bud said, nodding toward Ruth.

Wally had finally crawled to his horse and pulled his shotgun down. The men were not paying much attention to him. Most men would have been dead but pure meanness kept Wally alive. Crowder called Ruth over to the horses to inquire of Golden Gal's ownership. All the men seemed impressed by the gorgeous mare. Bud was handcuffed, standing to the side. He saw Wally slowly maneuvering himself and knew what he meant to do.

He wasn't inclined to warn these men who were going to imprison him and maybe hang him. His hopes were for Wally to achieve his goal and do harm to at least the one so ready to condemn him to the hanging tree. Bud didn't trust these lawmen. He knew they'd just as soon hang him as to take him back to a jail. Ruth was wearily trying to explain how she, a Negro, owned such a fine animal, when she glanced at Bud. She saw he was occupied watching something. Following his gaze she saw it was Wally he was looking at so intently. Wally had retrieved his shotgun and was trying to sit up to aim it. She gasped. At that moment Wally took aim at Preston. A whip wrapped around his wrist, causing him to yelp in pain as a blast went off wildly in the air when the shotgun dropped from his hands. Wally fell back. Bo came from behind a tree, attached to the other end of the whip. He kicked the shotgun from Wally's reach. Ruth couldn't believe her eyes. Bo couldn't see her since she was surrounded by the posse.

Wally looked up in his bloody weakened condition and swore when he recognized Bo.

Preston moved in closer to Wally, looking down at him. "You fiend. You shall die for what you did to Caroline. You will die slow and suffer like you've caused her to suffer. There will be no swift end for you, you raving lunatic, but a long, lingering, painful death you will have." He spoke as though pronouncing sentence, then kicked Wally in the side where he'd been stabbed. Wally yowled in agony and slumped to the ground. Bo stepped out into the clearing.

"What brings you out here?" the deputy asked him, smiling.

"Got to thinking about my wife gone and all and thought maybe she got captured by the slave catchers. Decided to come out here and check to see."

"Thought you said she left you on her own."

"I thought she did, but after you came saying what you did, I got to thinking. I wanted to make sure Ruth had not been captured and was being held prisoner. She's free, you know."

Wally's eye opened and his blurred vision surveyed his position. Bo was standing in front of him with his back to him. Hatred welled up enough to give him enough maniacal determination. He looked to his left, spotting a knife on the ground not far from his hand. He slowly wrapped his fingers around the handle. Moaning with pain, he still rallied enough to leap up and stab at the back of Bo's leg.

Ruth screamed when she saw Bo buckle and drop and the two men started tumbling. Wally's arm went up to stab Bo a second time. Bo landed a powerful blow and the knife fell out of Wally's hand. Bo sprang into action, punching his foe with one furious blow after another. Wally was helpless to fight back, his last vestige of energy spent. After a while, Bo had to hold up the man's limp body to receive each subsequent blow. He beat the almost-dead Wally with pent-up rage that shocked everyone witnessing it. Ruth ran to him, as did the others. Preston stood perfectly still, his inaction proving his support for Bo's dispensing of justice. Bo was still hitting Wally almost mindlessly, removed from awareness of his surroundings. Crowder finally grabbed hold of Bo's arm. "Awright, awright, that's enough, boy! Let him go!"

When Bo released Wally, it was evident the man was dead. Ruth was standing behind him, frightened. He knew he'd heard her voice and he was relieved to see her. He stood up and saw her battered face.

Bo looked menacingly at the other men, then back at Ruth. "Who did this to you?" he demanded.

She pointed to Wally's lifeless body. "He did."

Bo grabbed her tight and held on, thanking God she was alive and free. Then he broke his hold and asked, "Did he . . ." He choked on the words.

"No, but he would exceptin' he shot him," she pointed to Preston. She lowered her eyes in shame.

Crowder examined Wally's body. "Well, he won't be violatin' no more womenfolk or catching slaves either. He's dead as a rock."

"Saves us one hanging," Elsley mumbled, looking at Bud.

Bud was terrified. "I ain't violated no woman ever in my life. I tried to keep him away from this one here." He looked over at Ruth. "Tell them. Tell them how I tried to help you and keep you safe."

Ruth gazed at him coldly and remained silent.

The deputy grabbed Bud and shoved him toward the horses. "Get moving. You think we're dumb enough to believe you're so kindhearted to a wench you was about to sell back into slavery?"

"Please, tell them the truth! I can't hang. I got a wife and children!"

"Shut up or I'll have you swingin' right here and now," Elsley snapped.

"No hanging now, I told you. We're taking him in and have a legal trial first," Crowder insisted. He said to Bud, "You're under arrest for kidnapping free citizens and for the theft of lawfully owned slave property."

Ruth turned her back on Bud's pleading face. Bo held her close, glowering at Bud. He was happy to have her in his arms again and forced himself to focus on that. "I'm so thankful you're safe. I was going crazy worrying about you. I don't care what happened in the past. You're my wife and I love you. I want you home with me no matter what you did. I forgive you anything and everything just like the Lord forgave me. You mean the world to me. Please come home and stay and be my wife. I promise from my heart to be your husband in every way. Tell me you'll come home."

Ruth cried softly, her face buried in his shoulder. "Take me home, Bo, and I ain't never ever gonna leave ya."

➤ ➤ ➤ ➤ ➤ ➤

This trial was going to be a scandalous affair, the *Jerusalem Dispatch* had informed its readers.

The impending trial was discussed for two months before the circuit court judge arrived. Bud's wife and children had come to Jerusalem. Having few resources, they stayed in an abandoned farmhouse owned by Bud's lawyer. Marjorie, Bud's wife, was a mousy little woman with drab features. She cried inconsolably about Bud's situation. As a religious woman, she couldn't believe the terrible things her husband was accused of doing.

Many of the good citizens of Jerusalem took pity on Marjorie and her family. To be sure, many could not blame Bud for seeking to earn money by catching runaways; it was legal, and after all, they reasoned, slaves were property that should rightfully be returned to their owners. Stealing slaves from their owners was another matter entirely. Theft of someone's slave was wrong, just as stealing a buggy or a cow would be. And kidnapping free blacks in order to sell them into slavery . . . most citizens didn't cotton to such doings.

Marjorie went to church and endeared herself with devout believers. She told the congregation of their financial struggles, giving that as a reason why Bud was so desperate to make money.

The many struggling farmers in Southampton identified easily with that plight. The pastor preached about forgiveness and Christian compassion to sway any hardened hearts to change their condemning minds. The locals donated clothing and food to the family, and several ladies came and helped fix up the abandoned farmhouse with curtains and old furniture. The Ladies Aid committee gave the family warm coats and blankets. Some of the men fixed the holes in the roof to keep the rain and snow out and chopped plenty of wood for fire.

Marjorie was grateful for all the help and expressed it continually. The show of Christian kindness made her hopeful for a good outcome.

"They're feeling guilty, that's all," Bud told her spitefully. "They know I shouldn't be in here and they're making it right by helping you and the children."

"They're mostly good people, Bud. The jury will give you a fair trial. You will be set free. I can feel it."

"You think so? You didn't see them fellas the day Wally was killed."

"That Wally was a devil. He should have been stopped. I don't understand how you took up with a man like that. You're a decent person and you had no business traveling with an animal like him. That's why you're in here, why we're all sufferin' so."

"I know and I'm sorry. I made a stupid mistake and I may end up paying for it with my life."

"Don't say that. Slave catching doesn't require hanging. Kidnapping coloreds shouldn't either. After all, they was just colored."

Sheriff Crowder didn't care about Bud one way or the other. Wally had been the ringleader of their twosome, and Wally was dead. Good riddance. Crowder had been deliberately vague about the facts surrounding Wally's death in his report—too many people would look unkindly on a black woman stabbing him in the side and a black man pummeling him until he was dead no matter what despicable acts the man had done. That is, if they believed the word of blacks, which was not likely. As for the stranger from out of town shootin' him in the back . . . well, Preston couldn't even claim self-defense. He was avenging the attack on his fiancée; said Wally had defiled her. Crowder would have done the same thing if that animal had so much as touched his wife. And even though that free black Bo only got involved to protect his woman, not everyone would believe him if Bud said otherwise.

When the trial finally got under way, only Bud was left to answer for his and Wally's crimes. Bud was positively identified as having been seen with Wally several times, including the capture of Mara. Several slave owners testified about the theft of their slaves and identified as their property the missing men and women Bud and Wally had taken.

The trial took a full day and a half, and the next day, nearing four o'clock, the men of the jury announced their verdict. Bud was found guilty of kidnapping free citizens and of unlawful acquisition and selling of slave property. The judge sentenced him to one year in the Virginia State Penitentiary, never to come back to the state of Virginia after his release. The prison was located outside of Richmond, overlooking the James River.

➤ ➤ ➤ ➤ ➤ ➤

When Bo and Ruth heard about the verdict and sentence the next day, more than anything they were glad it was over. There was enough to think about, and they wanted the whole ordeal to be in the past. The trial kept it in the present, ever looming over their lives, but it didn't stop them from growing closer to each other and more deeply in love.

As the months rolled by, things somewhat settled down. Caroline Cane and her fiancé left for Savannah to get a boat to Europe, glad to get away from the place of their horrible experience. Bud's wife and children moved to Richmond to be near him in prison.

As spring ushered in new life, the events from that autumn were forgotten. Farmers and plantation owners alike were busy with a new year of planting, to coax as much bounty from the earth as possible. The days were busy, and evenings were peaceful times of rest from the toils of the day.

Twenty-Four

Southampton County, Virginia,
August 21, 1831

While crickets were clicking and frogs croaked their last nightly seranades not long before dawn, a band of eight slaves crept through the Travis household.

The pleasant predawn sounds were interrupted by blood-curdling screams, as five members of the family were bludgeoned . . . including an infant in a cradle.

The group of slaves roamed the premises, searching for more effective weapons. Riding away with the few Travis farm horses, they took four rifles, several old muskets, and gunpowder, and were on their way to the next mission in freedom's massacre.

Their leader, Prophet Nat Turner, had struck the first life-ending blow at his current master's home. The men moved into their murderous tasks with no hesitation. Nat had evolved from a slave to a preacher, a preacher to a prophet, and now a commanding general and executioner. He guided his men, focusing on the their objective of raising freedom's voice as they slipped through the final vestiges of the dark. They were not looting for personal gain or seeking carnal pleasure. They were soldiers in a campaign for a just cause by means of a deadly message for both victims and perpetrators. The men vowed they'd spare no white people on their route to the town of Jerusalem no more than fifteen miles away.

They walked away from one house failing to kill the inhabitants because the owner saw them coming and barricaded himself inside. Deciding it was not worth the risk of raising an alarm, they moved on. However, they deliberately bypassed two other farms. One was the Giles Reese farm where Turner's wife and three children were slaves. The other was the farm of his childhood friend John Clark Turner. No other residences were spared. They carried out their grisly deeds efficiently, leaving no white survivors. Slaves at the farms were given the choice of either taking up arms and joining the resistance or standing aside, not interfering in any way.

The army began to increase as more slaves joined the rebels. By the time Turner and half his band reached the Porter farm, it was deserted. Turner knew the rebellion would no longer have the advantage of surprise attacks. The word was out and circulating.

Five miles from Jerusalem at the Harris farm, General Turner came together with his soldiers, he had strategically split up. It was ten in the morning. He was awed to see forty mounted and armed men ready to slaughter and fight for freedom at his command. Those who were drinking too much apple brandy were duly reprimanded. "We needs ta give up dis rebellin' en go back why we kin," one slave called out at the end of General Nat's harsh dressing-down. The general looked at the man with disdain, but the slave would not be quiet. "We ain't able ta beat dem white folks en he knows it!" the slave continued, turning to face the other rebels.

"Who are you? What's your name?" Turner asked. He looked angry as he jumped off his horse.

"I's Aaron," the slave proclaimed.

"Has the effects of drinking made you a coward?" Turner accused.

"Naw, I ain't been drinking dat much en I ain't no coward, but I knows we ain't gonna win agin dem white folks."

"Have you no faith for our cause of freedom?"

"I's in Norfolk wit my massah at de last war in 1812 en seed all dem white soldiers. Hunnerds and hunnerds a 'em all fightin' to de death. We cain't outdo dem no matter what. I knows how fierce dey fights en dey is more a dem den us. Ya'd know dis is hopeless if ya been in war like me."

"Nothing is hopeless with God. All things are possible with God. Don't you know that?"

"Iffin God is behind dis."

Turner stood tall, facing the men under his command. "You doubt the Lord's hand in this fight for freedom?"

Aaron looked down and kicked the dirt, then looked back up at their leader. "I's don' rightly know fo' sure but I tink dis might be a fool's errand."

"This army has no need for the weakhearted. If you don't have the hunger for freedom like the rest of us, go home. If you value your life as a slave more than this quest for liberty, you don't belong in this fight." Turner's voice thundered with his declaration.

"I wans freedom. I wans it bad as any man here," Aaron

insisted. "But dis ain't gonna git none a us no freedom. All we's gonna git is dirt graves."

"Better dead den livin'as slaves!" someone yelled from atop a horse in the crowd of men behind Turner.

Aaron walked away shaking his head. "Dem white folks is jes too many," he mumbled.

"Death from this life is its own freedom!" Turner shouted, looking around at all the men. The boisterous affirmations from the insurgents were a mix of enthusiastic agreement and foolhardy intoxication. However, Nat Turner understood what the contrary slave was saying all too well. He knew the large number of Virginia militia would come against them, and the United States military would join forces with them if needed. This knowledge did not dull his tenacity to forge ahead in pursuit of an end to slavery, an end to the system that denied him and his race basic human dignity the founders of the United States proclaimed as every person's unalienable right. The constitution he'd read stated all men were created equal. The militant preacher knew he and the other rebels were all likely to be killed, but he had to continue, not for himself only but for the cause of something greater. Nat Turner believed with all his heart that this was his purpose in life, a calling. It was this belief that fueled his actions.

At every homestead they attacked with speed and gained more recruits. The plan was to hold out in the town of Jerusalem and hope more slaves would come and join the rebellion. Their army actually had sixty soldiers by noontime, but the rumor that rushed through the area was five hundred slaves were riding toward Jerusalem to murder all the white people; British troops were landing. The church bells in Jerusalem rang out a warning.

Letters for assistance went out with lone riders to as far away as Petersburg and Richmond. White families took up arms and barricaded themselves in or armed themselves, fleeing from their isolated farms and rushing to town for safety in numbers.

One plantation housed a school. The Waller Plantation spread out for many acres, comprising much land and utilizing many slaves. The rebels killed ten on the property that day and threw their bodies onto a pile. Some of the slaves were emotionally repulsed by what they had done. The gruesome sight of slain children was not an easy horror to digest. General Nat spoke of it in terms of a balance of justice for countless innocent African babies callously murdered or snatched from their mother's suckling breasts by a heartless slave owner.

❧ ❧ ❧ ❧ ❧ ❧

Prosperity stayed with Bo, although many farmers in Tidewater were struggling harder than ever. His fields were doing exceptionally well in spite of the drought conditions. He'd been able to enlarge his stock with a goat and a cow and save money toward buying more slaves to set free. The dry weather had taken a turn by mid-July. Rain finally nourished the ground, giving farmers hope to save their withering crops. Ruth's garden sprang to abundant life. The peach, apple, and pear trees started bearing healthy fruit.

Bo was in the north barn working on a broken cider press he was giving to Jethro and Mara. Ruth was hoeing in her vegetable garden nearby when the white men came riding up hard in a large number. Heart pounding, she ran to the barn to get Bo. He met them by the cabbage patch. Sheriff Crowder headed the pack with his usual arrogant manner, and looked around cautiously. The men with him looked stern, even grave.

They were heavily armed. Bo knew most of them by face if not by name. He knew there must be big trouble for this many men to be riding with the sheriff.

"You been here all day?" Crowder asked with an uncharacteristic sharpness.

"Yes, sir, I'm trying to fix my busted cider press. Why, what's happened?"

"Hundreds of slaves in this county are on a rampage killing white folks, that's what happened."

Ruth gasped. Bo's eyes widened. "Has nothing to do with us, Sheriff."

"They're said to be heading Jerusalem way, but I heard some more slaves from all over are planning on joining up with them after they kill a bunch of folks 'round here. You know anything 'bout that, boy?"

"No, sir," Bo assured him.

"Some of the slaves are already missing from their farms. Reckon they're headed to the swamp. Just as well, 'cause they're going to die with the rest of them murderin' dogs." Crowder spit on the ground.

"I don't know nothing about it. Why come here asking me?"

"Figure if we was having a slave revolt in these parts, it would take somebody like you to organize it. Them others too dumb to band together on their own. Some slave preacher named Nat Turner said to be the ringleader," Crowder said. Ruth gasped again. Crowder looked over at her. "You know him?"

Bo stepped in quickly to explain. "We heard him preach once, that's all. He's supposed to be a man of God, ain't he?"

"He'll need God when they catch up to him. Lived on the Travis farm and killed Travis and the whole household, women and children alike, even killed the innocent baby in the cradle. Went to the next farm doing the same thing. Place after place they been killing folks, old or young, it don't matter. Folks say they make sure to kill every white person in the house. If any more slaves get to killing folks around here, we're ready for them." Crowder's eyes narrowed.

Bo responded, "I'm not for killing, Sheriff. I have nothing to do with any killing. Me and my wife have been here all day."

"Do you know of any slaves talkin' about revoltin'?" Lindley Myers asked, moving up from behind the sheriff.

"I don't get involved in such matters, so I wouldn't know anything 'bout any of it."

"How we know he's telling the truth?" Lindley questioned.

Crowder threw up his hand. "I believe him. This here one ain't no fool. He knows his place and he knows if he tries killing white folks, his life is over. Besides he's already been freed, why should he revolt?" Crowder started up his horse. "We're wasting time here, let's ride. He don't know nuthin'." The dozen men rode off slowly.

When they were out of sight, Bo went to the barn and sat on a bale of hay. He ran his hand across his hair. "If Rooster and them are involved in this, they're going to die."

"They knew de risks all along," Ruth said, standing over him with her hand on his shoulder.

"But what good is it doing? What will be accomplished this way? They won't get their freedom, and more than likely innocent folks are going to die because of it."

"You think de sheriff gonna come back here?"

"I don't know, but no one is safe when white folks get scared. They'll kill us all if that's what it takes for them to feel safe."

"What it gonna take for us ta ever feel safe?" Ruth wondered aloud.

Twenty-Five

Bo's heart was sorrowful as he helped cut the heavy hemp to take the bodies down. Rooster, Mississippi Mel, young Tommy, Joby Peterman, Ned Scatters, Luke Crowe, and Josh Ellis had been hanging all day near Swamp Road. A group of men decided to give them decent burials before the buzzards took to feasting from the dangling corpses.

The posse caught the mutinous crew trying to make their way into the marshy part of the swamp to hide. Rooster and his rebels had killed all the whites on the Peterman Plantation twelve miles from the east end of Swamp Road. Clyde Peterman was a mean man known for being particularly cruel to his dozen slaves. The only Caucasian spared was an indentured servant they tied up but apparently not well enough. The terrified servant worked himself free and fled for help after they left. By the time they reached the neighboring Ellis farm, the Ellises were barricaded in their house and armed. The Peterman servant had gotten there first. Two of the seven men hanged near Swamp Road were slaves at the Peterman Plantation and two others from the Ellis farm who had opted to join the insurgence.

News spread fast in the Tidewater region about the rebellion in Southampton and the local murderous revolt. People began to panic in Norfolk, Chesapeake, Portsmouth, and Sussex. The slave army aggressively reigned its terror for the better part of the day. As the white militias rallied, the rebels' success waned. Turner's troops were dispersed, intoxicated, and by the next day in full retreat and hiding. The remaining soldiers were eventually overpowered in battles, captured and dwindling back, few in number. Many were captured, mutilated, and killed.

The insurrectionists were never able to occupy the town of Jerusalem as planned. Once the word got out, sizeable groups of angry white men traveled the roads, terrifying slaves who knew nothing of the rebellion. Many masters killed their own slaves out of fury or fear. Beyond the first few days after Nat Turner's revolt, the retaliatory effect was an echo of terror. Slaves were murdered for merely walking down the road at the wrong time and place.

The very next day after the revolt had been satisfactorily crushed, a young slave girl was brutally killed by a mob while picking berries for her mistress. She was deaf and didn't know there had been a revolt. Some slaves were hanged from trees and their bodies left to rot in the hot sun. Others were shot dead, and many lay strewn along the route to Richmond. Two military detachments from North Carolina slaughtered almost fifty people. Over a dozen were decapitated, their heads displayed on poles along the roadsides.

A militia riding out from Richmond was made up of military men and law enforcers who vowed to put an end to any further uprisings before it would spread to its borders. Panic levels were high. The whites feared more violent revolts and murders; the blacks feared unjust retaliation.

Weeks after the revolt was squelched and some of the guilty parties jailed or hanged, slaves were still being terrorized. In total, fifty men stood trial, and twenty-one of them were hanged. As many as thirty more so-called legal executions took place in neighboring counties and into North Carolina. The staggering number of lives lost due to the revolt was approximately sixty whites and two hundred fifty blacks. General Nat Turner eluded capture for over two months without ever leaving Southampton County.

Even the eventual capture of Nat Turner did not bring satisfaction to those determined to quell any further uprising. The Southampton revolt, the consequential trials and hangings dominated newspapers, pulpits, and conversations for a long time to come.

Written accounts and word of mouth told as much detail as could be given about the short trial of Nat Turner. People both black and white gathered in their segregated crowds on town streets, in stores, on roadsides, and in meeting halls to hear the tale of the unremorseful black prisoner who led a small army of slaves in a murderous bid for freedom. To everyone's surprise, Turner insisted on pleading not guilty, stating to his defense attorney, the judge, and entire courtroom he felt no guilt at all. Judge Cobb's sentence was preceded by a long-winded monologue against slave rebellion. It became a common occurrence for men to imitate the judge's impassioned pronouncement and gavel banging, "The judgment of this court is that you, on Friday next between 10 a.m. and 2 p.m. be hung by the neck until you are dead! *bam* dead! *bam*, dead! *bam* And may the Lord have mercy on your soul."

An almost festive atmosphere, complete with servings of fried chicken, biscuits, rhubarb and pumpkin pies, was in the air among the spectators who gathered at the edge of town for the hanging. Liquor jugs were emptying out fast. Emotions were wired and expectations high for a satisfying exhibition. A crisp autumn day served up the perfect climate for the end of the dastardly crime of violent slave revolt. Adults and children alike waited anxiously to see the sentence carried out, but no Negroes were present out of fear of stirring up more reprisal.

Southampton's hanging tree stood tall, strong, and ready to terminate the life of any who were unfortunate enough to be hoisted from its outstretched limbs. That tree had been the busy implement of the legal system since Nat Turner's revolt.

After a sizeable crowd had assembled, a wagon flanked front and rear with armed men on horseback rolled toward the infamous tree. Prophet Nat Turner no longer looked like an indestructible general for his people. Neither was he the monster white folks described. He was a short muscular man with handsome African features. He didn't foam at the mouth or spout violent rhetoric at the white faces around him. He was as he'd always been: resolute, composed, disciplined.

Once the wagon appeared, the crowd grew silent. Gaiety and chatter ceased as an ominous spirit fell. Turner, bound with chains, refused the privilege of making a final statement with a simple shake of his head. He looked up at the beauty of a clear autumn sky with soft billows of fluffy cumulus clouds. Taking in the wonder of God's creation, the God he hoped soon to see, he said, "I am ready." They placed the thick rope tightly around his neck. He didn't move or make a sound. His face remained stone, utterly unflinching. He looked up toward the sky one last time and closed his eyes. The men pulled the rope, and Turner's body was yanked off his feet. Some of the spectators gasped and groaned, but not a sound came from Nat Turner.

Prophet Nat's final act of rebellion was to die without uttering a word of regret. He died with as much courage, determination, and defiance in his soul as the day he led the slave uprising.

The relationship between masters and slaves, whites and blacks changed drastically all over the South. In Virginia it was even more pronounced because the government officials went to work passing laws making life for blacks more restrictive. It became unlawful to teach blacks—whether enslaved or free—to read, and blacks were prohibited from holding religious meetings without the presence of a white clergyman. Curfews were enforced, and movements of slaves were closely monitored.

Slave owners didn't sleep so peacefully at night, and slaves walked on eggshells for fear of their masters' animosity. Things would never be quite the same even after the horrors of the deadly rebellion were somewhat blunted in people's minds.

The stark reality was bloodily exposed; Africans were not content to be beasts of burden and would not always tolerate living as slaves. The most fearful yet simplistic part of the message the revolt sent out was that slaves were willing to fight and die for their freedom.

❧ ❧ ❧ ❧ ❧ ❧

Folks stayed close to home as much as possible in the aftermath of the revolt, but out of necessity life began to slowly return to normalcy as much as possible. It was a few days after the hanging of Nat Turner when Bo went to Branche's Emporium.

"And what do you want?" Cheasley asked after the only other customer had left the store. Cheasley was not wearing his usual cordial smile. His hostile countenance caught Bo off guard.

"I need a few things here on this list."

Cheasley snatched the paper from his hands, grumbling under his breath. "Flour and sugar, lamp oil, pound of five penny nails . . . wait here." Cheasley turned his back to Bo, but swung around abruptly. "And don't touch anything. You go stand over in the corner there and stay put. Mind your ways while I fill this order and don't touch anything. I don't want my white customers complaining 'bout you fingering the merchandise."

"Yes, sir." Bo dared not speak out against the insult. Cheasley had never talked to him so antagonistically. He retreated to the designated corner and kept quiet. He was seething, but he understood what brought about the change in attitude. Peter Dilworth and his wife, Elaine, came into the emporium. Peter was a red-faced portly man always chewing on a cigar. Elaine was a skinny, pinched-faced woman who had at least four inches of height over her husband. As soon as they walked in, she snatched his hat off his head, complaining he was ill-mannered. Cheasley immediately dropped Bo's list on the counter. "Good morning, Pete . . . Miss Elaine. What can I get you folks today?"

Elaine went straight to the display of ladies' hats on the far side, closer to where Bo stood. Peter glanced over at Bo and sauntered up to the counter. "I need some cigars," he whispered.

Elaine called after him, "And Pete, don't you dare buy any

of those overpriced foreign ones. You and those smelly ole expensive wrapped cigars . . . they all make me nauseated. I don't care how much they cost. You ought to give them up altogether and just chew tobacco like other men."

"Yes, dear," Peter said, then winked. Cheasley nodded knowingly.

Elaine looked at Bo standing awkwardly in the corner, hat in hand staring down at the floor. "Bo Peace, is that you?"

He slowly looked up. "Yes ma'am, Mrs. Dilworth, it's me."

She smiled. "Well, how you do? Been a long spell since I set eyes on you."

"Yes, ma'am, it has. I'm doing fine, ma'am." He smiled back nervously and dropped his gaze again.

Peter frowned at Cheasley and turned toward his wife. "Elaine, get over here now." She looked at him puzzled, but she didn't speak. Peter beckoned to her anxiously. "You heard me, get over here and stop chatting with slaves."

"Peter Dilworth, what has gotten into you?"

Peter moved over, grabbed Elaine by the arm, and pulled her to the counter where Cheasley stood scowling at Bo. "Please do as I say, and don't talk back for once in your life."

"Have you lost your senses?" Elaine queried.

"No, but I think you have. Standing there making small talk with one of them murderin' blackies. Have you forgotten what they did, killing all those people in their beds?"

She snatched her arm loose. "Bo didn't kill anybody, and you know it."

"He's one of them and they can't be trusted, none of them."

"Don't be a fool, Peter. You already sold off most our slaves. Now you're afraid to speak to Bo. Bo is a good man and you always said so before—"

"Before they took to murderin' us in out beds. I don't care if it's Bo or not . . . he's a slave just like those men who killed—"

"I'm not a slave, sir. I'm a free Negro," Bo said, calming himself with a deep breath.

Peter's eyes widened as he turned to face Bo. "You dare talk back to me? You a no-count slave have the audacity to contradict me, a white man?" He snatched his wife's arm again. "Don't you ever presume to speak to my wife or me again or I'll have you arrested and horse whipped!"

"But I spoke to him first," Elaine pointed out.

"Would you let me handle things for once in your life before he comes to our house and bludgeons us in our sleep one night."

"No, sir, I wouldn't harm an innocent soul as God is my witness . . ."

"That's it, let's go. I won't tolerate no sassin' from slaves. I don't care who they are, or how free they think they are. That's what's wrong, we've been too tolerant of you people and now you think you're as good as we are. Freein' up slaves and givin' them land . . . should hang them all!" He looked at Cheasley. "I'll be back when your place is free from them kind." He took his wife's elbow, walked to the door, and left.

Cheasley was angry, but didn't say a word as he assembled Bo's order. He recorded the costs in his ledger and looked over at Bo. "You already owe five dollars on the books and your new purchases total twelve dollars and twenty-five cents. So your total is seventeen dollars and twenty-five cents."

"I got ten dollars cash and the rest on credit if you please." Bo started toward the counter, taking his money out of his pocket.

"No credit; cash on the barrelhead."

"But I always pay, don't I?"

"I don't care. That was how it used to be. From now on, no credit and that's final. You want anything from my store, you pay cash up front for it. Unless you have barter goods, you pay cash, and that's final."

"But why, sir? I pay regular. You said so yourself."

"Don't argue with me, black boy! It's cash or nothing!"

"All I have is twelve dollars and . . ."

"Five dollars of that pays off your balance, so you can get seven dollars worth of merchandise. What do you want me to put back?" Cheasley's eyes were impatient and cold.

"Well, if I have to, let me think—"

"Don't take all day about it," Cheasley growled. "Come in here upsetting my white customers."

"Just give me twice as much flour and sugar and three times the nails. Put the rest back." Bo strained to cover his anger.

Cheasley rolled his eyes. "Durn coloreds think they can come in my place asking for credit. No more credit."

Bo dropped his head, avoiding the man's eyes. "Yes, sir, Mister Branche. No more credit."

"And from now on, you come in my store with your list and wait out back by the barrels for me to fill it. Don't be talking to my good customers starting trouble, saying you're free either. Nobody cares that you got papers saying you're free, 'cause long as you're black in this country, you will never be equal to any white man. Do you understand, boy?"

"Yes, sir, I understand."

➤ ➤ ➤ ➤ ➤ ➤

George Maitland sat across from a man who was unknown to Bo. There was no hostility or distrust on the stranger's face.

Bo noticed right off because these days it was odd in Southampton to see a white man smiling cordially at a black man. George had requested him to come up to his manor, but Bo did not know why. In light of recent events and ensuing attitudes, he feared the worst. He was still depressed by his treatment at Branche's Emporium; not just by the proprietor but Peter Dilworth's abusive behavior added offense. It was especially hurtful because he had always been so kind to Bo, both he and his wife. He wondered what other reactions from the uprising were about to change the life he had become accustomed to.

He stood in the chilly study, apprehensive, although George in his usual friendly gesture invited him to take a seat. Getting up to stoke the dying fire and add logs, he said, "Bo, I want you to meet my friend Albert Fields from Pennsylvania. He's a Quaker and active leader of an abolitionist organization there." Albert extended his hand, which also surprised Bo.

Shaking hands, Bo respectfully said, "Nice to meet you, sir." He was curious about the distinguished older gentleman who worked in the cause of freeing slaves.

Fields's smile was warm and sincere. "It's my pleasure to meet you, young man. I've heard some impressive things about you."

George looked at Bo and started explaining. "Albert's organization is arranging for escaped slaves to leave the East and travel north to Canada and west to the free territories out there. It will be hard travels, but worth it to start a new life as free people. Families will be able to stay together and own land when they get settled."

Bo looked at the white-haired Fields, then back at George. "Sounds good, sir." He knew there was more.

Fields nodded. "Glad you feel that way, because George says you're the man for the job of leading them."

Bo blinked. "Taking folks to Canada?"

"Or out west. The choice is yours."

"I've never been west of Virginia in my life, let alone all the way north up to Canada."

"It doesn't matter. We'll arrange everything. There will be two guides with you. All you have to do is lead the wagons to freedom. They need someone who can read and handle business—someone educated like you. They also need a godly man of strength and exceptional character, a free African to inspire them. A few of them will already be free but not many of them. We help slaves escape from as far away as Florida and Louisiana. More will join up as you cross toward the northwest. It won't be an easy trip or always safe, mind you."

George realized Bo's reluctance and spoke up. "You just think about it for now. You have plenty of time to make up your mind. I thought perhaps you were ready for a change, an adventure."

"You will be well compensated, I can assure you," Mr. Fields added. "Our covert group is made up of some very wealthy gentlemen who are not in a position to openly speak out against slavery, so they fight in secret with their financial contributions. We are able to pay you a handsome sum for your service."

Bo scratched his head and looked down thoughtfully. "Things are not good in these parts anymore. Mister Branche is demanding cash from me from now on, and I haven't done anything wrong to him and always paid my bill. I'm a good customer. He always told me so but that doesn't matter now. He's doing it out of spite. Since the slave revolt, folks' most hateful mean natures have come out, and I think they're going to stay that way for a long time."

"We got the news up in Philadelphia, and people who had

281

slaves there were scared out of their wits. I know it cost a lot of poor souls their lives, but it gave our cause a boost as to why slavery should be abolished. The opinion that Africans are content being slaves and ill-fitted to do anything else but be subservient is losing ground fast. People aren't so willing to purchase slaves if they're scared of being murdered by them."

"It'll be a long time before folks around here forget what happened. Maybe moving on is the best option for you," George said, looking at Bo.

"You mean never come back?"

"That would make the most sense."

"I thought I was just supposed to lead the wagon train and come back home."

"Of course if that's how you want to do it, you may, but it seems to me an awful lot of your life spent traveling. George said you're an especially good farmer," Albert pointed out. "You can get land out west and farm there just as well. It's wide-open in those territories. Plenty of land for everyone."

"Does 'everyone' include us?"

"It certainly does, young man. We've already established a small settlement of former slaves on the west side of the Mississippi River. This is how we'll do it if you go. The wagon train will be led down here from Lancaster, Pennsylvania, by a relative of mine, Jonas Silvers, a wagon trail master, and Sam Pitts, a free Negro associate from Delaware."

"With them along what do you need me for?"

"Jonas is not going all the way. He's coming back to Pennsylvania. Sam will connect with you, and you two leave together for the far northwest territory along with James Kettlemen. Sam and James will be a big help on the trail. They've been west before, several times as a matter of fact, but this trip is the far-thest west they've gone."

"Don't decide now," George advised. "Think about it for a while. Talk it over with Ruth and some of the others on the farm whose opinions you respect. Albert and his wife are coming for Thanksgiving celebration and you can give him your decision then."

"I'll think hard on it and pray till then, Mister Maitland, but what about my farm?"

"Don't worry about the farm. I'll buy it back from you at a fair price."

"But the folks who live there—"

"They can stay if they want and work it for me. I have no need to change much, but I have a feeling most of them will follow you, Bo."

"No need in folks following me, sir. They better do like I do and follow Jesus."

Twenty-Six

It was Bo and Ruth's first anniversary. It had been a tumultuous twelve months, but things were settling into a good life for them. Ruth had never been so happy. She was especially cheerful all that week.

Bo thought she expected something extra special for a gift. He'd gotten Rebecca Greene to make the selection of a store-bought dress and accessories. He decided that should please her.

The anniversary fell on Sunday, and they hurried home from worship service. They brought with them the meal Naomi had prepared so Ruth wouldn't have to cook that day. After setting the table, they sat down waiting for the food to heat up. Bo looked at her dreamily. She was as beautiful as he'd ever seen her, even more so. She'd put on a few pounds, but her figure was still shapely and her temperament was different. "I cain't wait. I want to give you your present now," she exclaimed.

"You didn't have to get me a present. You're gift enough for me."

Ruth loved Bo's sweet talk now more than ever. "Dis a . . . I mean, this is a special gift."

"Oh?" Bo looked around but he didn't see a package.

Ruth stood up and walked over to him, smiling. She sat close to him and kissed him. "Put your hand here," she said, moving his hand to her belly. "Notice anything different?"

"You mean how you're filling out real nice? Yeah, I noticed lately and I like it. You look good. You were a bit too skinny when you first got here. Now you look good and healthy with some meat on your bones."

"So you's saying I looked too po'ly befo'?"

"Just a bit poorly." Bo laughed and kissed her neck. "But you looked good just the same."

"Humph, we'll see how you like it when I'm wide as a barn wit dis baby . . . I mean, with the baby."

Bo froze before slowly turning his head to look in her eyes. They were joyful and full of life like never before. "Are you saying . . .?"

"I sho am; we's havin' a baby!" Ruth threw her arms around his neck excitedly. She knew Bo wanted a family but because he thought she couldn't have any more children, he never talked about it. One day she had overheard Bo and Naomi talking. Naomi was inquiring about the prospect of children. Bo told her the situation and how he would be so happy to have children by such a beautiful wife. He lamented that he'd been denied the privilege from two wives and was determined to accept that he was not meant to have any offspring. Naomi had been sympathetic and told him not to give up hope. Ruth was heartbroken and began praying for a miracle. Believing in a risen Savior was new to her at that time. She had the enthusiasm and faith of a new follower of Christ, a faith strongly encouraged by her husband.

"How can you be with child? You said you couldn't . . ."

She put her fingers to his lips. "That's what that no 'count doctor said. It was almost two years of them trying to breed me and nothing happened, so I believed it. I still believe I was ruined fo' givin' birth, but you said God kin do anything and He kin . . . I mean He can! He fixed what was wrong cause believe me, I's havin' a baby. I's sho of it. I wanted ta be sure fo' I tol' ya . . . I mean, before I told you. I wanted to be sure," she repeated, giggling.

"We're really having a baby?"

"Yeah."

Bo sprang to his feet with Ruth still in his arms. "Thank You, Jesus, thank You!" He spun her around.

"Hallelujah, thank You, Jesus! You's everything Bo said You was. You forgave my sins, gave me freedom, a good man, and a home. Now Ya blessing me to have a baby wit my man. I believes in the goodness of the Lord if I ain't never did befo'. I believe!"

Bo put Ruth on her feet. "I guess that settles the question of traveling out west."

Ruth looked at his disappointed expression. It told her Bo wanted to take the opportunity and he was ready to leave Southampton. She took his hand and looked into his eyes. "No it don't, if they is willing ta wait till I give birth, we should go."

A frightened look suddenly flashed across his face. "How do you feel about having another baby, Ruth?"

Her smile faded when she understood what he was really asking. "It's all right, Bo. I's happy to be totin' yo' child. You a good husband and I know ya want a family. We's gonna be a real family wit dis here youngun'. I wants dis baby . . . for de first time I's got a baby I really wanna have and no man kin take it from me. Dis . . . This baby gonna have a good life."

He looked relieved and smiled again. "I didn't mean to—"

"Don't fret none, I knows ya didn't mean ta hurt my feel-ins'. You was worried but don't worry. It's gonna be fine. I know it is."

"So have you thought any more about us leaving here and going west?"

"Some, I did. Makes me no never mine if we go or stay. Long as I's . . . I'm with you. If ya think we should leave dis place, den we leave. I will follow you anywhere you wanna go. Your life is my life like your God is now my God. Let nothing but death separate us ever, Bo . . . nothin'."

"It's going to be a real hard trip and take a long time to get there but when we do, there will be land a plenty for all of us and a new start. I feel like we need a new start."

"Won't you miss your friends here?"

"We'll be making new friends and a new home there. Things are not so good here anymore since all the trouble, and the white folks are not prospering so they will get more resent-ful. They're getting meaner and meaner toward Negroes and us especially 'cause the Lord is keeping us. I believe the Lord is leading us out of Southampton. For me to help escaped slaves and free blacks start a new life is a great thing to do. We get to start fresh too and with a baby. That does change things, though."

"No, it don't. I want dis baby to live free. We can go wit our baby and start a life in dat new territory where it can grow up happier and really free."

Bo saw a sad look come over her face. "What's wrong?"

"You said once you would try and buy Willie Boy from the Stanleys if you could. Will ya still try fo' me? I want him to go wit us and live free and be in our family . . . if he's still dere. I want my son fo' keeps if I's going so far away."

"I'll ask Mister Maitland if he can arrange for him to be bought. I'll do all I can to get your son for you—for us to be a family."

Ruth flung her arms around his neck. "You's the best husband in the world, Bo Peace. Jesus sho was good ta me putting you in my life."

Twenty-Seven

May 1835

*B*o's covered wagon reached the hilltop first. He got out, looking around as the other wagons slowly ascended. The caravan had started out with twenty-five wagons. Only twelve had withstood the arduous twenty-one-month journey to Oregon.

The first folks to leave did so at the beginning. They were not prepared for the trek across country and by the time they reached Kentucky relinquished their wagon to a pair of anxious runaway slaves who stayed the distance. Four wagons carrying ten people remained in northern Missouri, having had more than enough of the covered wagon experience. Five dropped out two months later, opting to homestead in a colored town called Emersonville that had sprung up some years before. The final four families who cut their journey short did so in Wyoming. A lone wagon carrying one courageous family west joined them at the start of the Oregon Country. Bo felt it was worth all the time and hardship they endured to reach this wondrous new frontier. Oregon was not yet an American territory. Shared with Britain and its ownership unsettled, Oregon offered untapped opportunity to those daring and smart enough to settle its unclaimed land. Traders were starting to pour into the area. It had vast untapped growth potential.

Ruth stood beside Bo proud and elated with what she saw. Naomi sat on the wagon holding their son, Obadiah, on her lap, with Willie Boy snuggled beside her. She was in awe of the spectacle before her. "I sho wish ya could see dis here place, Ephraim," she whispered. "Land for as far as de eye kin see. Trees so big en so tall they can almost reach de heavens."

Stretched out before them were the tall green grass and the clearest bluest sky imaginable as a backdrop. The mammoth trees were clustered through the landscape. It was different but more beautiful than Bo ever imagined. He let out a relieved sigh and sent up a prayer of gratitude. Ruth linked her arm inside his and asked, "Ya ever seed trees so big en purty?"

"Never in my life but I'm not surprised. We serve a big God who creates big beauty." He kissed her nose. "He made you, didn't He? It makes sense He'd make some really big beautiful trees. Sam said they're called Sequoias after the Indians, and Redwoods, the biggest trees in the country, maybe in the whole world."

"We's startin' a new life in dis beautiful place wit our new family. In spite all it took to git here, I's so happy."

Sam Pitts rode up on his horse next to their wagon. "Well, Brother Peace, what do you think of this Oregon country?"

"I think it's better then I ever thought it would be." Bo smiled. "I've been free for years, but for some reason I feel freer now than I ever did in my life. This is a good place, a

God-touched place. Here a man can really be free."

Naomi was rocking Obadiah when she called out, "Comin' here were God's plan all along! Ya was born fo' dis day!"

Willie Boy looked up at Naomi with sleepy eyes. "Mee Maw, we in Oregon yet?"

"We sho nuff is, sweet boy." He laid his head back against her and closed his eyes peacefully. She whispered to herself, "De Lord's been gettin' ya ready fo' dis a long time, Bodine Peace."

Bo looked up into the sky with a spirit of gratefulness, triumph, and contentment. "First thing before the winter sets in, we build a place for worship to honor the God who got us here."

Epilogue

*B*o and Ruth's family grew to five more children by 1846 when the treaty with Britain was signed. The treaty made Oregon an American territory and validated American sovereignty to the Pacific Northwest.

Oregon's streams, lakes, and rivers had an abundance of fish and beaver. Wildlife was plentiful all over the vast untamed region. Trappers, traders, and explorers were attracted to the land. The ex-slaves of the wagon train appropriately named their settlement Freedom. Freedom was located in central Oregon in the region that would one day form the eastern tail of Deschutes County.

When the school was built, its first student was an anxious Ruth Peace. The schoolmarm position was held by Maggie Ghering, the wife of an ex-slave, Paul Ghering, from North Carolina. He was the settlement's preacher. The Gherings were among the original group of the wagon train. Maggie helped Ruth improve her reading and writing skills Bo had started, and taught her basic arithmetic. Ruth took her additional education seriously and learned well enough to later teach some of the Indians to read.

The preacher, Paul Ghering, helped build what was appropriately called FREEDOM'S FIRST HOUSE OF WORSHIP. The settlement ballooned into a town. Bo was as successful a farmer in Oregon as he had been in Virginia. Although the climate was very different, the agrarian anointing was still on him.

The caravan of slaves had formed a community that made fast friends with the natives. It was the peaceful Sahaptin Indians who helped the black settlers survive the first brutal Oregon winter, and Bo learned from the Paiutes how to be an expert trapper of beaver and trade pelts. When the word got out, Freedom grew with more escaped slaves, European immigrants, and free blacks migrating for over a decade.

Bo became an important man in Freedom and throughout the territory. He was respected by most for his godly character, agricultural ability, and leadership qualities. He ministered to the Indians and became their unofficial advocate to the United States Bureau of Indian Affairs. He set up trading posts for them and farmed his own land beyond anyone's expectations.

Oregon continued to grow, as did a lot of the North Pacific, which included Northern California and Washington State. When gold was discovered, miners flooded in to ravage the land for the precious commodity. Freedom kept its integrity, and through Bo's leadership kept the gold diggers away from their slice of paradise. He fought against the tribal lands being used to excavate gold as well.

The town of Freedom thrived until the government allocated it as part of a reservation for the Indians. The Indians were at odds with the white man's dishonest governing, and wars broke out. Blacks and whites began to disperse and move farther west toward the coast. Bo and Ruth never left their home, because they loved it. They lived harmoniously among their Indian neighbors and through each territorial change until their deaths in the 1890s. Living well past the Civil War and being witness to the national emancipation of slavery sealed their faith in a liberating, prayer-answering God.

Their children eventually followed their own paths to California, Nevada, Texas, and Illinois. Only Willie Boy stayed in the vicinity of Freedom, Oregon. His children and children's children remained there until after the 1930s Great Depression, after which they were scattered across the country as far east as Virginia, coming full circle of their bloodline's origin.

The redemption of Ruth from bondage to freedom—freedom of body, soul, and spirit—had been multiplied more than a hundredfold.

Excerpt from

Son of a Preacherman

by Marlene Banks

August 1920
Greenwood District
Tulsa, Oklahoma

Benny wondered if she could ever stand up to the strain of greeting customers and chatting pleasantly, knowing what they were thinking.

As she considered ways of escaping the commitment she'd been pressured into, someone's loud throat-clearing interrupted her thoughts. He got her attention, and she looked into the man's crafty, widespread eyes.

"Morning, Benny, surprised to see you here. Where's your mother?" the man asked with an irritating affability.

"Good morning, Mr. Grapnel. She went to the reservation today and asked me to work in the shop for her." Her response was polite but dry.

"I need to speak to your father. Thought Ella would be here so I could find out if he's in town before I go out to the ranch."

"He's at the ranch, sir."

Grapnel frowned. "Blast it. Guess I'll have to drive on out there."

"He's awful busy. They're getting cattle ready for market. Maybe you should wait till next week," Benny suggested.

"I've got an offer on that Boxwood Flats property I know he can't refuse, and it won't wait."

"You might as well not bother, sir. You'd be wasting your time since he's already told you he won't sell it to you."

"It's not me that's buying, little gal, but a businessman from Texarkana wants it."

"My father's going to say no just the same. He's already told you he wouldn't sell one acre of land to you or your associates. So why keep coming around asking?"

Grapnel's face reddened. "Your father's a stubborn fool. If he's smart he'll sell that piece of land while he's still got something worth selling.

"What's that supposed to mean?" Benny wanted to know.

Grapnel pointed his finger in her face. "It means you coloreds are getting too high and mighty. You better remember your place, gal. I don't care how much oil money your family's got. You might be doing well now, but that doesn't mean you always will. Things change."

"Please remove your finger from my face, Mr. Grapnel," Benny said firmly. "How dare you come here to do business and make threats! My father will never sell to you or your friends."

Grapnel's finger moved in closer. "You better watch your tongue, missy. Be careful how you talk to white folks or somebody's gonna teach the little teacher a lesson she won't forget."

Fear clamped down on Benny, but she stood her ground.

"I asked you to remove your finger from my face," she reminded him.

"Why, you uppity . . ." He swung his raised hand back.

"I wouldn't do that if I were you, mister. The lady asked you nicely to move your hand out of her face. A gentleman would do that just as nicely as she requested," a deep voice cautioned. Grapnel's head swung to the right, and his eyes bugged at the powerful black man standing in the drugstore doorway whose eyes were pinned menacingly on him. "The best advice I can give you right now, sir, is to step back right now and walk away."

Grapnel withdrew his hand grudgingly, scowling at Benny. "Better watch your step, girlie," he warned as he hurried off.

Relieved but surprised by the stranger's assistance, Benny stared at the handsome man with the commanding air.

"Are you all right?" he asked, stepping closer.

"Yes. Yes. I'm fine, thank you," she replied, feeling awkward. "Thank you for your help."

"Glad to. My name's William Ray Matthias but call me Billy Ray. And you are?" He held out his hand.

Benny was staring at his remarkable good looks and large hands. The top of her head reached only to his broad shoulders. Catching herself, she answered.

"My name's Benjamina, but folks call me Benny. Benny Freeman." She stretched out her arm to shake his hand. His massive grip swallowed her hand with an enthusiastic gusto that startled her.

Billy Ray took in Benny from head to toe. She was not flashy in appearance like a lot of Tulsa women he'd seen, but lovely in a dignified way. She was naturally pretty with thick, dark hair braided on both sides and pinned into a knot at the nape of her neck. The style gave her a less youthful look than he would have preferred. Yet it didn't detract from her beautiful face and flawless golden brown skin. Her brown, almond-shaped eyes were appealing though they held a hint of sadness. Her figure was definitely notable in a puffy, fitted cotton blouse the color of dandelions. Her waist was belted to reveal its small size and her shapeliness. He glanced down at her feet where he saw shoes made of the shiny new-style patent leather peeking out from under an expensive-looking emerald green skirt. Everything about her seemed poised and sophisticated, and he liked what he saw.

"Did you say Freeman? We met an Earl Freeman a few days ago. Are you related?"

"He's my father."

"What a coincidence. He offered to help us get settled. Even said he'd give us a few head of cattle once our fence gets repaired. He's very generous."

Benny smiled faintly. "Yes, he is." Billy Ray's eyes were so penetrating they made her nervous. "You just moved here?" she asked, hoping to divert his stare.

"Yes, ma'am. We moved from Durham, North Carolina."

"That's funny; we're getting a new preacher from North Carolina."

"That would be *my* father." He beamed at her.

Benny looked back at him while taking note of his fine-looking dark skin and shiny black hair. It was cut fashionably low, but she could see the distinct waviness. Billy Ray's huge build was overwhelming, and she had to be mindful not to gawk.

"Do you work here?" he asked, breaking an uncomfortable silence

"Sort of—this is my mother's shop. I'm just helping out today. I teach school."

298

She glanced out the window at a few rambunctious youth who were crossing the street on their way to school and looked down.

"At least I did teach," she mumbled. Billy Ray started buttoning the white jacket he was wearing. "You work in the pharmacy?" she asked.

"My brother and I own it. Or at least we will once we pay off the bank. We bought it from Mr. Andrews last month. My brother's a physician and I'm a pharmacist."

"I had no idea Mr. Andrews sold this place.

"That's what everyone keeps saying. He must have kept it secret for some reason. He said he didn't want anyone to know until the sale was final and he was gone."

"I can't imagine why."

"He seemed in an awful hurry to leave here and move to North Carolina."

"He left?" Benny hadn't heard that.

"Yeah, he and his family left two days ago on the train. He told my father he felt things were getting too tense in Tulsa, which turned out well for us. It was a sweet deal because he bought our family's house in Durham. If you ask me, things are always tense when our people make money and start living successfully on our own. Same problem took place in Durham."

Benny was surprised. "He sold his house?"

"My father bought his house in Eagles Pointe since it's near the church. That's where my family and I live. My brother plans to get his own place here in Greenwood. He's not much for living out away from town. Well, actually it's not him so much as his wife, who wants to live in the city where there's more excitement and more goings on that keep a busybody like her happy." Billy Ray chuckled. "My brother intends on setting up practice where he can see more patients and be near the hospital. I guess Eagles Pointe is too remote."

"My family lives in Eagles Pointe."

"Your father told us. Glad to know we're neighbors."

To Benny his friendly nature seemed excessive, but genuine. The school bell rang in the distance. Benny flipped the CLOSED sign hanging on the door to OPEN.

"It's time for me to get to work," she explained.

"Me too. I've got a load of boxes to unpack. Supplies came in late yesterday. I'm supposed to be putting things together with my brother, but it's nicer talking to you." The look he flashed her was flirty and bold. He walked to the door of the pharmacy and glanced back.

"Have a good day, Benny. Hope to see you again."

"I suppose you'll see me Sunday in church. Is your father preaching, or is Pastor Richmond?"

"My father's giving his first sermon. I think Pastor Richmond is saying his good-byes to the congregation. He's leaving for the reservation next week."

Son of a Preacherman

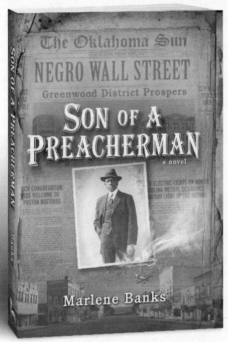

A historical romance novel set in the 1920s in Tulsa, Oklahoma, depicting the segregated life of African Americans in Northern Tulsa and the tensions leading up to the Tulsa Race Riots. Billy Ray Matthias is the handsome son of the church's new pastor. Benny is the daughter of the oil-rich Freeman family. He's convinced she's the woman God has for him, but she's hesitant about getting involved in a relationship. As Billy Ray's pursuit of Benny intensifies, so does the political and social climate in the Greenwood District, an affluent African American neighborhood. When tensions come to a head and violence breaks out, Billy Ray and Benny are caught up in the heat of chaos. He vows to keep her safe, but will she let him? Will faith in God be enough to sustain the people of Greenwood as their lives are forever changed by deadly acts of hatred?

LIFT EVERY VOICE BOOKS

lifteveryvoicebooks.com

Lift Every Voice Books

Lift every voice and sing
Till earth and heaven ring,
Ring with the harmonies of Liberty;
Let our rejoicing rise
High as the listening skies,
Let it resound loud as the rolling sea.
Sing a song full of the faith that the dark past has taught us,
Sing a song full of the hope that the present has brought us,
Facing the rising sun of our new day begun
Let us march on till victory is won.

The Black National Anthem, written by James Weldon Johnson in 1900, captures the essence of Lift Every Voice Books. Lift Every Voice Books is an imprint of Moody Publishers that celebrates a rich culture and great heritage of faith, based on the foundation of eternal truth—God's Word. We endeavor to restore the fabric of the African-American soul and reclaim the indomitable spirit that kept our forefathers true to God in spite of insurmountable odds.

We are Lift Every Voice Books—Christ-centered books and resources for restoring the African-American soul.

For more information on other books and products
written and produced from a biblical perspective, go to
www.lifteveryvoicebooks.com or write to:

Lift Every Voice Books
820 N. LaSalle Boulevard
Chicago, IL 60610
www.lifteveryvoicebooks.com